D0435575

THE HIVE

THE HIVE

MELISSA SCHOLES YOUNG

Turner Publishing Company
Nashville, Tennessee

www.turnerpublishing.com

The Hive

Author photo: Colleen Dolak

Jacket designer: Lauren Peters-Collaer

Jacket artist: Andrea Akers

Text designer: Tim Holtz

Library of Congress Cataloging-in-Publication Data

9781684426430 Hardcover
9781684426454 eBook

Printed in the United States of America

I'll try and be what he loves to call me, "a little woman," and not be rough and wild, but do my duty here instead of wanting to be somewhere else.

—Louisa May Alcott
Little Women

For my daughters, Isabelle and Piper,
sisters always

In memory of Debbie Scholes Catlett,
a beloved queen bee

Also by Melissa Scholes Young

FICTION

Flood

Scrap Metal Baby

EDITED VOLUMES

Furious Gravity

Grace in Darkness

PROLOGUE

Fehler Sisters

It was mid-July on a sweltering Missouri afternoon, and the sun couldn't find a single cloud to hide behind. Waterfowl ducked beneath the river's surface, and whip-poor-wills sang their melancholy from lush trees waving above. The stale air stank of soil and algae mixed with coconut sunscreen. The muddy water of the Mississippi River wasn't worried with the Fehler family's survival, but the sisters were.

Sunshine baked the wooden dock and kissed the Fehler sisters' freckles. Just as they had the summer before and the one before that one too, the sisters wore bikinis, faded tops and bottoms passed down and among them. The river assaulted the elastic, and the blistering light faded the floral colors, but still the camp swimwear endured.

"It came too close for me," Tammy said, dangling her legs off the dock. "We almost lost everything." She flexed her feet in the sticky air. A rotten piece of debris hung from her pinky toe. Tammy shook it off, and the current swept it away. "Everything that mattered, anyway."

"It was never that close," Maggie insisted. She swatted a mosquito on Tammy's thigh, leaving a thin trail of crimson bug blood. "Besides, nobody would want this old fishing camp. It's a mess."

"But it's our mess," Kate said, looking up and down her row of sisters.

"It was too close for Mom," Jules added. "She was itching to be done with it all. The family business and the business of the family. All of it."

"At least we're still together," Maggie said. "That's what Dad cared about."

Sipping green glass bottles of soda, the sisters agreed but they'd never know the true feelings of their father.

One year ago they'd sat on this same dock, months before their family broke and they were left with only the fragments of the whole they'd once been. Now they were making their first camp trip solo as sisters. They were still sorting out who brought what and how the family worked now.

Jules dove into the brown water alone and waded her way back up. Maggie and Tammy held hands, nudging each other's hips, and jumped off the dock together. Kate ran at her sisters, waited in vain for her parents to call after them, and then belly flopped in the middle of their wake with a splash.

The Fehler Family Fish Camp had been handed down for three generations, a burden both beloved and neglected. It was a simple single-wide trailer on stilts with rusted panels that had maybe once been painted white. The camp sat at the meeting of the Mighty Mississippi and the Ohio River on the lap of Fort Defiance Park. Robbie, their dad, liked to remind them all it was once called Camp Defiance during the Civil War and had been commanded by General Ulysses S. Grant. Jules would roll her eyes and tell him that glorifying a war fought for slavery was oppressive. Before they began bantering about erasing history versus righting historical wrongs, Grace, their mother, would hold up her hand and say, "Enough." By the time they loaded the car for these trips, Grace had made dozens of decisions. She sought a truce, even if it wouldn't hold.

The trailer's living room and kitchen combination reeked of rancid catfish and bitter beer. The two miniature bedrooms housed four sets of built-in bunk beds with narrow strips of peeling, dingy vinyl between the lofts. The Fehlers ran to camp most summer weekends and squeezed in a few fall trips before the chill arrived and the leaves crisped in the Missouri Valley. At camp, the sisters learned to bait hooks, pull fish traps from the muck, and dig burrs out of bare feet. They knew which bunks were theirs because they'd carved their names in the frames as a tradition on their fifth birthdays. On their annual inaugural trip, as spring rounded the corner to summer, Grace cut notches in the wooden stairs to measure her daughters' growth. She added initials and the date while the sisters raced ahead, peeling off Catholic school uniforms and pulling on mismatched swimsuit pieces from a communal wicker basket before jumping off the dock into the cool relief of the muddy water. The family dog chased them, cautioning their courage with a bark and cheering on their unleashed animal freedom.

The promise of the camp brought hope; it lifted the family's spirits to pile in the car after the last day of school and travel toward the water. Each trip the Fehler family wished they would roast marshmallows for s'mores and finally catch fireflies without fighting over which sister had more. They would leave the family pest control business behind and not talk about how to cover the quarterly tax bill or whether they should pay for their employees' cell phones. But first, they had to drive the forty-six miles from Cape Girardeau, Missouri, to Cairo, Illinois, snaking the Mississippi River's gritty coast to put in the boat.

On their way, they had to quote their favorite scenes from *Adventures of Huckleberry Finn*, when Huck and Jim float past Cairo in the fog and miss their transfer to the Ohio River and Jim's independence. Tammy would pull out the dog-eared paperback tucked in the back of the driver's seat. "'Jim said it made him all over trembly and feverish to be so close to freedom.'"

Kate took over. "'Well, I can tell you it made me all over trembly and feverish, too, to hear him, because I begun to get it through my head that he WAS most free—and who was to blame for it? Why, ME.'"

Then Jules would look out the window at the water and say, "'Maybe we went by Cairo in the fog that night.'"

Maggie didn't want to finish with the sadness of the chapter, so she chose a different Huck line. "'Jim said that bees won't sting idiots, but I didn't believe that, because I tried them lots of times myself and they wouldn't sting me,'" and they all giggled because bug girls knew how to handle bees. They also knew the hive's survival mattered more than any puncture. Like Huck, the girls would sacrifice to save each other. Like Huck, they loved their pap, even when he disappointed them.

Each trip, Robbie insisted they coordinate bathroom breaks for the drive, but they had to stop at least twice. Even as they grew from children to teens to young adults, their trips were the same. Maggie would say they should have checked the road conditions. Jules got carsick. Someone else would say planning took away from the adventure, probably Tammy. Kate didn't say much; she was lost in her own thoughts and passed around their mom's latest creation of homemade granola bars. Their brindle pit bull, Nacho, would whine from the back seat and lick their hands for crumbs.

Robbie promised that if they could all hold it, they would be cooking hot dogs over a fire in time for supper, but they usually settled for grilled cheese sandwiches on the dock as the sun set.

Nacho ran after the bunnies in the bushes hoping to find his own dinner, relieved to be released from the car.

Who knew which family camp trip would be the one they'd remember most? The pieces of the weekends and years might add up to an entirely different story. Maybe they'd each remember separate parts, or the same ones in different patterns. Perhaps as grief and joy intersected, they'd learn that the whole mattered more than the portions. Nacho could have told them that. Dogs know that the only moment that matters is this one you're living.

PART I

Honeycomb

There's a contribution in him from every ancestor he ever had. In him there's atoms of priests, soldiers, crusaders, poets, and sweet and gracious women.

—Mark Twain
The American Claimant

1

Maggie

Like her dad, Maggie drank her coffee black. She preferred a bit of milk, but everyone learned to drink coffee black at Fehler Family Exterminating. Even new employees who once took sugar or powdered creamer relented by the second week of work. No one actually knew why. It's the way things were done. The way things had always been done. And you didn't question tradition. It was a fourth-generation pest control business; they were still around for a reason.

Maggie's dad was the guy who brought the bugs to school. When she'd been in fourth grade at Blessed Family Catholic School, Mrs. Snyder had met Robbie at the door and helped him carry the cages into the classroom. He'd brought in hissing cockroaches, an ant colony with glass on both sides, a display of dead butterflies, their wings pinned permanently open, termites in their mud tubing, and one tarantula named Hairy. Robbie's uniform was a hunter-green long-sleeve button-down shirt with *Fehler Family Exterminating* sewn in white on a sunny-yellow patch over his pocket. Because he owned only three uniform shirts—buy two, get one free—Grace, who resented doing laundry midweek off schedule, had taught Maggie at an early age to retrieve the shirts wet from the dryer and hang them damp to avoid fading, shrinkage, and perpetual ironing.

Maggie's classmates had loved the bug guy and the bugs. His arrival was a tornado in her tense Catholic school. Maggie had even put away her highlighters, which she kept lined up on her desk for annotations, in honor of his visit. Girls screamed and recoiled in their chairs, while boys jumped out of their seats and spun around on the carpet to get closer to the bugs. Mrs. Snyder flailed her arms for control and shouted warnings, but it was useless. They quieted down only when she had introduced Maggie's dad. "Boys and girls, this is Mr. Fehler, owner and operator of Fehler Family Exterminating." Then everyone had turned and stared at Maggie. There's only one family in Cape Girardeau, Missouri, with that name. The Fehler family had been in the pest control business since 1938, and Maggie would be a fourth-generation bug girl. Her fate was so easily assumed that she never questioned or minded it. She liked to know what was coming.

At this cue, Robbie would introduce the bugs one by one. "The roach is the *Gromphadorhina portentosa.* You may call the butterfly a *Danaus plexippus. Camponotus pennsylvanicus* is an ant." They'd peer into the cages and squeal when he let the cockroaches run up and down his arm. Maggie had felt their fear was silly. She knew what lived in their homes and under their pillows and crawled across them while they slept. She had been raised knowing and armed with chemical prevention.

"Do you bring these bugs to your customers' houses?" Hillary Carlson had asked.

Robbie smiled. "That would be good for business, huh?"

Maggie got the joke. Her classmates didn't. Her dad winked at her.

"No. We get the bugs out of your house," he said. "Or at least we find them and make sure they don't bother you anymore."

"Where'd you get the butterflies?" Noah Michaels asked. "I like to kill bugs too," he added.

"My wife and I collected them on our honeymoon," Robbie said. Maggie knew the story well. A young Grace and Robbie had spent their romantic week on the beaches in Georgia hunting insects for his entomology class project. Robbie was a sophomore in college. Grace was eighteen and pregnant. She'd said the butterflies along their path were a sign from God. She'd insisted on only capturing dead ones, and the orange monarchs, blue and green morphos, and brown buckeyes had kept their color all these years. The project, six display cases of pinned insects with their scientific names, hung proudly in the foyer of the business office downtown. It was the last assignment he completed before quitting Southeast Missouri State University and becoming a bug guy full time.

"We got bugs," Martin Lamont said, scratching the dozens of small red bites on his arms. "Bed bugs."

"Give us a call then. Fehlers' will take care of all your pest control needs." Robbie had sounded just like the commercial on the local radio station. "Martin, we haven't seen bed bugs in a long time. DDT did too good of a job, if you know what I mean." Maggie was able to tell by Martin's face that he didn't.

Maggie was proud to be the bug guy's daughter. Spiders and hissing cockroaches increased her social status. Also, children liked Robbie. He was a kidder. He was a hugger, at least a pull-you-into-a-headlock-knuckle-punch kind of hugger. Kids love that stuff.

When the bug guy visited Maggie's classroom, she was famous for the first fifteen minutes. Then the kids realized that her dad *killed* bugs. For a living. He climbed underneath strangers' houses with his flashlight, found out where the bugs were coming in, and sprayed chemicals into the crevices to stop them. In the Fehler home, it was honorable, hard work, and Maggie hadn't questioned her future as much as how she might sort out her own place.

"Does he come home all dirty?" Spencer Willett asked, swinging from the monkey bars at recess. The bug guy had left after lunch, but kids talked about him for the rest of the day.

"Nope," Maggie lied. "He looks like he did today." She liked his professional uniform. He was a licensed pest control technician with a paper that said so. He was so official that the sisters weren't allowed to hug Robbie at the door after work; he had to shower first. He usually smelled of Dursban or Lorsban, chemicals now banned by the EPA. He often had peanut butter glue boards for catching mice stuffed into his back pocket. Chemicals. Sweat. Heat. If he wore a bee suit, he undressed in the front yard. Allergy tests had revealed that Grace was allergic to insect dust. An after-work kiss would send her into a sneezing fit.

"Do you like bugs too, Maggie?"

"No. Not really." Which was finally the truth. She didn't just *like* them, she loved them, mostly because they were reliable.

She still felt the same way ten years later.

Maggie beat her dad to work by one freshly brewed pot. "Coffee," Robbie said, inhaling deeply as he walked through the front door of their dated, familiar office. Maggie had heard the story of her mom insisting the building—it was only four rooms—be gutted after her parents' butcher shop had to close. Once they'd installed new vinyl floors in the bathroom and storage rooms and industrial carpet in the rest, she'd decorated the front office with rose-patterned wallpaper. The desk chairs were navy blue, and the carpet was a boring beige. Dried flower arrangements hung on the walls next to benign landscape portraits from Walmart. She imagined her mom thought it a bit fancy. It was good enough. Customers rarely came in; it was pest control, so the business went to them.

Robbie studied the dry-erase board of daily technicians and geography. "Routes full?" he asked.

Maggie stood next to him assessing the route board. "Johnson's in Jefferson City. Termite inspections. Bowers has Springfield today. Re-treats, mostly, but I asked him to swing by the vo-tech school, too, and check the glue boards."

"No organophosphates at the schools," Robbie said.

"I know, Dad."

"You think you know everything, huh?" It was a joke. It came out sharp. Maggie winced. She had been stuck to his hip at work since she was nine years old. "Name me an organophosphate, smarty-pants."

"Diazinon."

Robbie sipped his coffee and nodded.

Maggie looked back up at the route board. "Terrell is doing monthlies over in Jackson all day. I asked him to take Shorty with him, show him some bait stations before he gets his own route. One day."

"He'll learn. They all do." Robbie drained his coffee and held it out to his daughter for more. "Then they quit. Or steal your stuff and tell everyone else how you do it." Maggie pretended she was tidying up with her dry eraser and ignored the cup. Her mom once told her, "You start doing stuff for a man that they can do themselves and they'll never let you stop. Don't start is my advice." Maggie thought it a bit of a contradiction considering how little her mom let their dad do at home.

"We should talk about Jenn, Dad," Maggie said.

"Jenn who?"

"The one at the front desk. With the short skirts. We hired her last week."

"And?"

"And she sassed another customer. Someone called for a re-treat saying the rain had washed away all the chemicals, and she reminded them they hadn't paid their last bill."

Robbie squinted and sipped his coffee. "I like Jenn. She's easy on the eyes."

"We've talked about this, Dad. You can't say things like that anymore. People are sensitive, and Jenn might consider that harassment. Actually, it is harassment." Maggie put her hands on her hips like she was talking to a toddler. Sometimes she felt that way too. "The account was overdue three days. She should have scheduled the re-treat and had the tech collect at the time of service."

"She ain't pregnant is she? Our insurance premiums will go through the roof."

"Not that I know of. It's illegal to ask things like that."

Robbie put his empty coffee mug on a nearby desk, oblivious to who would clean it up after him. "Why should I pay for someone to have a baby? No one is paying for me to have a baby."

Maggie didn't point out the obvious flaw in her dad's thinking. She had bigger battles. "Dad," she said, using her mother's same worn-out tone.

"I thought you were managing the office. I thought you wanted more responsibility. Sounds like your problem, not mine, kiddo." Behind every crowded route board, every noncompete employee clause, and every school account banning pesticides, Maggie knew there was the question of succession. In a family business, someone is always ready to take over, but that someone is usually a son. Her grandfather had given her dad two pieces of advice: "Make sure to have enough FU money—you know, so you can say Fuck You and quit—and get yourself a boy to manage all those girls." The one thing her dad wanted more than a bug girl was a son. Maggie didn't feel like apologizing, though; she had work to do.

"Fine," she said. "I'll talk to her. I know how to handle the office, Dad. What I said was that I wanted to help make more sales decisions, do more strategic planning."

"Strategic what? Two years of Mississippi College and you're ready to run the business? By the time I was ten I'd inched into the crawl spaces of most of Cape Girardeau's houses. I could *smell* termites."

"It's an investment," Maggie said an hour later in their morning sales meeting. "We can start with three bug heaters. Each treats three thousand square feet. That'll cover most homes in Cape Girardeau. Jefferson City is crawling with them too. I can only imagine St. Louis and Columbia. All those college kids and their parents bring new batches all the time. The hotels can't keep up."

"What's wrong with the way we been doing it? Seems to have worked for more than seventy-five years. But what do we old guys know, huh?" Robbie elbowed Billy, who wiggled his eyebrows in agreement. "You feminists are fixing everything for us."

This wasn't an issue of feminism, unless feminism meant running a business well, making enough money to pay your employees, and serving your community. Jules would say everything was an issue of feminism, and Maggie wondered if she was right. She wasn't sure what gender had to do with her business plan.

It was never clear if her dad dismissed her because she was a woman or because she was his daughter. Maggie didn't think it mattered. She would keep claiming her place until he was proud and impressed enough to notice. She'd be steady and push forward. Maggie couldn't help but believe in a better future, even as the recession grew worse and the town built to panic around her. Her little corner looked bright. And when she organized her planner day into thirty-minute rainbow blocks, she felt she was accomplishing something.

Maggie looked down at the highlighted sections in her notebook—which she'd covered with clear tape for durability—and felt calm courage. Blue for electronic specifics, yellow for insect data, pink for labor needs, and green for potential income.

"The fans are 120 volts, and they're rated at 7.5 amps," she continued. "That's plenty—4,500 CFM at 500,000 BTU will kill bed bugs. It's guaranteed. Think of the chemicals we'll save."

"Save? Sounds like you want to spend." Robbie leaned back in the maroon leather chair Maggie's grandpa had bought. It had a black swivel base that sometimes made its occupant wobble in an un-boss-like kind of way. For decades that single expensive chair butted up against a card table. Salesmen were relegated to folding chairs. Cheap wood paneling separated the conference room from the front office, but everyone could hear everyone's business. An air freshener with a customized Fehler Family Exterminating label provided the sales meeting with an ocean breeze. If Maggie replaced it before her dad did, she chose clementine, though it didn't actually smell like oranges. "This ain't the time to be spending, Mags. There's the recession. Everyone knows it's going to get worse before it gets better, especially if the Republicans lose the House. Healthcare costs are doubling for businesses. What we have to pay to insure these people and their families is highway robbery. We're always one accident away from being broke."

Maggie wanted to say *these people* are our employees. *These people* are like family. We take care of them because their work keeps us in business. That's what she believed, and it's what she needed to believe her dad did too. The health insurance they offered was so basic it was practically useless. They couldn't offer dental, and the medical policy had a low cap on each sickness or injury. It wasn't health insurance for the ill; it was merely a prayer for the healthy. Maggie had seen the costs for Billy's daughter who had Lupus and knew she needed better care than their policy would cover. She slid her open notebook across the table to her dad. "Like I said, it's an investment. Did you read my business plan? The heaters will pay for themselves in three months. The sales team will have plenty of work."

"But if we eliminate bed bugs, aren't we eliminating customers?" Travis asked. With five months of sales records under his belt, he was the hotshot. He'd moved to town six months ago from Hannibal with what Maggie assumed was a phony resume. The old-timers, Billy and Dave, threw away his business cards when he wasn't looking, and Travis was often fumbling in his shirt pocket for one. He had placed an order for more cards, but Robbie said he would have to pay for them himself.

"Ain't killing bugs kind of the point?" Billy said. He scratched his bald head and rubbed his thumb on the side of his coffee cup.

Robbie drained his cup and inspected the bottom of his mug for more. "Bed bugs aren't going anywhere. There's plenty of bugs to kill. You're right to want happy customers. But you're wrong to think something like heat is going to work better than chemicals."

Jenn brought in a new pot of coffee and refilled everyone's mug. When she bent over, the men ogled her indiscreetly. Maggie looked to her own simple black slacks and Fehler Family Exterminating polo. Maybe she would offer Jenn a shirt too, for coverage.

"Bed bug pesticide resistance is increasing dramatically," Maggie said.

"It's what? Speak up. You can't be a leader when you whisper, Margaret."

"I don't need to shout to be heard, Dad." Maggie blushed but she didn't back down. "This is the future not the present. It's in my business plan."

"Well, kiddo, maybe we can't afford your business plan. Maybe we need to buy land instead. Can't rent forever."

Maggie wondered if that was the only sticking point. Fehler

Family Exterminating had previously occupied an office and a garage that Robbie's dad had purchased in 1952 with a savings bond he bought before the war. The building was cheap because it was too close to the Mississippi River on the Illinois side. When the flood of 1968 hit, their chemicals threatened the surrounding farmland. Southeast Missouri State University funded an Army Corps of Engineers rerouting project for the Mississippi River because they wanted to grow their campus into the floodplain. The EPA said Fehlers' had to move too. The family and employees spent three days driving back and forth before they closed the bridges, but it was better than being stuck due to rising waters. In 1987, when her parents married, Grace's folks gifted them their family's butcher shop. It had been closed for years and was decrepit, but it was something. Maggie's grandparents couldn't afford the taxes on it anyway. She liked to think this made them even more of a family affair because it bound them all together, but her dad didn't give any credit for the contribution. He grumbled because the property wasn't big enough to build a garage on and he had to rent space in the lot next door for storage. Robbie had never shared how much the warehouse rental cost nor how in debt the business became under his father, but when the recession hit in 2007, there were months Robbie couldn't make the rent. They were still recovering. Robbie blamed it on the Democrats and their expensive regulations, rising insurance premiums, taxes, and the liberals' war on small businesses, but Maggie didn't see it that way.

"Hey," Jenn interrupted. "Your wife's not answering the business line at the house. Customers say it's ringing and ringing. Where is she anyway?"

"That's probably none of your goddamn business," Robbie said. Travis scribbled on his notepad. Billy studied the ceiling. Dave excused himself to the bathroom.

"I'll check after lunch," Maggie said. "Maybe they're getting a busy signal. Mornings are usually hectic."

"We done here?" Travis asked. "I got calls to make."

Maggie packed her binder and lined her highlighters back up in their package, arranging their fluorescence exactly as they'd arrived. She wished the American brands were more effective, but she'd resigned herself to the Korean highlighters she'd once received from a Secret Santa for their superiority in ink brightness. The package included eleven markers—one in gray she hadn't found a need for yet—compared to the measly six Sharpie offered. As a lefty, Maggie felt her tools mattered even more. She slid the cold coffee back across the table at Jenn as Robbie finished his.

Her dad needed to have the last word. "Jenn, your coffee is shit. Learn to make a better pot or you're out of a job. You can spend the rest of the day teaching her, Maggie. That'll keep you busy so you don't have to do no more bed bug research."

"Whatever you say, Dad," Maggie replied, but she had no intention of following her dad's orders.

2

Grace

Grace knew she'd be the one to save them all in the end. Certainly she couldn't count on Robbie, but she'd be prepared. She'd rescue her daughters too, even if they were ungrateful. Grace made lists. She also made plans and contingency plans and worst-case scenario plans. Surviving was all that mattered. It was life or death, and Grace chose to live and to fight for her family because no one else would.

As a kindred prepper, sometimes Kate would join Grace on the front lines in the cellar basement and help with inventory. One time she'd even caught her favorite daughter watching *Doomsday Preppers* and Grace thought, *Finally, someone gets me*, even though most of the preppers on TV were just showing off. Some of them thought it was a game. It wasn't. She preferred the term *survivalist* to *prepper* because surviving this marriage, this family business, and this life was a war she knew how to win.

The lists she wrote clarified the daily battle plan before she holed up on the front lines in her basement for real work. Most mornings she mentally prepped on her front porch with her notepad and a fresh cup of coffee. Survival schemes blurred into grocery lists and home repair to-dos and errands to run. She recorded the daily weather forecast for each family member's location. Clouds, rain, flood stages, snow, and ice were her love language. It's not that Grace didn't notice sunshine, but she saw the threats to her family more acutely.

The sounds of the neighborhood soothed her as she plotted, especially the peaceful seconds after the school buses carried the kids away. The houses sighed. Nacho stretched out on the rug by the front door. He'd let Grace know when their mailman, Jerry, dropped grocery flyers and bills in the slot or if an intruder tried to storm their castle. The mat at their threshold read *Welcome*, but no one really was. Even the distant call of the Thompsons' leaf blower brought calm. Maybe they were finally clearing the woodpile that was surely the cause of the recent chipmunk infestation. When the bird feeder rush hour chatter began, Grace made a note to refill the hummingbird nectar. She understood their spastic energy and territorial intensity. The tornado of tiny wings calmed her. She checked her list again and saw *duct tape* crossed off. So why wasn't it where she'd left it on her workbench? Nothing could highjack a day of prepping more than low supplies.

Grace yelled into the garage where she thought her husband was: "Robbie, did you take my duct tape again?" She didn't bother checking, just opened the door a slit and screamed again. "I bought a three-pack last week at Walmart, and two are missing!"

Robbie didn't answer. He was probably there behind the tool bench, in a lawn chair with a beer, but she couldn't see him without coming into the garage. Grace never came into the garage, and Robbie agreed not to go near the cellar. Their arrangement worked, mostly. Even when he said he was listening, he wasn't. He stared vacantly and agreed with a passive "okay," which Grace had learned meant nothing. Robbie rarely did what he said he would. After his heart attack a few years back, he promised to give up hamburgers but hadn't. Avoidance was his life's motto. He'd decided any disagreement was a criticism. *He is so fragile*, Grace thought. Early on, it was his vulnerability and shyness about his emotions that she found attractive. Now he thought her a nag whenever she spoke up. He should have married someone docile, someone without something to say. She thought he resented the tiny building her family had given them, even though it had kept them afloat. Loyalty was tricky. Sometimes you hate the thing you need the most. Grace had opinions, and because she felt unwanted in the business, she was using her smarts to prepare them for the inevitability of the world collapsing. There was no other way to live.

In the garage, Robbie usually busied himself with his ham radio, calling out to other operators as "Bug Guy." Beside his handheld and microphone was the framed license he'd earned from the FCC that allowed him to communicate on the amateur bands. Grace would have been annoyed by his hobby, but she was counting on his skill in crisis. She'd read it was the ham radio contact that kept New York City agencies in touch when their command center was destroyed on 9/11. At least, it was a contribution.

In the cellar, Grace began where she always began by unpacking and repacking the Bug Out Bags. It was a daily, meditative ritual. Among friends, Grace called them BOBs. First things first: grab and run. The blogs claimed that hunkering down and defending was the primary line of defense, but survivalists like her preferred an escape route. Her family rarely took her efforts seriously and never helped prepare—except for Kate, sometimes.

Grace didn't like the idea of relying on chemical concoctions, but the idea of being stuck indefinitely in a perfectly stocked cellar with her husband made her stash Valium. She'd peeled off the prescription label and wrote Emergency Use in a black Sharpie. Then she added MOM ONLY underneath. She'd decided not to share any Valium with Jules when she forced her to take an extra BOB with her to college. "What if it happens when you're away?" Grace had insisted. "You won't be prepared, and then what?"

"I'm hoping not to make it through the apocalypse, Mom," Jules had said, tossing the BOB on top of the rest of the boxes in her hatchback. "That's my plan. That and college so I can get out of this shithole town."

Grace had watched Jules's hot-pink The Princess Saves Herself bumper sticker get smaller and smaller. She'd wanted to take Jules to college together. There had been a 70 percent chance of rain that day. She'd wanted to move her daughter into her dorm like they do on the commercials, but Jules would have none of it. She packed herself and barely said goodbye. "It's only three hours away. It's not that big of a deal." But neither Grace nor Robbie had earned college degrees and it *was* a big deal, even if Jules was too stubborn to know it. Just like her dad. Three hours wasn't that far, Grace knew, except when a natural disaster hit or civil unrest broke out.

Jules was the daughter Grace worried about most and understood the least. Even as a toddler, she couldn't be contained. She was often trying to hurt herself by climbing things, like ladders in Robbie's garage, and stuffing herself into places, like the fireplace full of ash, and throwing herself in the way of things, like Maggie's new birthday bike. Jules was an unpredictable storm, and college was her latest forecast. Grace had watched her drive away in awe, lightning and all.

In the basement, Grace cranked up the volume of *The Rush Limbaugh Show* and shook out the contents of the six BOBs onto the worktable. She ran her hands over each carefully marked plastic bag. Seeing through the bags made her checklist easier, but sometimes she liked to unpack them and reorganize. It felt like an accomplishment in her otherwise mundane day. "The government is not going to save you," Rush explained, and Grace listened. She was a

God-fearing Catholic and believed the Bible when Isaiah said "the Lord will come in fire, and his chariots like the stormwind; To wreak his anger in burning rage and his rebuke in fiery flames." Grace's own mother had taught her that you do what you have to in order to survive, especially with limited resources. It was that simple, said the Good Book. At least now she could afford a few provisions. Grace would be ready. She'd hide until the first wave of violence ended. It could take years. Then she and her daughters would emerge, BOBs restocked on their backs, and do whatever they had to do. Her tribe would prevail. She assumed Robbie would trail behind them or take credit for the whole thing. He had skills, it was true, but what Grace wanted most was a partner, an equal match, someone as devoted as she was to surviving. She'd made a list of her husband's liabilities, and it wore her out. As far as she could tell, loving her kids too much was her only real weakness. She was prepared to do anything to save them.

Grace saw threats everywhere, which is what made BOBs so essential and challenging. Each BOB had the basics:

- folding shovel
- Marine Raider Bowie knife
- Gerber multi-tool
- fire starter items
- flashlight
- first aid kit (with QuikClot)
- crank radio
- rope
- water
- bottle with filter
- food bag (replaced once per year)
- hygiene items

- utensils
- bowl
- sewing kit
- work gloves
- extra socks
- tarp
- compass
- batteries
- Bible
- bullets

But she added a few extras for each:

- a journal with pencils for Jules, who liked to scribble
- a key chain stuffed animal for Kate, who, even at twelve, still slept with her army of dolls
- a romance novel for Tammy
- maps and markers to keep Maggie's mind occupied
- a full flask for Robbie
- lipstick and night cream in the secret pocket of her personal BOB

Grace patted her .38 Special, tucked in an underarm holster, and stroked the loaded Ruger 10/22. Robbie preferred his 9 mm Glock G19 and never left home without it. His one big contribution, besides funding their preparation, was devising the code phrase Grace agreed to for when the Shit Hit The Fan—SHTF for short among preppers—and they needed to bolt. "How 'bout 'It's time for business'?" Robbie offered, and she'd nodded because it was perfect, even if he'd come up with it.

Grace repacked each labeled bag and loaded them back onto

the metal shelves that lined the basement walls. By her count, their pantry could last them two years if they used the generator sparingly, but they'd have to barter for gas. She'd stocked dozens of Jim Beam bottles for trade. She'd buried two propane tanks in the backyard. They could live on Grace's garden alone for years, unless the marauders raided it. She canned every ounce she could and fed them the rest to save on the grocery bill. Of course Robbie would have to go out hunting some, and she'd be the one to dress and cook the meat. She'd watched her own father take an animal apart from nose to tail and use every inch. Secretly, Grace suspected that most survivalists wanted to test their prepping skills just to show the government how little they needed their help. She made her family do drills, but she already knew that they'd survive because she made sure they were ready. Her lists. Her plans. Her mental strength and will. Grace was on alert because she had to be. She was a survivor, and she alone would save her family. It was her calling in life, her greatest responsibility.

She scanned the shelves again thinking maybe she'd already brought the duct tape down and had blamed Robbie for nothing. When she couldn't locate the extra rolls, she fumed all over again, stomped up the stairs, and called the office.

"Fehler Family Exterminating, Jenn speaking."

"Jenn who?" Grace asked, sipping a lukewarm cup of coffee.

"Jenn-I'm-new-here-what's-it-to-you?"

"Huh. You're something, aren't you? This is Mrs. Fehler. I need you to send over a technician with two rolls of duct tape." She smashed the phone between her ear and shoulder and cleaned out the coffeepot with her free hands.

"You want to speak to Mr. Fehler?"

"No. I want you to call one of the guys from the back room. Trust me—whoever is back there isn't doing anything useful. Put two rolls of duct tape from the stockroom in his hands, and tell him to drive to my house."

"Hold on. I'll get Maggie."

Grace was in the basement loading the flashlights with batteries, testing them, and unloading them again, when Travis came down the steps ten minutes later. He hadn't knocked. He paused at the base of the stairs, spun a roll of duct tape in each hand, and parked them at his waist like six-shooters. "Heard somebody needs to be taped up," he said, blowing on a roll like it was smoking.

"Seriously, Travis? They sent you?" Her face twitched into a smile, but she busied herself testing the flints. Her mother had once told her, "Never look too available, especially when it comes to men. They prefer the chase."

"Ain't you glad to see me, Grace?" Travis pleaded like a puppy. His friendly, wide smile pulled down into a pout. He puffed up his chest and focused his soft brown eyes on her. He was good at sales. Getting him hired at Fehlers' was surprisingly easy and mostly convenient. Robbie vastly underappreciated his skills, but Grace saw his value.

"I'm glad to see you—just not in my house."

"Don't see nobody home."

Grace looked at her watch. "Kate and Tammy's school bus will be here in exactly twenty-seven minutes."

Travis closed the space between them, dropped to his knees in front of Grace's waist, and offered the duct tape. Grace took both rolls and stacked them neatly. She leaned away to cross the tape off her list again. Then Travis rose, put his hands around her backside, and laid Grace out on the workbench. "You are so strong," he said, sliding his hands up her plump thighs. She kissed him back, thrilled that when the world ended, basic instincts would prevail.

She blushed to have someone else in control. She trusted Travis, and he made her feel safe in a world where she never felt safe. He admired her lists and carefully considered the details of each of her plans. When Travis had joined their local preppers assembly, she knew immediately that he took survival as seriously as she did. Robbie had been skipping the meetings for months, and Grace had to go alone.

Maybe Robbie would perish first and this affair wouldn't even be a sin. She'd said extra Hail Marys on her rosary every night since it began. She'd even broken it off a few times, hating how calm she felt with Travis. When the end of the world came, she'd pray on her knees and repent, she promised. But first, this.

Grace undressed him quickly to get the smell of his uniform out of her nose. The last thing she wanted to think about right now was the family business or the business of the family. This was about endurance and survival. Together, they could do both. Travis strengthened the hive, even as he threatened it. This was how she made sure her daughters would be safe. Her checklist fell to the floor, and the duct tape soon followed.

3

Tammy

Fifty cars or more waited on the weekends to hear the little boy's ghost scream. The dirt road outside Screaming Johnny's, or what was left of the burned-out Old School Baptist Church, was littered with soda cans and cheeseburger wrappers. Church hadn't been held in the abandoned building on the outskirts of Cape Girardeau since 1913, but townies like Tammy and her boyfriend, Wade, still came for services.

They'd met on Memorial Day at the Dairy Queen off Kings Highway, where she worked the drive-through. She'd handed Wade a triple-dipped cone with extra sprinkles, and he kept coming back for more napkins until she said she'd go out with him. She was used to the attention. Tammy knew she was the prettiest of the sisters; men had leered at her from a much too early age and called her a "little flirt" as she hammed it up, popped out a hip, and blew old-timers kisses. Meeting Wade and dating boys was easy for Tammy. It made her feel powerful in a house where she wasn't. But Wade was both eager and earnest. She liked his honesty, and it flattered her that he always wanted to know more about what she was reading. Tammy preferred mysteries and romances mostly, sometimes motivational self-help stuff and financial how-tos, but she certainly didn't share that with Wade. When he helped her practice answering possible questions she might get asked in the Miss Cape Girardeau Pageant, Wade really listened. He didn't only nod along. He'd pause and then ask more questions like he was fascinated by everything she had to say.

Tammy thought it was cute that Wade had vacuumed his car for their four-month anniversary night and propped up a single red rose in the ashtray. It showed he cared. She'd decided to tell him that night. She knew he'd be there for her, no matter what.

"For me?" Tammy said, sliding into the beige bucket seat and snatching up the rose. She tossed the umbrellas and stupid rain poncho her mom had forced on her into the back seat, then clenched the rose between her teeth and growled like she'd seen Kim Kardashian do on TV. Tammy loved Kim's glamour and poutiness, and she practiced puckering her lips in the mirror the same.

At least three TVs perpetually blared in the Fehlers' house, usually on different channels. Grace studied FOX News and answered the customer calls that came in from Fehler Family Exterminating on a separate phone line—when she felt like it, anyway, and wasn't busy in a tizzy over the end of the world. Tammy and her sisters fought over *Gilmore Girls* reruns and *Project Runway*. If her dad made it home from work at a decent hour, which he rarely did, he called out the letters on *Wheel of Fortune* with his first beer of the night. Tammy didn't even like TV except for *Keeping Up with the Kardashians*; she thought of the show as more of an instructional business model rather than a vapid reality show. Sure, she loved the fashion, but she also saw that Kim's shrewd ways equaled money, and what was wrong with that? Tammy could see herself making money one day—not the kind of barely surviving her parents did in the family business, but real money and certainly not as a bug girl.

Wade took the rose out of her mouth and kissed her. Tammy could tell he was anxious to do a lot more.

"Wait, Wade. My dad is still watching from the window. *Wheel of Fortune* just finished, and he's got nothing better to do. Next he'll get his shotgun and stand on the porch as a joke. Let's go somewhere. You said you'd take me to Screaming Johnny's."

"The line is crazy. We'll waste all my gas."

"You promised. It's our anniversary!" Tears stung Tammy's eyes, and it surprised her.

"Calm down." On the car radio, the local sports update cut into Taylor Swift's "Our Song." The Cape Girardeau High Miners had lost again to the Troy Panthers: 17 to 0. Embarrassing. No one in Cape Girardeau felt much like celebrating, not even Tammy and Wade's Catholic school friends who were often rowdier than the public school ones. Wade's brother had texted that the barn party at Schmitty's had an almost empty beer keg and three bottles of peach schnapps—for the girls. It had to be at least a little better to drive through the cemetery and see if they heard Screaming Johnny.

She wanted to remember this night and have a real talk with Wade, to see how strong their relationship was.

"You promised," she whined again, running her hand over his biceps. He flexed beneath her fingers. She told herself not to get emotional, but she couldn't stop how she was feeling. Not anymore. Not really ever.

Twenty minutes later, Wade pulled up in line behind a pickup and killed the engine. "It'll be awhile, I'm sure," he said. A loud crack in the sky, like a bat hitting a ball in the sweet spot, made Wade jump. Tammy smiled at his scare but didn't tease him. Maggie had once told her, "Boys hate when you call them wimps, and then they do stupid stuff to prove they're not."

Tammy listened to the rain beat on the roof like kids throwing tantrums. She pressed her hands against it to feel the vibrations and rhythm. Then she pointed to the vehicle in front. "That's Aiden Conley's truck—but that ain't his girl." She folded her legs underneath her for a better view. "Can't quite see." She rolled down her window and stretched her neck. Wet hair blanketed her face. She closed her eyes against the rain.

"Roll that up!" Wade called. "You're going to get the seat wet!"

"But I think I hear something." Rumor was that "Johnny" was an eight-year-old boy who'd played too close to an open water well. Even after he drowned and folks filled the hole with dirt, he kept screaming. The story didn't scare Tammy; it excited her.

Wade tugged on her jean pocket and then pulled her back in the car by her shoulders. "It's not a ghost. Those seats are genuine pleather."

"All you care about is this stupid car. You don't even care about me!"

Wade reached across her lap and rolled up the window. "That's not true and you know it." He lowered his voice to a whisper. "You're my girl, Tammy."

"Whatever." Tammy flipped the radio off. She didn't feel like his girl. She felt bloated and worried. What if she told him and he was super mad?

Wade inched the car forward one spot. There were still dozens in front of them. The line stretched around the turn in the road. Screaming Johnny's wasn't even in sight yet. "I told you there'd be a line."

"At least we can cuddle," she said, climbing halfway over into Wade's lap. He stuck his hand up her shirt and cut the engine again. She was glad she'd shaved her armpits in case he brushed them with his groping. Tammy stopped him just before he unhooked her bra. Her breasts ached, and she didn't want anyone touching them. "First, I got to say something."

"Uh-huh," he mumbled and unbuttoned the top of her jeans.

"No, wait," Tammy said. Then she whispered in his ear, "I think I'm pregnant." She wasn't sure. She'd missed her period, but she hadn't taken a test yet. She couldn't tell her mom. She hadn't even told Maggie yet, and all the sisters went to her first.

Wade pulled back his hands like Tammy's skin was on fire. "No way."

"Maybe."

"Tammy, you don't 'maybe' a baby."

"I'm late."

"How late?"

"A month." Tammy had been tallying up the weeks since Wade's uncle's farm, after the summer flooding. It was entirely possible. Probable, even. But she had been flicking the thought away each time it crept in.

"Shit."

Tammy looked out the window at the rain and wondered whether Kim K. had had an abortion and whether she felt guilty about it as a sort-of Catholic. If she was going to do it, she shouldn't have even told Wade. None of it felt real; it couldn't be. A knock on the driver's window startled them both. She covered her unbuttoned pants and slid back across to her seat. "Car's stalled up ahead," Aiden said when Wade rolled down the glass. "It's going to be awhile. Pass it on."

It was Wade's turn to get wet and tell the car behind them. He sprinted through the rain. Soaked, he climbed back into the car and pulled a Cardinals fleece blanket from the back seat. "Here," he said, spreading the baseball bird logo smooth on her lap and tucking the blanket around her. They both settled in for the wait. Wade opened his mouth to say something else, but Tammy was already crying. She didn't even necessarily know why she was crying. The maybe baby, of course, but everything felt so big these days. Usually it was Jules who was all ragey, but Tammy was pissed and then sad all at the same time when the toilet paper roll ran out this morning and she couldn't reach another from the stool. She'd had to call Maggie in to save her, which of course she did.

"I don't want to get stuck in Cape, Wade. Not like this." She wiped her snot on the blanket. "If I'm pregnant, that's it. That's my whole future. I can't be Miss Cape with a big, fat belly, you jerk." She knew she should care more about a possible pregnancy than a pageant, but she didn't. Not yet.

Wade shook his head, either at the snot or at what Tammy had said. He tucked a wet curl behind her ear and traced her jawline with his finger.

"You're going to have to work at Fehlers', you know?" she said. "You've got to get a job."

"I will," he said, taking her hand.

"Or else . . ."

"Or else what?"

"You know."

Wade punched the steering wheel with his palm. The rain beaded in straight lines on Tammy's window, but it was a quiet pitter-patter now. Wade had said he was practically guaranteed a basketball scholarship. He'd made the varsity team his freshman year. The whole town had told him he was that good. But it didn't matter how good he was if he was going to be a daddy. Tammy knew a lot of townies who were has-beens. They'd had babies young too.

"Goddamn it," Tammy said, thinking he'd handled the news better than she expected. "In all my dreams, I never wanted to be a bug girl."

4

Kate

It was the Assumption of the Blessed Virgin Mary, and Kate and her sisters wore corsages of lilies their dad bought yesterday at Save A Lot half-priced. He'd pinned them on clumsily above each chest, almost centered, or resting awkwardly on a shoulder. Grace took them from his shaky hands and did it herself. "You drink too much coffee," she mumbled with pins pressed between her lips. She moved Kate's pink bud from her shoulder to a spot above her heart. Kate saw fury in her mom's face. She'd heard her up all night in the cellar basement with the radio blaring, shelving and reshelving, packing and repacking, prepping when she couldn't sleep from the worry. Grace flung off the dried baby's breath and greenery, letting them fall to the floor, and eyed Robbie until he understood he should pick them up. "Can't you get the elastic wrists next time?"

Kate noticed the tiny pinpricks her dad's attempt left in her black sweater, but she didn't mind. She thought it was sweet the way he remembered flowers. That's how she felt, but she sided with her mom instead; it was safer and expected. "Yeah, Dad. It's weird. Like you're taking us all to the prom or something." Kate slipped Nacho a piece of bacon leftover from breakfast. She had other secrets too.

"We're late. Again," Maggie said a few minutes later as she rushed into the room in a peach skirt paired with a floppy white blouse, paused for the pinning, and grabbed car keys off the tiled art project Jules had made in kindergarten. In the brightest red she could find, Jules had splashed *Mom* and *Dad* and *Sissy* above the key hooks. The Fehler family refused to use their assigned hooks, though, so Maggie and Tammy mixed up keys and blamed each other. Both had a set of keys to the used Chevy Impala they were supposed to share, but Tammy mostly grabbed rides with Wade. For Christmas last year, Kate had bought all her sisters key chains with bedazzled letters—*M*, *J*, *T*, and *K* for her future driving self—but the system brought only momentary harmony.

"I'm ready," Kate announced. "Dad is already in the car." She'd seen him slip out. Kate tracked the members of her hive and noted their moods. Sometimes, when they were apart, she wished she had echolocation, not only for navigation and foraging, but so she could jam signals between them that would avoid fights later. She saw and heard, even when her sisters and parents didn't speak.

"Of course he is," Grace sneered. "Didn't even think to run the dishwasher."

Tammy came into the kitchen still in her pajamas. "I'll do it, Mom. It's my turn to load."

"Why aren't you dressed? I am not going to walk in after Father Tom's procession again, especially with the O'Neils watching."

Tammy shrugged and turned to lean heavily on the counter. Kate saw her sister plead with Maggie. Whatever the ask was it wasn't about her outfit. Tammy looked good in anything. She could wear a potato sack and the whole church would look at only her. Kate preferred neutrals and steered clear of Tammy's hand-me-downs. Too many loud colors. Too many low necks and short skirts. She had little to fill the shirts with anyway. None of it mattered when the Earth was about to expire. She found it hard to take fashion seriously with the recent setback on the Doomsday Clock. Only her mother understood that humans are dismantling our planet and we have to face those consequences. Her sisters ignored it. She couldn't even convince Tammy to stop drinking out of disposable plastic bottles.

Grace put her hands on her hips. "God doesn't care what you wear to church! Except a sweater. It's chilly. Everyone grab an extra sweater." Kate knew there were extra heat sources in each BOB in the back of the truck. They'd never freeze. Not with the Earth warming so rapidly.

"It's probably her period again, Mom. She was hogging the bathroom. You go on. I'll drive her. Save us a seat," Maggie said. Kate thought there might be more. She'd been studying Tammy extra close, even charting and timing her bathroom visits in her diary. Kate liked data and predictions. It helped regulate temperatures and outcomes. She cataloged the real threats: climate change, deforestation, pollution, loss of biodiversity, melting polar ice caps, rising sea levels, oceanic dead zones, and population growth. Her mom's prepping could save them from only some of these, but at least it was something.

In the front seat of the truck, Kate tucked herself between her parents and pretended, for a moment, that she was an only child, swimming in their adoration. She thought her mom, who was herself the middle daughter of four brothers, understood how hard it was to be seen in a crowded family that was also a family business. Grace had grown up in her father's butcher shop with her own mother working the front counter as cashier. With all her brothers off in Vietnam, Grace told her that she had learned to be useful, mopping blood off the floors, salting carcasses, and wrapping cuts of meat for sale. Kate didn't blame her for not wanting to work at

Fehlers'. Her mom wanted to be more than labor. Prepping was her purpose, her calling. Kate had seen her grandparents only in pictures. They both fell to the flu months after her birth. Poor people weren't that healthy. Their black-and-white portraits in the hallway of family pictures rarely spoke up. And if they had spoken, Kate would have been the only one listening. She absolutely believed in ghosts. She couldn't say exactly why, but they didn't scare her at all.

Ten minutes after Father Tom had read the first scripture, Maggie and Tammy slipped into the pew during the responsorial psalm and crawled over their mom, kissing her cheek for forgiveness and slipping Kate a piece of gum. Robbie had refused to scoot over from his post. He sat at the end of the pew, as Kate knew the men in Blessed Family Catholic Church tended to do. He hung his hairy arm over the aisle, as if he might reach out and punch the incense fumes Father Tom had just swung in their direction. He nodded at Mr. O'Neil across the aisle, and Kate saw him return a smirk. He, too, was a rooster guarding precious, unruly hens.

The O'Neils had the curse of four daughters also, and each had arrived and been baptized almost simultaneously with the Fehler sisters. Two were now off to college. Two remained but sat with enough distance between them that Kate guessed how their morning went. Robbie wrinkled his brow at the sisters as he carefully moved a peppermint candy around in his mouth. There was a tiny "click" as the candy settled on enamel. Kate wondered if Mr. O'Neil liked mints too. She knew from CCD class with Ashley, the daughter closest to her age, that he certainly liked beer and lots of it. So did Father Tom. Sometimes they even drank together, but Kate assumed whatever you did in the presence of a priest wasn't a sin.

Mrs. Randolph's voice sounded like a dying bird behind them. She gurgled and chirped through pursed lips a beat behind the choir. Everything about her reminded Kate of a coil: tightly wound hair, narrow glasses, taut shoulders. Mrs. Vicker, equally pinched, sat to the left and a pew in front and cleaned out the contents of her purse onto the bench. She made a production of searching for her checkbook and writing out the numbers, coughing at the task. Black fuzz framed the line of her lips, and the hacking caused her chin whiskers to wiggle, seemingly in time with the hymn, "Be Not Afraid."

Kate had to pee. She hadn't gone before they left the house because she wanted to be the first sister to the truck, hoping someone might notice. She couldn't hold it any longer, all that orange juice she'd gulped for breakfast. "Sorry," she whispered to her mom. "Sorry," she said scooting past her dad. "Sorry," she nodded to the usher who held the door for her exit. Jules always said, "You don't need to apologize for breathing, Kate," but Kate couldn't help it. That her parents' fourth and final try resulted in a girl made apology her life's motto.

In the bathroom, Kate sat on the handicap toilet as two church elders washed their hands and gossiped. "Well, that one is completely out of control. Her poor parents," one of them said.

"My sister is the secretary at the high school. She said the oldest one is decent but the rest are trouble. That middle one is fast. I'll bet their parents wished they were boys," the other one answered. "At least boys can't get pregnant."

"Amen to that. Seems like such a godly family. Don't know what went wrong!"

"I know. I know. Poor things. And that mother."

"Butcher's daughter. My mother used to get her meat there."

"At least she was raised in the church."

"They sent one off to college, yeah?"

"I think so, but the youngest kind of looks like a boy."

Kate had heard enough, and she had to get back to their pew. She swung the stall door wide. The women stared like she was intruding on their private conversation, which she was. Kate swallowed an apology. "Excuse me," she said, moving to the sink, where she washed her hands twice to show that her mother had raised her right and bit her tongue not to apologize for taking so long. Her cheeks burned like *she* was the one in the wrong. Kate didn't care about the stupid things the stupid ladies said, but she hated the attention. It embarrassed her and made her want to hide, but a tiny smile also creeped onto her face that these old biddies had said she blended in like a boy.

Back in the pew, Kate mouthed the Nicene Creed and reached into her mom's purse for the check she'd deposit in the Offertory basket when the usher slid the woven basket on a stick her way. But the checkbook with its smooth gray cover wasn't there. Her hand settled on something hard and cold instead. Her mom poked the small of Tammy's back, urging her to sit up straight. Kate brought the plastic ivory purse into her lap for a closer inspection and straightened her own back like a board. Tucked beneath Grace's cherry lip balm and breath mints was a pistol. Kate knew guns. She'd shot her dad's rifle plenty at aluminum cans on posts on the side of the road in the country. She'd seen a handgun in the glove compartment wrapped tight in a plaid kitchen towel. But this was church; this was something different. When did her mom start carrying a gun? Why did she bring it to Mass? Wasn't she scared it might go off during the gospel? Missouri had open carry laws—she'd learned that in school—but still.

Feeling the gun made Kate remember the time she'd had strep throat and her mom had told her a story about sneaking around. "I was thinking," Grace had said in the soft voice she reserved for her daughters' fevers, nightmares, tummy aches, and scorching hot summer days, “how one Christmas morning—my brothers must have been little, five, seven, eight, nine—we unwrapped all the presents under the tree early. I could still see the moon outside over the barn. Anyway, Mama and Daddy came out in their nightclothes and found us already playing with the toys—airplanes, trucks, wheelie things for boys that I had to play with too. Mama stood there, and Daddy walked straight out the front door and sat in his cold car until lunch. It was out of gas. They'd spent the gas money on our Christmas presents. So Daddy was stuck with us, and we weren't even that sorry.” The story had made Kate sad. Her mom's wanting had an edge, like she couldn't trust anyone in the whole world. Grace lived on the defensive, anticipating the next attack. Kate felt the same way when her science teacher reviewed the impact of climate change even though he wasn't allowed to call it global warming. They all knew what it was. Their parents had ruined the planet for them.

“Get out of there,” Grace said, swatting Kate's hands. “I haven't written the check yet.” She zipped the purse and placed it on the other side of the bench. “Don't snoop and don't sneak. How many times have I told you that?”

Kate didn't say anything. She had questions that wouldn't be answered. She accepted the loopy cursive paper for *fifteen dollars* made out to *Blessed Family*, placed the paper in the basket when an usher waved it under her nose, and stared at the bloody body of Jesus hanging above the alter.

5
Jules

Jules didn't want to go to the Fehler Family Fish Camp for the weekend. She had a paper due for Introduction to Accounting, and she'd just picked up her reserved copy of *The Collected Poems of Emily Dickinson* from the library. She'd be missing a major meeting of the Young Republicans and she was considering running for president next semester if Sean, the senior who'd already announced his candidacy, had mono as rumored. Maybe she had started the rumor. Maybe she wasn't even a Republican anymore. She'd been raised conservative, but she didn't feel conservative. She'd been raised Catholic, but she found all religion bullshit. She couldn't stop poking at things, her mom said, but Jules didn't see why that was so bad.

"The only thing I ask, Jules," Robbie insisted when he'd promised to pay her tuition to the University of Missouri, "is that you try to join us at the camp once a month. That's it. If Mississippi River Metro Business College isn't good enough for you, fancy pants, fine, but don't forget where you're from." Jules doubted a couple hundred miles north on I-55 and I-70 would give her proper amnesia. In the Fehler family, she was the rebel, the risk taker. Her outsides rarely matched her insides. She was as stubborn as her dad, and her mom rarely missed a chance to throw shade on her for it. She was also as anxious as her mom, and her dad liked to tell her just to calm down.

For all his teasing, though, Robbie was the one who helped her apply to college. He sat at the kitchen table filling out financial aid forms, even as he complained about the government in his business. When she got her admission letter, her mom bought her the purple Doc Martens combat boots Jules had begged for since her sophomore year in high school. She could talk Grace into anything if it was for survival.

Robbie had thought classes three days a week meant Jules might come home to work in the office the other days. "It's not like you're going to be busy. I saw your schedule. You could even do sales calls up there. Expand our territory a little, you know?"

Jules had rolled her eyes. "Those are my study days—for research and papers." Robbie also pestered her for taking Lit 110: Introduction to Poetry and for papering her dorm walls with vintage Equal Rights Amendment posters. "But the Republicans supported the ERA before the Democrats, Dad," Jules had explained, taping the corners tight. "Ask Eisenhower. Or Ford." She turned up the volume on Coldplay and alphabetized her poetry collections: Gwendolyn Brooks, Lucille Clifton, Carol Ann Duffy, Audre Lorde, Adrienne Rich, Anne Sexton. It was nice to have friends on her desk who understood Jules's own demons.

"But why are you even taking it if it's not a business class? You're a business major. Business is what Fehlers do." *It may not be what I do*, Jules thought but couldn't say. He was paying her bill. Maggie was always telling her to stop stirring up trouble; Jules recommended Maggie stir up a little of her own.

On her dorm room wall, she hung her navy Mary Daly poster—"Beyond God the Father: Toward a Philosophy of Women's Liberation." Jules's parents told her the saying was blasphemous and made her move it from her sisters' shared bathroom to over her bed, as if feminism might be contagious. "It's a Gen Ed. I told you. It's required." She had explained the Gen Ed program, extensively, to her mom and dad, but they complained that it was stupid to pay for those credits at university when she could take the same class at the community college for half the price. Jules knew it wasn't the same class. Half of those classes were online and taught by underpaid part-time faculty. But she was still learning how to navigate college herself and couldn't convince her parents. It wasn't only that they'd never been to university; it was that Jules was now living in a foreign land, and she was learning a language they'd never speak. And she liked it.

Just as Jules was trying to muster up a tickle in her throat that might excuse her from family camp, her phone buzzed. It was Niko. His third text that morning: we need to talk plz call.

She'd sworn off relationships when she went to college. She didn't want the distractions. meet me at mconalds now, she typed back. She had enough time for fries and a strawberry milkshake before her drive home.

Niko was waiting. He'd already ordered her food. She sniffed melted cheese and imagined the juicy burger. As a newly converted vegetarian, she hadn't quite mastered McDonald's without a burger.

"What's up?" Jules asked, straddling the plastic yellow stool.

Niko held out a Happy Meal Lego Batman toy. He'd paid the extra dollar because it might make her smile. Jules worried about the waste, especially during the recession, which Maggie reminded her of relentlessly. "S'up with you?" he asked back, raising his eyebrows. "You left early, didn't leave a note, and ignored my calls."

"Keeping it casual. Isn't that what you said?" Jules had spent the night before in his room at an off-campus party in the house he rented with four guys. A keg of PBR in the kitchen, red Solo cups, Bruno Mars booming in her chest while she wished it were Kendrick Lamar, and the inevitable knock of police at 2:00 a.m. *It all seemed like such a cliché,* Jules thought, *except the Niko part.* Nothing about Niko was a cliché. Everything he did was original, and Jules was struggling to keep it cool.

"It may have been what I said, at first, but it's not what I meant. Not now."

"Not now, why?" Jules dipped her fries in the frothy ice cream. Salty and sweet, her favorite combination.

Niko swiped a fry. "Because I like you."

Jules kept her eyes on her shake and didn't respond. If she looked up, she'd give herself away. It felt good to be liked, especially by someone as badass as Niko, but falling for a guy the first month on campus was not in her plans. Figuring a way out of her inevitable Fehler future and finding artsy friends was first on her agenda. But then Niko came along. "I told you about my family. We have this camp thing this weekend."

"I can come with you, if you want," Niko offered. "It'd take me five minutes to pack."

She thought of Niko's delicious king bed and then pictured double sets of bunk beds at the camp. "My sisters would eat you alive. My parents might have a fit."

"Why? Girls love me."

"Because you're Black, Niko."

Jules didn't lower her voice the way her family did when they discussed race. "It's not *all* colored people," Robbie had once clarified over a debate about the politics of welfare, "it's only *some* of them." She'd asked who "them" was, but her dad had told her to wash the dishes and clean up, as if domesticity was a punishment. She didn't move from the dinner table. "Actually, corporations take more welfare than individuals. Welfare fraud is a misconception.

We think it's higher than it really is. The media perpetuates these stereotypes too," she'd said, but he ignored her and slid his plate across the table. Jules cleaned the kitchen but left his plate exactly where it was. "It's 'people of color,' Dad. No one says 'colored people' anymore." She knew it fell on deaf ears. Robbie used outdated language because the world hadn't changed much for him. He hadn't had a reason to change, and he considered the world order just right.

She'd decided not to whisper at all anymore. Or apologize. Why did so many of her classmates start their sentences with "I'm sorry but . . ."? What were they sorry for? Her mother had taught her how to behave, too, but when Niko called her dangerous, she felt fierce. He said a lot of other nice things about a lot of her parts, but Jules was suspicious of compliments.

"Actually, I'm biracial. My dad is Black, but my mom is Japanese American."

"Where I'm from, you're Black." Jules said, like she was looking at him for the first time. She wanted to trace his wide cheekbones and thick brow and sketch them in her journal.

Niko cleared his throat. "Yeah, well where I'm from, you are what you tell people you are." There was an edge to his voice that Jules found sexy. He had a calm authority, and she was stunned by his confidence. Niko did look different with clothes on. She wasn't distracted by muscle lines and toned abs. She hadn't wondered about his eyes before, how they reminded her of the cool Mississippi mud off her family's dock. She liked how Niko carried himself in a slow, calm saunter.

"You can tell them my roommate is from Old Appleton. He says it's practically the same town as yours."

"Old Appleton wishes it was," Jules said. She'd been there once after a wrong turn on a dirt road with her prom date. The most interesting thing about the night had been the sign on Highway

61 declaring Apple Creek. Her prom date had wanted to make out, but Jules had little interest in foreplay or Charles "Chaz" Murphy III. Even his name was lame. Chaz lasted twelve seconds when she'd gone down on him in the front seat of his car. What a waste of the perfectly good condom she'd swiped from a box she'd found in Maggie's room—like her sister, the good Catholic girl, was going to use them. After, Jules lied about her curfew so she could go home early and google the history of Apple Creek: Founded in 1824. Pierre Louis Lorimier. Named for Riviere a la Pomme. In 1982 a flood destroyed McClain Mill and their original bridge. The prom was lame too. She'd fought an urge to leave the stupid dance and walk to the bus station, to go anywhere but where she was.

The farthest she'd ever been from Missouri was her junior year trip to Washington, D.C. Staring at the Lincoln Memorial, Jules learned if you hug the side of a tall building, you never even feel the rain. If you duck under someone's umbrella on H Street, you can tell if they had garlic and onions for last night's dinner. When she and her classmates got caught in the downpour, they all looked like wet puppies. Jules was intoxicated by the anonymity of the city. She'd wandered into a bookstore, found a poetry section, and was overwhelmed when all the words on the page added up to exactly what she'd felt and seen and couldn't say. A panic attack rose in her chest, but it was the first time anxiety was exhilarating rather than debilitating. She couldn't wait to get out of Cape and Fehler Family Exterminating and the trap it promised.

"Wait," Niko held up his hand like a stop sign and pushed the rest of the fries toward her. "We should . . . you know, talk."

"What's there to talk about?" Jules crossed her arms and felt down into her sleeves where her scars were. The smooth skin from clean cuts soothed her. "We've been hanging out only a week. Or so."

Jules knew it had been four weeks because it was the last time she cut herself. Niko had declared himself a literature major with an emphasis on Harlem Renaissance writers, and Jules had asked for his number. She'd never been to the West Coast and certainly couldn't imagine a place like Portland, Oregon, but she liked how far away his hometown sounded. Niko's hands were often on her, resting on her knee, touching her shoulder, his fingers playing with her palm. It was how he inhabited his body and the space around him that electrified her. He'd traced the red lines on her inner thigh and noted their symmetry. She had a feeling he knew what they were, but neither of them said anything. With Niko, a bit of the angst in her belly was gone. She wasn't in *love* love; she felt relief and release. It was hard to explain. She didn't want to think about it too much, didn't want to dampen the urgency he seemed to feel for her. Maybe Niko was in *love* love, or maybe he was enjoying the chase and he'd be gone once she gave him more attention. Jules thought the game was exhausting though.

Niko didn't take his eyes off her. "Come on. You could teach me to fish."

"You've never gone fishing? Seriously?"

"I'm a fast learner."

Which was entirely true, Jules knew, especially in bed. He seemed to enjoy watching her pleasure more than his own. "You'd be bored. All we talk about is the business."

"What kind of business?"

"My family is in the pest control business." She expected Niko to not understand, but he did. In fact, he leaned in to listen. "It's corny and weird, I know. But it's what my family does. Fourth generation. We kill bugs. It pays the bills. I thought I told you all that."

"Work is work. I respect that. And you barely tell me anything." Niko was right. Jules did often redirect the conversation. She was fascinated by Niko's story. His father was a musician, and his mother was a therapist. They'd lived in Brazil. They spoke three languages. Niko was raised far from the life she'd known on the banks of the Mississippi River.

"The business talk leads to fights anyway. Usually Maggie—that's my oldest sister—has to fix it all."

Niko used her straw to spear the Day-Glo maraschino cherry. Then he finished her milkshake without asking. Gathering her things, she got up to leave. "I gotta run. You can finish my fries," she called over her shoulder and bumped open the glass door with her backside.

"Jules?" Niko called. "I'll miss you." The Lego Batman held up his arms toward her.

She stopped in the parking lot and made a beating heart with hands pumping toward him. Then she watched him lean back on the plastic bench like he owned the whole damn place.

6

Grace

Grace was knitting in the front seat while Robbie drove. At least she was *trying* to knit; the needles kept slipping, and she had to stop and hunt around on the floorboards of the truck to find them. She was determined to increase her skill set, and she'd decided knitting was one way. Last week at her survivalist meeting they'd discussed abilities they could trade or barter when their stockpiles ran out. Travis had shared that he'd recently taken up beer brewing; Grace was proud of his potential and hoped his skill building was going better than hers. Knitting wasn't coming naturally, but she'd managed something that might be a sock or maybe a baby's hat. She'd need to use her duct tape, though, to hold the sides together. Her mother had always said, "Do and make do," and Grace tried to, especially in her marriage.

Grace had loved Robbie since they were kids. "When you marry at eighteen, you grow up together. That's how it works," her mother had said. "You stay. You endure." Grace couldn't explain any of this to Travis, and she'd barely tried. He wasn't begging her to run off into the sunset. Theirs was a necessary partnership with benefits. She'd seen a few sunsets in life, and they were mostly hot and sticky with swarms of biting flies.

She couldn't rationalize her devotion or her anger, but they were both solely directed at Robbie. They were stuck together, in this swarm, and it wasn't always bad. Like their daughters. Like the silly family camp that Grace adored. She loved being on the water and away with her people where life was simpler, more manageable for the boiling down, and safer because they were far from the threats of the world. Besides, they had their BOBs and she'd stocked the cramped camp as best she could. There was more to do and her fears multiplied daily, especially with the election and all the talk about the economy crashing. Grace could feel the buzz building to a frenzy.

"Can you believe it? Three seventy-two. That's ridiculous," Robbie said, passing another gas station on their way to camp.

"Sure beats the four dollars and eleven cents we were paying all summer," Grace answered. "Aunt Jane said they were paying double up in St. Louis."

Gas prices were safe territory for a rocky marriage of twenty-one years. She didn't have the heart to tell Robbie that one day his bug killing skills would be worthless. He'd probably need to learn how to cook grubs for dinner instead.

"Look at that. Three eighty-four. Unbelievable." He nodded out the window at a Speedway gas station. There wasn't a single car at the pumps.

"The nerve. It'll be worse if Obama wins. The whole damn economy will probably collapse." Grace wanted to broach the subject of something bigger. Getting Robbie outraged about the election and gas prices was a good way to start. They'd cataloged the way the country was going to hell and the media dismissed the Midwest. One day they'd get their candidate and all the folks who thought the middle of the country didn't matter would have to listen. The news covered the coasts and ignored the middle. Robbie's resentment grew. These days, he blamed everything on Washington. "So, at my prep meeting last week, we talked about alternative bases, like places to get to that are already stocked. If we lived in the country, it'd be different, but what with the neighbors so close, we might want to think about something else."

"Something else? Like what? You've got us stocked for years in our basement, Gracie. What more do you want?" Robbie turned up the weather report on the radio. She knew he was hoping for good fishing weather. They were hosting the company party at camp the next day and rain would push them all into the house, which could barely hold the Fehlers.

Kate spoke up from the back seat, "Bees are preppers too. When they're getting ready to swarm, worker bees make these things called queen cups. The queen lays eggs in them—you know, to make all the baby bees—and they store the cups until they're capped. But here's the thing—they keep a remnant colony stocked too. Like a base camp with supplies."

"That's right," Robbie nodded, as if he'd said it himself.

Grace saw Kate's proud face and decided it was best to build on that. "See? Like Kate said. Just hear me out. I was thinking since we've got all that land at the camp. You know your father would have wanted us safe. That's why he bought up all the acres. So we could bury something out there, like a storage container or something. They're cheap enough. The hole isn't, of course, but the unit itself isn't much. I could help with the digging until we need a backhoe."

"Still sounds expensive. It's a tough time to be spending. Recession and all. But you know we have got to hold on until we can fix this country." Robbie kept his eyes on the road, but he reached over to Grace's lap and held her hand. She didn't pull away, like she usually did, brushing him off because she was too busy. Four kids were a lot of work, especially with each adding to her prepping.

But besides failing at knitting and worrying about the economy, there wasn't much else to do in the passenger seat than rub Robbie's calloused fingers. She knew he worked hard at the office. His hands showed it. He and Maggie covered whatever needed doing, especially when they couldn't find reliable people to hire.

Grace was raised to labor. They'd earned what they had, and they deserved it. The government took plenty of it as it was. Why should they have to pay for someone else's problems? They had plenty of their own. Father Tom preached about helping others, but when would they help themselves? She took a lotion sample they were giving out free at Walmart last week from her purse and began working shea butter into her husband's thumb. "Don't make me smell all girly," he said, but he kept his hand with her.

She moved on to his gnarly knuckles and their many creases. "I could even start digging it myself this weekend if you help me scout the spot. Just to get it started. Think about it, okay, Robbie?"

He chewed on the inside of his cheek like he was considering it. "I will. I'll think on it."

"Great." Grace felt better about her failed knitting already. "And I've got everything organized for the fish fry. You'll barely need to lift a finger." She pulled her list out of her purse: *potato salad, corn on the cob, coleslaw, green beans, strawberry shortcake*. She'd raided her garden for most of the groceries, but she'd have Kate make a sponge cake tomorrow for the dessert. Maggie could cook the potatoes. Tammy would grill the corn. She'd task Jules with strawberry slicing. "You'll need to defrost some fish tonight, Robbie, and catch some fresh tomorrow. What time did you tell folks?"

"I said we'd eat at five, so I expect they'll show up early for free beer. You know how they are." She'd watched him stack extra cases of beer in the bed of the truck. She'd tossed in concentrated cans of lemonade and extra sun tea bags. Grace reminded him to stop for bags of ice to pack the coolers tonight so they'd be chilled by tomorrow for the annual Fehler Family Exterminating Picnic.

"Free beers seems the least we can do for our employees," Maggie piped up from the back seat. "The fish fry is fun, especially the horseshoe tournament. Just the thing to say thanks."

"Don't forget," he said. "I always win." Robbie glanced in the rearview mirror at his daughters, and for a moment Grace wasn't at all sorry she married him.

Grace always made homemade donuts at camp. It was their last weekend together for the season. Before they grew into teenagers who slept until noon, the girls would line up at the counter blowing on the hot dough balls, begging Grace for their favorite toppings. Maggie's was chocolate syrup, Jules preferred them simple with a quick powdered sugar dip, Tammy wanted sprinkles, and Kate rolled hers in the leftovers and called it an "everything donut."

This morning, only Kate was up early enough. At camp, Kate sometimes woke up even before Grace. She said she liked the quiet pace of the morning on the river before her sisters trampled the day. Kate was often early, three weeks exactly to her own birth. The baby of the family and four years later than the rest, Kate was mostly unsupervised. Grace trusted her more. She'd already seen what her kids would and wouldn't do, and she'd raised them right.

Grace set out the cinnamon and sugar and dumped the donuts from the deep fryer onto a paper towel in front of Kate. "Quick, before the grease gets all soaked up and the sugar won't stick."

"Got it, Mom. I'm rolling. They're still hot, though." Kate fanned her fingers in the air and licked the sugar off her thumb.

Grace peered over her reading glasses. "The heat makes the sugar melt. That's the glaze. Keep going." She dipped another batch into the fryer and reeled back from the oil that splattered. "Your dad said you did good work with the billing envelopes last month. How much did he pay you?"

"Not enough. Twenty bucks. Took all afternoon. He made me lick them. I even got a paper cut on my tongue." Kate stuck out her tongue to show her, and she glanced at it for good measure.

Grace hid her grin. She couldn't see an injury, but she knew it hurt less if she pretended to care. She'd been telling Robbie for years about electronic billing, but he insisted customers liked the way they'd always done things. It gave Kate a job, too, now that Jules wasn't running the billing for the company anymore. *Kids need to work*, she thought. *They should learn to earn their own. That way they don't expect handouts.*

"Even with my babysitting money, I'm only halfway there."

"Did you ask Santa?" Grace had seen her dog-earing the Penny boards in her skating magazine. She'd been riding a regular skateboard since she was eight, but the petite Pennys were what her friends rode in the parking lot at the mall.

"Stop, Mom. I'm not a kid anymore."

"They look dangerous to me. You'll need a helmet."

"I know. You've told me a million times."

"If you listened, I probably wouldn't tell you a million times. You should be prepared." She leaned over the counter and brushed the cinnamon sugar from Kate's chin. "Try rolling as many as you eat."

The girls' bedroom door creaked open, and Tammy came out in an oversized T-shirt with the Cape Girardeau Miners basketball logo. Her hair was a nest like she'd been wrestling with her sheets all night. She stumbled to the other barstool and laid her head on the cool kitchen counter. Kate slid the donuts closer. Tammy coughed and turned her face the other way.

"Coffee?" Grace asked, cupping both hands around her mug that read Teenage Daughter Survivor. The girls had stuffed it in her stocking for Christmas one year. She liked to say it made Robbie's coffee almost bearable, but truthfully, she was grateful he made their morning brew. If only he could learn to clean out the pot and empty the grounds rather than letting it go gummy and stale. What if they lost power and water when the pot wasn't clean? Grace wanted to be one step ahead of disorder.

Tammy shook her head at the coffee like it was poison. "Do we have any Sprite?" She picked up a donut and took a tentative bite. Usually, she inhaled more than her share, even after Maggie insisted they divide them evenly.

"Robbie!" Grace called out the trailer kitchen window. She assumed he was outside somewhere fussing over his fish stuff. "Bring in the cooler. Tammy wants a soda."

"God, Mom. Stop screaming," Tammy whispered, rubbing her temples. Then she bolted to the porch and puked over the railing. Kate brought her a roll of paper towels. Tammy wiped her mouth and limped back to her bed with Grace close behind.

"You better not be getting a stomach bug, you hear me? I told you to wash your hands. Is Wade sick too?" Grace leaned over the pillow to press her lips to Tammy's forehead. She hadn't needed a thermometer in years. "You're not hot. Did you eat something bad? Lord, I hope you feel better in time for the fish fry."

Tammy whimpered and curled into a ball. She looked like her baby self for a second. An idea flickered in Grace's mind, but she quickly pushed it away. Her daughter was probably just sick. She didn't like that idea either. She didn't want to be inside taking care of her. She'd done more than her share over the years. Robbie was useless when it came to sick kids. He sympathized so much he'd throw up too and she would have more to clean up.

"I want to sleep, Mom," Tammy said.

Grace hesitated. She had other plans—hole digging plans—for

her day. The office folks would be arriving late afternoon, but she'd prepped the meal already and would delegate the rest. Hopefully, they wouldn't linger. She worried they would. "Well, let me know if you need something. I'll be out back. Just holler."

She looked in on Jules, who was snoring in the top bunk. She had arrived late to camp with a pile of books, nodded at their questions about college, and begged off to bed with the promise of a full report in the morning. Grace had a feeling there would be more avoidance. Jules wanted to stay at college, but Robbie wanted the family together, even if he was off fishing all day.

Grace understood the desire to run away. When she became a mother, staying put was the hardest part. They needed her. She loved them fiercely, but it all became so claustrophobic so quick. Before she knew it, she had four babies of her own while she was still a baby herself.

She had established a birthday breakfast in bed tradition for the girls to mark her love for them and another year she hadn't run away. She'd heard and seen on TV fancy hotels that delivered room service. The night before, Grace would crawl into bed with the birthday girl and take her breakfast order. She'd deliver her order the next morning on a white-tiled tray with her favorite blue vase filled with freshly cut flowers from her back garden. She'd assemble the sisters and drag Robbie in too, while they sang "Happy Birthday." Whatever her little women wanted: french toast with caramel sauce, blueberry muffins, chocolate pancakes, western omelets with peppers, chives, cheddar, and salsa. She said they could have anything. Jules, who hated breakfast food, often ordered homemade soup, usually cheddar broccoli or potato, and Grace obliged. She added Hallmark cards to their trays that said the things she couldn't quite bring herself to express. Those card writers did it better than she could anyway. She hoped her exterior demonstrations might hide her interior ambivalence.

Despite her many flaws, maybe they'd remember that their mom made birthdays a treat.

Back in the kitchen, Maggie was plating the rest of the donuts and hiding them in the microwave. "I can still see them in there," Robbie said, leaning over her shoulder and grabbing a handful. He'd put on what he called "baby weight" with each subsequent pregnancy. Grace ran and lifted weights at the YMCA to lose hers—the prepper training included regimented workouts—but Robbie's gut looked like he was ready to deliver their fifth child.

"Your cholesterol numbers can see them too," Grace muttered on her way out the screen door. She slipped a donut to Nacho and walked down the dirt road, grateful that the sun wasn't too bright yet.

Grace was looking for a place to begin. Far enough from the camp that it wouldn't be discovered, but close enough to the road for delivery and installation. Near the river would be good, but the ground was sandy there and less likely to hold the tank. She'd have to have someone come out and do an actual assessment, but she wanted to see how far she could dig down without hitting water. They'd need a filtration system for sure, and she didn't want to tell Robbie how much that would cost. She'd brought two shovels, a mental focus to protect her family, and gardening gloves.

On her third scoop, Maggie and Kate walked down the road, Nacho weaving between their legs. They stopped when they saw Grace digging. Maggie threw her arm around Kate and pulled her in to say something. Grace couldn't hear them, but she could imagine.

"Did you all clean up the kitchen?" Grace called, resting both arms on the handle. "I made a list of chores for the picnic too."

"We left it for Jules," Kate reported, "in exchange for not telling you about all of her hickeys."

"How classy for a college girl," Maggie said.

Grace shrugged it off. She was used to the teasing among the sisters and knew how harsh they could be if anyone else did the same. She was happy Jules had made it to college without getting pregnant first. Her own path may have looked very different if Robbie hadn't been so handsy in high school. Her mother had suggested Grace could do worse than Robbie and began sewing a wedding dress. "How's Tammy?"

"She seemed better. Said it was a stomach bug. A quick one," Kate said. "She said Wade's coming out later for the picnic."

Maggie cocked her eyebrows. "Did she share that good news with Dad? He's not the biggest fan."

"I guess we can ask her." Grace nodded as Tammy and Jules came into view at the end of the long dirt road. Nacho ran back to herd up the other sisters. Jules picked up a stick and threw it for him. He sprinted after it. Nacho obeyed Kate best, but he had a soft spot for Jules; he often licked her most—like it was his job to clean her, the most fragile of the puppies.

"What are you doing anyway, Mom?" Kate asked, picking up the other shovel. "Wait. Is this for a base camp?" Her eyes lit up like she'd found an extra present under the tree at Christmas with her name on it.

Grace dug her spade in as far as she could and used her weight to push farther through the rocky sand. "We need a backup plan. Your father and I have started discussing whether to build a shelter out here too. Underground. I was scouting places for a hole—to bury a tanker." Grace's mother had always said, "If you don't know how to do something, start," so she pretended she knew exactly how this hole would turn out. She looked to the sky to see when the bright fluffy clouds might turn heavy and gray. There was a 30 percent chance of a thunderstorm, and the odds would increase when the temperature fell after sunset.

"A tanker? Like a fallout shelter? I am not living underground," Tammy said.

Grace blocked the sun with her glove. "Well, then, you won't live, honey. That's your choice."

Jules shook her head. "I'm not staying there either, unless you stock books, of course."

"Nobody is living there, right, Mom?" Maggie said. "You plan for the worst and hope for the best. It's not like the apocalypse is imminent." She prepared to throw another stick for Nacho, who started after it, but then hesitated to see if Maggie meant it. Then he ran after it on his mission.

Maggie's optimism made Grace itch a bit. As their mother, she had to balance doom and gloom with hope, but the reality of what they would face to survive was real. If her own family didn't take it seriously, why was Grace doing all this? "Maybe not. But the electric grid is never safe. And water is usually under threat. The news this morning reported an increased risk for an EMP."

"What's that?" Jules asked.

"Electromagnetic pulse. It's a weapon. Like they used in *The Matrix*. A low-level pulse could jam all of our electronics," Kate explained. Grace often talked about sanitation systems, power grids, airplanes—anything run by computers—going out.

"That's right, Kate," Grace beamed. "Then there's nuclear—"

"Anyway," Maggie interrupted, "Dad and I are taking the boat out. Who's game?"

The sisters turned together and started walking back to the dock. It was a better offer than helping their mother dig a hole for nothing in the middle of nowhere.

Grace watched them go, lazily arm in arm with playful nudges, and then she dug faster. She wasn't sure this was the right spot, but she didn't want to move locations while her daughters might see her error.

"Dig, Nacho," she commanded, but he looked at her like it was a setup. He'd been yelled at enough to know the consequences of digging a hole. Then Nacho barked and ran toward the dirt stirred up on the road by Travis's truck as it barreled up and came to a stop by Grace's puny hole. "What the hell?" she asked when he rolled down his window. "You're kind of early for the fish fry, you know."

"I thought I'd lend a hand." Travis nodded and removed his Fehler Family Exterminating ball cap. On the cap was a bee, its stinger the stem of the capital F in "Fehler." He hung his arm out the window. "Is Robbie around?"

"Went fishing. I'm the only one working."

Travis pulled the truck to the side of the road, climbed out of the cab, and picked up the extra shovel.

"You play baseball?" She dug her spade in the dirt and tossed a pile over her shoulder, wanting to impress him with her strength. Travis suddenly seemed so young. He didn't ask what they were digging; he just joined in.

"It's a men's league at the YMCA. What's wrong with baseball?"

"Nothing. I didn't know Fehlers' sponsored a team."

"Robbie probably doesn't know either. Maggie set it up. It was part of her branding and local marketing strategy."

They labored together over the hole, sweating and flirting, until the bass boat motor interrupted them. It was probably Robbie and the girls returning for more bait. Or lunch. She'd told Jules it was her turn to make the sandwiches, but Jules said she was out of the rotation since she didn't live at home anymore. She'd been trying that trick plenty, and Grace was tired of it. Sometimes it took her more work to get others to do the work. It'd be easier to do it all herself, but they needed chores and to know how to take care of each other. What if something happened to her? It was her duty to teach them what she knew about surviving too. Kate would probably get stuck with sandwich duty. Or maybe Maggie made them last night. She could count on Maggie.

Travis shoveled three more heaping scoops. The hole was almost knee-deep now, and Grace knew she couldn't have accomplished so much without his muscle. She was aroused just thinking of his level of persistence. It was definitely a useful trait. Grace imagined what it would be like if she and Travis were stuck together in the underground bunker. They'd strategize and catalog their rations. They'd make a daily schedule to keep themselves physically and mentally fit. And, of course, there'd be sex. It was a surprise to Grace to feel alive again with a man after all the years of routine, familiar rolls in bed with Robbie while babies interrupted them.

"At least you appreciate me," Travis said. He'd sweated through his shirt and thrown it into the bed of his truck.

"I do," Grace said.

Travis bent to lift a big boulder their digging had uncovered. He hefted it to the side of the road and tossed it into the brush. "My sales were a record last month, especially for initial treatments and termites. Maggie kept us updated on the white board in the break room."

"Wow," Grace said, like she did when one of her kids won another academic achievement award for good grades or got a piece of paper declaring them a good citizen. There were so many acknowledgments for so little these days. It was hard to get excited anymore, but she could tell Travis needed her praise. "Sales are hard during the summer."

"One of the other guys kept wiping my numbers off the board. Another drew a dick next to my name. Robbie thought it was funny."

Grace didn't need the tattling. She'd mediated plenty of family feuds in her day, and that was certainly not why she kept Travis around. Besides, it was a losing battle. She'd always take her husband's side. "Uh-huh."

"It seems like no matter what I do for Fehlers', it's never good enough." He was pouting like someone had taken his ball at the playground. Grace didn't want to see it. She needed him strong, not weary and wronged.

"I appreciate you, Travis. I really do." Grace put on her family business persona and patted his hand on the shovel. "I'm sorry it doesn't seem that way at the office. It's been a hard few years for the business, but I'm glad you're part of the team." It sounded stiff, even to her, but she meant it. He was more than good enough. He'd brought her back to life.

Travis cocked his head to the side, grinned shyly, and wiped sweat from his brow. "You're making an underground shelter, yeah?" Nacho circled them again and barked. Grace hadn't called him off yet.

"You get me," Grace said, shoveling another sandy scoop. "Quit!" She stomped in Nacho's direction, and he ran off into the bushes after a bunny's tail.

Hours later, when the sun began lowering itself from the midday heat, Travis followed Grace out to the dock where Robbie and Maggie were filleting their catch. "I got the big one!" Kate announced as they came around the porch corner together.

"Travis?" Robbie said, looking up from the filleting board with a bloody knife in his hand. "You're early."

"Yes, sir," Travis nodded. "I had some time and thought I'd offer to help."

"Give me a minute to finish up. Jules, take the knife."

"I'm a vegetarian." The family stared at Jules.

Maggie and Kate burst out laughing so hard they had to hold on to each other's arms to not fall over. Maybe they were laughing at Jules, but Grace knew it was most likely at her and Robbie and their speechlessness.

"A what?" Grace asked, shading her eyes from the sun glaring off the water.

"I'm not filleting that fish, and I'm sure not going to eat it. I'll eat the hush puppies instead. I'm not killing things that have done me no harm." Jules stomped off down the trailer steps, probably in search of Nacho, who was more sympathetic than her sisters and parents.

"Fine," Robbie said. "You caught the most anyway, Maggie. They're all yours."

"I can finish the fish, sir," Travis offered, reaching for the knife.

"You're our guest, Travis. This is family work," Robbie said, flinching. "Clean this up, Kate."

"Tammy has to help too!" Kate pointed her finger at her sister, who was quietly exiting the dock.

"Jesus Christ, you two. Just do it," Grace said in a low voice. "The business always comes first. It's a matter of survival." It came out mocking. She didn't mean it that way. She thought it was all too much sometimes. The family. Each of their needs. The business. So many ways they could die. And now this affair. What was she even doing? She turned back down the stairs toward her hole, leaving them all to sort it out, even Travis.

When Grace returned to camp, after a brisk walk with Nacho in the brush, Maggie had set up the porch near the river with streamers, paper plates, napkins, and cutlery. The corn was buttered in a heaping pile, and a layer of plastic protected the sweating coleslaw. "I made tartar sauce," Grace said, assessing the spread. "It's in the fridge." Kate ran to grab it and brought out a huge bowl of sugared strawberries. Jules sat snapping green beans and tossing the tops into the water. "How's Tammy?"

"Better," Maggie reported. "Wade's inside helping her make lemonade."

"Looks like this is under control. I'm going to take a quick shower. Travis, get yourself a drink and light those citronella torches, will you?" As Grace went into the trailer, she waved at Robbie standing in the driveway with his Bayou Classic Fish Cooker. The vat of oil met his waist where tongs hung from his belt hook. He was finishing a beer, and based on the cans at his feet it looked like he was well on his way into a six-pack.

Trucks began rolling up clouds of dust on the dirt road. Fresh from her shower, Grace handed out Popsicles to the kids and tried to remember each employee's spouse's name. She added large serving spoons to the dishes and refilled the drink pitchers. She was at her best when she was busy, and she didn't mind hosting if it meant Robbie was in a good mood about the hole she'd been digging. "Fish ready?" Grace called down the driveway where the salesmen were gathered with cases of beer littered in the gravel around the fryer.

Maggie stood nearby petting Nacho and inching closer to the action. "I'll bring some up, Mom," she called.

When the last tray of fried fish was dripping on paper towels, Robbie raised his beer to get their attention. Jenn, sporting a low-cut plaid bikini top, swayed into one of the route technicians. Kids played chase around the trailer stilts. The sun was finally setting, and it lit up the marshy banks of the Mississippi River. "A family business is a family. That's what we are, for better or for worse. We're in this together. We stick. We look out for each other. It's been a tough year for Fehlers'. Hell, it's been a tough couple of years for our country. But we're here, and we're glad y'all came today to enjoy Gracie's good food and the river's good fish. From all of us, thank you."

Grace dipped a spoon into the coleslaw to begin serving, but Robbie didn't seem finished with his little speech. The fish was getting cold. She said a quick prayer that he wouldn't get into politics.

"We have a chance to make this country ours again and to make it great again just like Reagan said. They haven't taken it all away yet, but they will." Maggie moved closer to Robbie. She reached out her hand to his elbow, but it was too late.

"Now, I'm not saying if you vote for Obama, you're fired." Jenn burst out laughing but quickly realized it wasn't a joke. Travis shuffled rocks at his feet. Jules stood square, facing her dad with her hands on her hips. Grace shot her a warning look.

"I'm saying you should educate yourself on the issues and think about who cares about what we care about—family, business, hard work, survival, and protecting those you love. Most of those folks out in Washington hate Middle America and us working-class folks." Maggie cracked open a can of beer and shoved it at Robbie, who took it gratefully and downed half of it. Grace passed out empty plates and gestured toward the food. Hawks circled above them. Jenn swatted a mosquito on Travis's bare back.

Robbie looked flustered that he was losing their attention. He wasn't done, but Grace knew he wanted the last word. Maggie stepped in and raised her iced tea. "Thanks again for sharing your afternoon with us. We're grateful you're a part of the Fehler family. Now, let's eat!" Robbie's mouth hung open like a fish.

Just after sunset, when they were rounding the porch with plastic trash bags and cleaning up, Grace whispered to Travis, "You shouldn't have beat Robbie at horseshoes. He'll make you pay for that."

"I won fair and square. It's not my fault the old man can't play like he used to."

She handed him a bursting bag to tie and haul away. "That old man is my old man. We're the same age, Travis."

"Oh," he said, swinging the trash over his shoulder and sneaking a peek down her cleavage. "Doesn't show." Grace wasn't sure if that was true, but it was nice to hear. She'd pulled off the whole picnic, and Robbie had barely thanked her. Now her daughters were gathered around the campfire roasting marshmallows and Robbie was asleep in a lawn chair. Maybe he was passed out. Grace gave Travis's ass a quick pat as he walked toward the truck.

7

Kate

The ten dollars Robbie promised her to be the official photographer when Maggie received the Cape Girardeau Chamber of Commerce Emerging Business Woman Award was enough to persuade Kate. At the rate she was saving, she'd have the Penny board before the first snow fell. She hoped when she debuted it, Lila would be there to watch. It was worth a night at a boring townie dinner with her family to have Lila look her way. She wasn't sure why she wanted her attention so much, but she knew that when she imagined doing aerials and kickflips to show off it was Lila's blue eyes and pouty lips she wanted to turn toward her. When Kate thought of Lila, she burned and blushed.

Kate was proud of her sister too. She looked up to Maggie. She imagined Maggie leading Fehler Family Exterminating one day and doing that bed bug expansion she kept bringing up. Her government teacher had read from the *Southeast Missourian* that at least three hotels out on the highway had to close due to beg bugs. Maybe Maggie could help them. She liked helping people, especially their employees. Maggie had a lot of other ideas too. Though when Maggie mentioned paid maternity leave and covering the health insurance premiums for employees, their mom had said, "Paid what?

You want to pay our secretaries to have babies?" It didn't make sense to Kate. She sat in church and listened to the gospel about carrying each other's burdens and sacrificing to please God but then saw folks in the church parking lot complaining about helping others. It didn't add up, but Maggie did.

The Chamber award was a big deal in town. She was glad that others in Cape Girardeau saw how great Maggie was too. What she wasn't going to do was wear a skirt, no matter how much Grace nagged, begged, or bribed. She settled for black slacks and a button-down white shirt, hand-me-downs from the year Jules tried and failed to play clarinet in middle school band. "You'll look like one of the waiters," Tammy had told her, but Kate cared so little about that stuff and couldn't see what was wrong with blending in.

The Cape Girardeau Chamber of Commerce held their Monday night meetings in a side room of the American Legion Hall. It was one of the only places in town besides the VFW that could seat their regular thirty-five attendees and their perspective members and the veterans didn't serve food, only beer. The Chamber dinners were dry, but most of Robbie's buddies went to Sandy's afterward for drafts, including Mr. O'Neil, who sometimes had to leave his car in the parking lot and ask one of the guys to drive him home. The American Legion Hall buffet on Chamber night was free if you brought along a guest who may or may not be interested in joining. Robbie complained on the drive that he thought $11.99 was too much for fried chicken, coleslaw, and mashed potatoes. KFC was cheaper and the biscuits were better. "How come you're paying me ten dollars when you're saving eleven ninety-nine by dragging me along?" Kate asked, wiping off the stupid lip gloss her mom had smeared on her as she was walking out the door.

"Because I'm a good businessman, that's why."

"She's right, Dad. You should give her all of it," Maggie said, smoothing her blue wrap dress and fingering the single pearl drop necklace her parents had given her at graduation. They'd promised each daughter the same, but Jules left hers at home still in the package when she'd left for college. Kate thought her sister looked too fancy, but it was Maggie's night so she had told her she was pretty. Maggie looked out the window. "Even smart businessmen know when to be generous and not cheap."

"If you want to get ahead in life, girls, you have to be smart," Robbie replied, turning the wheel sharply, as if he hadn't heard the knock at all. "And work hard. There's no substitute for hard work. No one gives you a free lunch, that's for sure."

Kate didn't mention that she was getting a free dinner that night. She also didn't say she was sure the company paid for his Chamber membership dues and all his meals out. She knew he put a lot under "business expenses" to avoid taxes. He believed in keeping his own salary low and paying himself in perks. Her dad always said, "Keep what's yours. Don't let the government take it from you. There are ways around the rules." In the back seat, Kate took a selfie and texted it to Lila din w/ fam-yeah! to match her sour face. Lila sent back a LOL, but Kate wanted more.

"Don't forget to save a seat for Mom," Maggie reminded them as they climbed out of the truck together. "She's picking Tammy up from cheerleading practice." Kate had overheard Tammy getting the "fat lecture" from their mom that morning. Apparently, she'd put on a few pounds and the coach was insisting she order a new uniform. A new fifty-eight-dollar uniform. Grace said she'd take out the skirt waist herself and told Tammy to stop eating all the Oreos.

"Well, look, it's little Katie all grown up!" Mrs. Michaels, the current Chamber president, said when Kate approached the head table where the special guests had been assigned. Mrs. Michaels put her hands on her hips, wrinkling her green pantsuit in the process, and looked Kate up and down.

Kate winced. She took a deep breath and said, "Hello, Mrs. Michaels. Good to see you again," and then she dove into her chair. The padding on her seat was once burgundy and now stained with something dark. The room smelled like cooking grease. It could certainly use a Fehlers' deodorizer. Kate rubbed the edges of the Penny board magazine ad in her pocket. She'd cut it out months ago and drawn hearts around the edge. She kept it near in case they had to Bug Out. It would remind her of the world before and all there was to want.

"And you, Maggie. Darling, we are *so* proud of *you*!" Mrs. Michaels took both of Maggie's shoulders and shimmied her a bit. She ignored Robbie, but he held out his hand to shake hers anyway. "Robbie." She nodded. "You must be so proud of your daughters. Look at them! Smart and gorgeous. You don't have to be both in life, ladies, but it sure don't hurt." Kate felt liquid inside, like her arms were jelly.

"I keep my shotgun close, that's for sure." Robbie nudged Mr. Michaels, who hadn't said a word. Mr. Michaels sipped his watered-down iced tea. His face did not look amused, but it was unclear if his disdain was for the beverage, the Chamber, or the company.

"Oh, Dad. You don't mean that," Maggie said, swatting at him to make sure they knew it was a joke. Kate wondered why it was her sister's job to smooth everything over for their dad.

"Thank you for the award," Maggie said, stepping in front of Robbie. "I'm honored, Mrs. Michaels, really I am."

"We're the ones who should be thanking you, Maggie. You've brought in more young people as members to our aging Chamber in one year than we've had in the previous decade. It's like Cape Girardeau has a future again. We owe that to you, little lady."

At five-foot-eight, Maggie towered over the petite Mrs. Michaels. Kate thought her oldest sister had the body of a supermodel, long and lean, and her face was distinguished like Virginia Woolf, whom she'd seen on the cover of one of Jules's books. Kate hoped she'd grow up to look the same, rather than the curves and soft faces of Jules and Tammy. The auburn hair and freckles weren't negotiable, she knew; it was only a matter of who had more, and so far, even though she pulled it back in a tight ponytail, Kate couldn't hide her curls. She was even a bit pleased that she had more red in her hair than the rest, but she didn't like to say so.

"Will you excuse us a minute? The little ladies' room calls," Maggie said, putting her napkin in her chair and reaching her hand to Kate. It was the first time Kate had smiled all night.

In the bathroom, Maggie checked her makeup and called to Kate over t he stall. "Dad's harmless. He means well. He can't understand how the world has changed. I see it for the better, but he doesn't."

"Yeah, but it's so embarrassing."

"It's hard for him. Grandpa was so strict and never praised Dad. I think he operates from a place still hurt by that. He gives me a lot more pats on the back than you see."

"I hope he makes tonight about you and not about him."

"Will you bring me some toilet paper to blot my lipstick? I try to tell Dad he has to change too, but he won't listen."

Kate flushed and brought the tissue to Maggie. "Then why do you do this? Any of this?" The fluorescent lights in the bathroom made their skin look gray. One of them flickered and buzzed like a bug zapper.

"It matters to me. The company matters. We serve this community. It's corny, I know, but I was raised to be a bug girl." Maggie offered some pale pink lipstick. Kate rolled her eyes, but she puckered up. "Here. Blot it." Maggie showed her how to wipe off enough with the tissue that it didn't smear. "See?" The tube read Girls Just Want to Have Fun, but Kate didn't feel like they were.

Kate looked at herself in the mirror. What was the point? She was a colt next to her sister. Kate's parts were all out of proportion and still sprouting. Maggie was perfect. "But things would be different? If you were in charge?"

"A lot would. But a lot wouldn't. Dad knows what he's doing, even if it doesn't seem so from the outside. He doesn't like to fix things that aren't broken. That's all. And from his vantage point, nothing is broken." Maggie took Kate's hair out of the ponytail and spread it on her shoulders.

Kate had to admit the lipstick gave her more color and her hair did look shiny and even redder in contrast to the lip color. *What would Lila say if she saw me like this?* She twitched with curiosity that she cared. Lila popping up in her mind was confusing.

"We should go," Maggie said, taking her hand again.

Grace had joined them back at the table, and Tammy was sitting in her cheerleading outfit beside her. "I told her to bring something to change into, but she never listens to me," Grace said, pecking Maggie on the cheek. "Sorry."

"Oh, you look adorable," Mrs. Michaels said, patting Tammy's knee. "You're cheering for your sister, aren't you? Get it?" Robbie smacked the table. Mr. Michael shook his empty tea glass at the waiter. Kate wondered if he had a flask in his pocket. The iced tea wasn't *that* good. "It's almost time. You ready, Maggie?"

Maggie nodded, but then her face broke into a huge grin and Kate turned to see Jules running toward them. "Surprise!" she said, folding herself into Maggie's arms.

"Well, looky there. Sweetie, it's good that you came home. It's a big night for our family!" Robbie said, trying to pull Jules in for a squeeze. She side-armed him like a football player but then relented. Kate wondered what anti-patriarchy T-shirt she was hiding under her Mizzou sweatshirt. At least her jeans didn't have holes in them; that would send their mom into a fit.

Grace patted the empty seat beside her. Kate realized she must have been saving it for Jules. Jules pecked Kate on the cheek and high-fived Tammy. "Nice outfit, Tammy."

Mrs. Michaels walked to the podium to welcome everyone. She gave a glowing speech about the contributions of Fehler Family Exterminating in the Cape Girardeau community. "I kind of wanted to be a bug girl too, when your dad brought in the bugs. Robbie, remember? We were in Mrs. Pool's class that year at Hills Crossing Elementary." The crowd laughed—many of them remembered the bug guy visiting their classes too. "But tonight is about this fine young woman, Maggie Fehler, and her own leadership in our community. Let's give her a round of applause!" Maggie blushed. Robbie waved to the crowd, but Grace leaned over and told him to put his hand down. He looked hurt.

"You know," Mrs. Michaels continued, "this is the year of the woman. I have high hopes for the future of our country when women like Sarah Palin and Maggie Fehler step forward and embrace leadership roles." Jules crunched loudly on the ice in her tea. "Maggie is a shining example of what hard work and persistence can do for a local business. Sure, she was raised right, and we're all grateful to the Fehler family for that. But Maggie was nominated for the Cape Girardeau Chamber of Commerce Emerging Business Woman Award because of her leadership in welcoming a new generation of Cape Girardeau leaders into our ranks and her service in speaking at numerous 4-H meetings around the area. I have high hopes for Maggie's future, and I look forward to her continued efforts in our own Chamber of Commerce." Robbie stuck his hand up again and waved to the crowd. Then he kept it in the air like he was waiting for the teacher to call on him. "Yes, Robbie? You want to say something?"

Robbie smiled. "I do, ma'am. On behalf of my daughter, if I may."

Mrs. Michaels waved him up to the microphone. "Make it quick," Kate heard her whisper.

"Our family is so honored tonight," Robbie began. "And look, we're all here together!" He spread his arms wide and indicated the table of Fehler women. "I'll admit it's a lot of estrogen in one house. And it's a long wait for a bathroom." He waited for laughs of sympathy, but people mostly readjusted their seating. His forehead was all sweaty, and he wiped at it. "But we're so proud of our Maggie. She's been working by my side since she was waist high, and she's learned so much from me."

Kate decided now was the moment to start taking pictures. It was easier to look through the lens than to watch Maggie's patient, pained face. Kate sensed a train wreck in the room that everyone saw coming but no one could stop.

"Who knows what the future of Fehler Family Exterminating will hold? But Maggie is a huge help!" A few claps followed as folks tried to figure out if Robbie was done—if that was all he could muster for his oldest daughter.

"Thank you, Robbie," Mrs. Michaels said, using her hip to move him to the side. Robbie stopped talking, but he didn't budge. It was clear he'd be standing up there as if the award was actually his. "And now, Maggie, will you join us up here?" Everyone clapped as Maggie walked up front to the podium. Mrs. Michaels brought out an engraved plaque from the podium's shelf. "It is my pleasure to award you"—Mrs. Michaels tried to nudge a bit more room in the lineup for Maggie as she held the plaque between them, Robbie put his hand on Maggie's elbow like she might need help holding it up, and Kate snapped another picture—"with the 2008 Cape Girardeau Chamber of Commerce Emerging Business Woman Award!"

Maggie hugged Mrs. Michaels. Robbie clutched his chest like he was so proud his heart may burst. The crowd clapped loudly, and Tammy put her fingers in her mouth and whistled inappropriately. Robbie continued leaning forward like he might be grabbing for the award. He reached out one arm, and Maggie caught him awkwardly. Then Robbie's face reddened like he was choking. Kate watched it all through her camera lens and couldn't stop taking pictures. The clapping slowed, and Mrs. Michael said, "Robbie, are you okay, honey?" loudly into the microphone. Robbie's eyes bulged, he grabbed his chest again, and then he fell to the floor as Grace ran to his side. Kate stopped taking pictures; her camera couldn't stop time. She reached for Jules's and Tammy's hands.

"I'll call nine-one-one," Mr. Michaels said, his first words of the evening.

PART II

Smoke Out

Grief, when it comes, is nothing like we expect it to be.

—Joan Didion
The Year of Magical Thinking

8

Tammy

The funeral was an event in Cape Girardeau, and the spectacle annoyed Tammy. Usually she enjoyed attention, but right now she hoped it would all go away. She wanted it not to be true: the baby, her dad's death, this funeral, the uncertainty of her family's future. Her dad made her feel safe, and now he was gone. He wouldn't be in the audience cheering for her at the Miss Cape Pageant. He wouldn't be there for her high school graduation or to walk her down the aisle on her wedding day. It wasn't fair at all.

She was tired of people's condolences and their well-intentioned pressing of tissues with wet hands. Robbie Fehler and Fehler Family Exterminating was a local institution. A good Catholic family. Everyone knew Robbie. Good-natured, kidder dad. Devoted husband. Damn fine businessman. *Remember that time Robbie Fehler did the dunking booth at the elementary school carnival? Who was there when he dressed up his car as a giant rat for the homecoming parade and made movable whiskers out of his windshield wipers? Don't forget his favorite ball cap too—the one with the beer bottle opener on the bill. Robbie could fish. He fed his whole family and all his employees single-handed from the Mississippi River.* Robbie Fehler was a community leader struck down in his prime. Sure, he'd had a heart attack a few years back, but who would have imagined another.

An extensive photo collage would play on a loop beside the guest book at the funeral home. Last night, Tammy and her sisters had culled their family albums for pictures, and it had gutted them. Robbie teaching each daughter how to fish with a Snoopy pole. Robbie in a full bee suit holding a beer. Robbie laughing at a holiday pageant when Tammy forgot the words to "Jingle Bells." Grace kept leaving the room. Such a public display of their business. Tammy could hear the town talking, *What would become of those little women without their father?*

Her mom mostly seemed stunned. She was normally prepared for anything, but now she could barely speak. Or maybe it was the Valium. Maybe she'd taken two. How are you supposed to act when your husband dies? Grace was usually scared about something, and this seemed to focus her fears. Tammy couldn't stand the thought of something happening to Wade, and they'd only been dating six months. Of course they were all in shock, Father Tom had told them at the emergency room. "Grief looks different for different people," he'd said, but it didn't feel reassuring to Tammy. Everything was blank. Her mind was swimming in mud. She kept seeing Robbie fall to the ground at the Chamber of Commerce dinner again and again.

Now was not the time to consider the baby, but how could she ignore it? Death brought life so close. She hadn't had a period in months. Tammy wasn't wondering about it anymore. She was grateful Maggie didn't notice she wasn't using her share of the stocked tampons. Since Jules had been away at Mizzou, she'd declared tampons part of the patriarchy; she now proudly left out her DivaCup like it was show-and-tell. Tammy thought Jules could try to be less of a spectacle sometimes. Kate was so private, none of them even knew if she'd gotten her period yet. But all the sisters noticed

Tammy was taking too long in their shared bathroom on the morning of Robbie's funeral.

"Seriously, Tammy? Come on." Maggie pounded again on the bathroom door. "Let me in!"

"Just a minute," Tammy called. Her voice was muffled in a bath towel she was using to cover her gagging. The fresh mountain breeze of their laundry detergent was making it worse. Usually she rushed to Wade's car in the mornings before school and could wait until he drove around the corner to puke out the door. Mr. Graham's grass wasn't growing so well with her morning fertilizer, but she had bigger problems. In the bathroom, Tammy took a deep breath, steadied herself against the sink, and flushed twice. Everything made her vomit these days. She threw up when they raced Robbie away in the ambulance. She puked in the waiting room's family bathroom. She almost lost her stomach when the doctor came out to tell her and her sisters that their dad couldn't be saved. Watching her dad's heart attack felt like it was happening to someone else. It couldn't be her. None of this was real, right? How could her future fall apart so fast?

"We're leaving in five minutes!" Grace shouted. She yelled like this was an ordinary morning instead of their dad's funeral. Her mom was walking around like a zombie, and watching her unhinged scared them all.

"How's Mom? Any better?" Tammy asked through the door. She washed her mouth out under the faucet and unlocked the door. She felt Maggie's hand on the other side and barely moved out of the way as her sister busted through.

"Not good," Maggie answered, opening and slamming vanity drawers in search of a hairbrush. Last Christmas, Kate had used their mom's label maker to designate the colors and owners of each brush, but three of the four sisters ignored the directions. Jules didn't like being told what to do. Tammy's hair needed twice the attention. Maggie grabbed whatever was left out of necessity.

Tammy watched Maggie in the mirror. Her sister was a whole head taller, but they had the same nose and same brown eyes. Fehler freckles too. Maggie's lashes were to die for, and they'd be amazing with mascara. But today was not a day for mascara. "How are you?" Tammy whispered.

"Tired. Shocked. Confused. I'm a mess. I couldn't sleep at all."

"I can't believe Dad's gone," Tammy said, "like I thought he'd live forever or something." She pushed her breasts up and wondered if it was too much cleavage for the occasion. They kept growing along with the baby.

Maggie leaned over the sink to steady herself. Tammy grabbed a tissue box and rubbed her back. Mrs. Harris had brought over six boxes of Puffs, the expensive kind that boasted built-in lotion, along with a pan of gooey lasagna. At the time, Grace said it was overkill, but the tissues were half gone and Tammy had eaten the noodles for lunch and dinner. It had been only two days since Robbie's heart attack. The nice nurse at the ER—her name tag read Laura—said their father was dead when he hit the industrial tiled floor of the American Legion Hall, but they had rushed him to the hospital anyway and did all the lifesaving heart jumpstarts for show. Laura said he hadn't suffered. She held Tammy's hand and seemed to know a lot. To distract Tammy, she told her about her own children—twins named Huck and Jim—and her husband, Sammy, who had been her high school sweetheart, like Robbie and Grace. "Sometimes you don't know the path life will take you on," Laura said, patting Tammy's hand. "It's like the Mississippi. Lovely and unpredictable. You hold on for the ride, white knuckles and all."

Tammy wanted to tell her about the baby. She seemed like someone she could trust. Maggie was busy with insurance paperwork,

Kate and Grace were clinging to each other in tears, and Jules was stone sitting in a metal chair in the waiting room gripping the armrests.

"Is it hard to be a parent?" Tammy had asked. Until that moment, she'd never considered the possibility of losing one. Your parents are always there, right? Clearly she'd been wrong.

Laura had smiled and handed her another tissue. "It is. But I wouldn't have it any other way. You don't know what you want until you can't have it."

"Like my dad."

"Like your dad. This will be hard. But you'll find out you're stronger than you think, certainly than you feel right now."

"Did you ever think about not becoming a mom? Like after you were pregnant." She knew her mom wouldn't agree to even consider a discussion about a you-know-what, and in Missouri a parent had to sign and come with her for the procedure after a seventy-two-hour waiting period. Probably by now it would have to be done in the hospital. Tammy guessed that not a single doctor in town would be willing anyway. She'd tried to find a Planned Parenthood—just to have someone to talk to—but there wasn't one for at least a hundred miles.

Laura had taken a deep breath and looked Tammy in the eye. "You can come talk to me later, maybe next week, if you want. Get through this first, okay? You're in shock. No sudden moves. My Aunt Betty always said that every problem has a solution. There isn't a right or wrong. Just a decision."

Maybe some things just were and worked themselves out on their own. *But Dad didn't get to decide any of this,* Tammy thought. She couldn't stop wanting her dad just not to have died. It was childish but so true it ached. Death couldn't be undone, but a pregnancy could.

Father Tom had performed the last rites at the hospital, which all the Fehler women thought Robbie would have hated, but no one stopped him. How could it hurt? In their kitchen, while Maggie poured more coffee for visitors, her mom reassured Mrs. Harris that indeed Robbie lived long enough for the ritual. Mrs. Harris crossed herself and said, "Then we'll see him in heaven." Tammy wasn't sure what she was supposed to feel, but she wasn't reassured by Mrs. Harris's version of death's reward. She didn't want her dad in heaven. She wanted him right here in this mess with the rest of them.

The mess might have gotten worse if Maggie hadn't reminded Tammy to call DQ to say she wouldn't be making her shift the night Robbie died. Amber, whom she didn't like, answered, and Tammy had been surprised by how nice she was on the phone. "You see to your people, you hear? Your Dairy Queen family is here whenever you need us. We're so sorry for your loss."

At the bathroom sink, Tammy watched tears fall down Maggie's cheeks into the basin. "I miss him so much. Isn't that weird?" Tammy said. "Like I think he's at work or something and he'll be home soon, you know?"

"I need to go to the office." Maggie blew her nose. "Thank God he died on a Friday and the routes were almost done so we didn't have to close more than one day." In any other family, Tammy knew this might be a horrible thing to say, but in theirs, it was true. The business came first. They couldn't not open and let the employees starve. They'd already given everyone today off for the funeral.

Tammy noticed Kate in the bathroom doorway then, so still and straight she might be trying to hold up the frame, but then the corners of her mouth twitched. The convenience of their dad's weekend death released the tension of the ridiculousness of what Maggie had just said. Tammy even smiled in the mirror at her sister. Jules huffed, "This family is so twisted," as she rushed past to the toilet, hiking her skirt and pulling down pantyhose as she went. The sisters turned to watch her struggle with the nylon.

"What?" Jules spat. "They're for Mom. She'd want me to wear goddamn pantyhose to hide my hairy legs." And then, that tenderness—her sister, a hippy in stockings, wanting to make her mom's pain a minute less—broke them all apart and back together again. Tammy was grateful. She cried so much then into Kate's shoulder that she thought she might throw up again. Something fluttered inside. Like wings. Or gills. Her hand instinctively palmed the place on her tummy where it happened, and she knew in that moment that it was hers, that it had to be, that Wade would have to do, that there were worse things in life, like loss, than a baby and someone to love. She was raw and ripe and bruised like a juicy apple that took on too much water hanging on its tree, but she was keeping her baby.

"This time God cares what you wear to church!" Grace screamed, and the sisters came rushing, one by one in the order of their birth, in various black skirts and sweaters and dresses; their mother's fury drained. "He'd be proud," she said. "Just look at you." They stood in the kitchen together, and Tammy assessed the dirty coffee mugs from too many visitors and the aluminum foiled casseroles from parishioners and sympathy cards sent from employees. The women waited for Robbie. "He's probably already in the car," Grace said, and then, "Damn it," as the funeral parlor's long black car pulled up so they didn't have to drive themselves from the service to the gravesite and then back to the church for the reception. It seemed like a lot of moving parts but it was how things were done, and Tammy thought her dad would at least appreciate the tradition.

After the funeral Mass, as they climbed out of the back seat of the car again at the gravesite, Jules whispered, "Are you high, Mom? You seem high."

"Shut your mouth, Julianna Marie. It's your father's funeral." Grace crossed herself and then seemed transfixed by the shiny surface of the rosary beads she moved around her hand as they lowered Robbie's body into the ground. Travis, one of the Fehler technicians, kept coming over to hug her mom, and it was creeping Tammy out. Then her mom lifted her head. "Who's that?"

Tammy looked up to see a handsome face in a full navy suit parting the crowd. Most of the men wore slacks or jeans, but this guy was gussied up. She looked around for Wade. He'd put on a tie and khakis, and he looked cute. Jules squeezed Tammy's hand and whispered, "Shit! Cover for me."

"Cover what? He's here for you?" Tammy said it too loud. This guy wasn't from Cape. And he was Black.

Maggie steered Grace toward the roses on top of Robbie's casket. Aunt Charlene, whom they hadn't seen in years, held Grace's hand. Her grown-up kids, Bryan and Missy, stood awkwardly to the side. Maggie took the roses out one by one and gave them to cousins and friends as they hugged goodbye. There was a ritual to it, a thing to do. The nice ER nurse Laura had told Tammy that the blessings of a funeral are that it must be done. Phone calls and arrangements and decisions give you a task to ease the grief that will come with the not doing. "Blessed Family's basement is open for a reception," they said again and again, and Tammy realized she was starving.

Tammy walked among the flowers and wrote down names for thank you notes, but she kept glancing at Jules and her visitor. He was tall and thin and freshly shaved. His hair was lush curls, and his smile was so bright that Tammy imagined him on the cover of their local orthodontist's brochure. Most of the crowd pretended to mingle and not stare. Jules hugged the guy and hung on too long for it to be friendly. He slid his hand down her back. He kissed her forehead in such a tender way that everyone knew that Robbie Fehler's wild daughter was dating a Black man and brought him to her daddy's funeral. Tsk-tsk. Tammy wanted to cheer her on. The danger made her feel suddenly alive. Angry Jules had a crush. Maybe it would soften her hard heart a bit. Maybe it would quiet her down and lighten her up. Clearly life is short. Why shouldn't you be happy? Being near this guy made Jules glow.

Back in the car on the way to the Blessed Family Church for the basement reception, Grace checked her makeup—or what was left of it. Tammy thought she'd never seen her mother so tired and wondered how they'd all get through the day. Maybe she could take the whole week off school. She wouldn't mind a week in bed. She was exhausted too. Growing a baby is hard work, she guessed. She decided she was going to tell Maggie. But then Maggie would probably insist on taking her to a doctor. Doctors were expensive and so were babies. An extra burden for her family when they didn't need any more. She'd have to go to a doctor soon anyway now that she'd decided. Had she decided? The flutter again. She'd decided. She was Catholic, after all. So was Wade. Robbie would have killed Wade, but there was no way Tammy could hurt this baby, not after she felt it kick. It was real now.

Jules and Grace sat facing each other. "What is your problem, Mom? Because he's Black?"

"Because your dad is dead, Jules. And none of us knew you had a boyfriend."

"This is probably not the moment to discuss any of this," Maggie said, rubbing her temples.

Jules passed her mother a bottle of water. "He's not my boyfriend."

"Then what is he? He's just a friend who shows up at your dad's funeral to make a scene? His hands were all over you. It's not good timing, Jules."

Kate leaned on Tammy's shoulder and looked out the window. The blue sky was full of puffy clouds. Tammy wondered if later they'd remember it a rainy, dreary day when in fact it was a gorgeous fall afternoon, crisp and bright and promising unexpected warmth. She knew she was supposed to be pissed because their mother was obviously pissed, but she was also curious. "What's his name? He's kind of hot, Jules."

"Niko. His name is Niko."

"Sounds foreign," Grace said, squinting like she'd licked a lemon.

Maggie rolled her eyes and opened the window for some air. Tammy felt the sunlight on her face, and it made her sleepy. She wondered if most pregnant women became narcoleptic.

Jules exploded. "How do you all not know how racist our family is?" Tammy didn't want to hear Jules right now push and poke everything. She never let up. She fought with Robbie all the time about politics. She said she wasn't even Catholic anymore. Since Jules had left, the house was calmer.

"Jesus, Mary, and Joseph, we are not racist. Remember that one Black guy, Larry? He worked for us for years. And the neighbor that used to live on the corner, Mrs. Jackson. Your dad loved her."

"Having one Black person work for you doesn't mean you're not racist. We are surrounded by sundown towns, and that legacy lives on."

Tammy thought Jules had a point, but she was not speaking up and defending her sister in this moment. Like her dad, she preferred to hide when the hive was stressed.

"He's a friend, Mom. He cares about me. Can you imagine how hard it was for him to show up? He's the only person of color in the whole crowd. We aren't exactly welcoming."

"We're almost at the church," Maggie said. "Can you two stop?"

"I had told him not to come to the funeral Mass, Mom," Jules whispered. "He's not Catholic." Then she ruined it with her snarky, "Happy?"

Grace put on her sunglasses. Jules closed her eyes. And they all settled into the car's buttery leather seats for a quiet cry.

Tammy thought she'd never seen so many layers of cream of mushroom soup in her whole life. There were rows and rows of gelatinous casseroles, each with a different topping: broccoli, shredded cheese, two with chunks of ham, several with crispy french onions, and one with fresh spinach that everyone was avoiding except Niko. He was making himself comfortable and shaking hands with Father Tom. Niko had a heaping plate of turkey sliders and coleslaw waiting for him once he finished his casserole sampler. The smells made Tammy's tummy gurgle with hunger and repulsion.

She headed for the bathroom and tucked herself into their favorite stall, the one with the elevated toilet. It felt like a throne. When they were little, her sisters used to fight over who got to climb up first. With her skirt bunched up around her waist, Tammy texted Wade. in bathroom. 1 min. go ahead & eat. get me iced tea. Wade's whole family was at the funeral, even his little brother. Their families had known each other for years through church, and Wade's dad had coached Maggie's softball team in high school. Robbie had always said, "Everybody knows everybody in Cape Girardeau. Sometimes twice." But he wouldn't be saying it again. Tammy worried that maybe he'd been in pain. Maybe a heart attack hurts. She knew his heart wasn't strong. He didn't take care of himself; he took care of them.

A twitch of resentment rose through her. He would never even meet this baby or know he had his first grandchild on the way, but then, she might not have even had the baby if he were alive. "Honey, we're so sorry about your daddy," Wade's mom had said, pulling Tammy into an awkward hug. She smelled like toasted marshmallows from her sweet potato casserole. Tammy wondered if she'd be so nice if she knew that her son had gotten his sixteen-year-old girlfriend pregnant and ruined his chances for a college basketball scholarship—not that one was actually forthcoming. She suspected it would be easier for the family to blame her for ruining his future than to face the fact that being a star of the Blessed Family Shamrocks basketball team meant little in other leagues. They probably wouldn't even consider what Tammy had planned or how she wanted to make something of herself too.

After pulling herself together in the bathroom, Tammy found Wade at the far food table. Her iced tea was now watery, but it soothed the syrupy taste in her mouth. "So where are you from?" Wade asked, passing Niko a can of Coke he'd filled halfway up with rum.

Niko smelled it, smiled, and took a swig. "I'm from Portland."

"No, I mean, you know . . . where are you *from* from?"

"God, Wade. Really?" Tammy acted outraged, but she was curious too. Niko wasn't exactly Black, but he sure wasn't White. His skin was a bronzed beige, and with his suit and sharp chin, he looked like a model Tammy had seen on the cover of *GQ*. Up close, he was even taller than she'd imagined. He might be six-foot-two. He stood straight, like he'd been raised with good manners. She wondered if Jules had slept with him yet. Probably, knowing Jules. "Sorry. He's so embarrassing," she added. Wade had his arm around her waist, hunched toward her, and she wondered if he'd still grow a few more inches.

Niko handed the can back, and Wade drained it. "Same place as you, bro. I've lived here my whole life."

Jules joined them with a plate of brownies. Her nose was so red from blowing it that Tammy thought she looked like a sad clown. The brownies looked good, though, and she suddenly wanted to eat them all. A fly buzzed near them, but she brushed it away before it could land on the brownies.

"Is that a bee?" Niko asked. He swatted at the empty air, clearly nervous at the possible threat. "I'm allergic."

Jules shook her head. "No, a common housefly. They like basements and brownies."

"I understand your dad was a beekeeper. Did he ever tell you about Rangkemi?"

"Rang who?" Wade said, ducking another fly.

"I did a paper on honey hunting earlier this semester," Niko told them. "Rangkemi is the guardian spirit of bees. There's this place in Nepal where the largest honeybees in the world, the Himalayan giant, make hallucinogenic honey. It's called 'mad honey,' and it's red because the bees eat the pollen of rhododendrons."

"Whoa." Wade nodded. "So you can, like, get high on honey?"

Tammy didn't want to get high. She wanted the brownies and her dad back. Robbie would have loved the "mad honey" story but not Jules's boyfriend who was telling it. She reached over to the plate and took the largest brownie.

Jules normally would have objected but not today. She handed the plate to her and went to get another. "You want some milk?" she asked, and when she met Tammy's eyes for an answer, they leaned into each other's arms. Niko reached over to hold Jules's hand in the huddle but accidentally grabbed Tammy's. She didn't pull away. Niko's hand felt friendly, the way she imagined a brother's might.

9

Maggie

Maggie decided to fake it. She'd always assumed she'd run Fehler Family Exterminating one day. She thought her dad expected that too, but they'd never talked about it, not concretely anyway. She was going to pretend she was in charge and carry on like it was business as usual. What other choice did she have? She was a bug girl.

She glanced at her mother and sisters as they sat waiting at Fehler Family Exterminating for the family's sometimes lawyer. Maybe Tammy would work with her. She didn't seem to have any other plans, and she liked the kind of nice things you'd need money for. She wasn't sure if Jules or Kate had any interest, but she knew her mother wanted none of it. Grace kept a respectful distance from the family business, happy to have her bills paid, proud when it served her, but resentful when it seeped into every hour of their day. Still, Maggie had asked her mother that morning if she wanted to be involved. "You know, in the business and stuff? With Dad gone, I mean."

"Do you need me?" Maggie could hear her mother trying. Her voice was strained and hoarse. "At the office?" Grace stared out her bedroom window toward the hives, working her rosary beads in her lap. "It's like watching the hives." She sounded all spacey, maybe medicated again. "Birds and bees have so much purpose in our survival." She laughed at her own joke. "The birds and the bees, get it?" Then her face cringed and tears came.

Maggie got the joke but didn't think it was funny, not right now anyway. And the last thing she wanted to discuss with her mom was the birds and the bees. Maggie had barely been kissed. That one time with Carlos, the foreign exchange student from Spain, hardly even counted. Boys mistook her reserve as disinterest, so she made it seem she was too busy with the business anyway. Besides, her parents hadn't made marriage look that desirable. It was an obligation, something you were supposed to do. And another round of "the way things have always been done." It didn't sit right with Maggie.

Mr. Bly strutted through the front door with two briefcases. Maggie noticed his beer gut had swollen since she'd seen him in her dad's office a few months ago, and he'd bathed in a gallon of Old Spice. He was ten minutes late.

Tammy whispered to Jules, "Show-off."

He shook everyone's hand. "My condolences," he said, pumping Maggie's palm too hard. They gathered around the conference table and left Robbie's chair empty. Finally, Kate rolled it out of the room and stuffed it into the storage closet. Grace looked relieved.

"Shall we start with house and personal assets?" Mr. Bly said. Maggie thought his voice sounded like an annoying game show host.

"Are you going to read it out loud?" Tammy asked.

"No," Mr. Bly said, "they only do that in the movies. The good news is that all the papers are in order and everything is up to date. As hard as this time is, Robbie made provisions to care for you all."

"Up to date?" Grace asked.

"Mr. Fehler recently updated his will. We'll get to that in a minute."

Jenn knocked on the conference room door. "The phones," she said, "they're ringing off the hook. I can't manage them all by myself. A lot of folks are calling to say they're sorry about Robbie." She turned toward Grace. "I mean, we're all sorry for your loss, Mrs. Fehler."

Maggie imagined that her mom was trying to restrain an eye roll. "Thank you, Jenn," Maggie said. "How about some coffee? Jules and Tammy, can you handle a few calls? Take messages and such." Her sisters sprinted from the room. Kate followed but looked back to Maggie and Grace for reassurance. Maggie nodded. It wasn't that her sisters didn't need to know but rather that the business and the family couldn't be separated in the conversation. Maggie wanted time to process what would happen next without her sisters expecting her to make everything alright. She wasn't sure she could, and her mom didn't seem to want to. The extent of Grace's involvement was checking in on the sisters before bed. She rubbed backs, brought more tissues, and cleaned up used ones, but she didn't have much more to give right now. Maggie didn't blame her. They were all walking wounded.

"So, as Mr. Fehler's attorney and the executor of his estate, I've already filed the will with probate. Just thought I'd start the ball rolling. I have an updated list of assets. None of these can be distributed until after probate, of course."

"Why did Robbie change his will? Why now?" Grace interrupted.

"That's not for me to say, ma'am."

"When did he call you?"

"Three months ago. Again, I'm so sorry for your loss, Mrs. Fehler."

Grace's face was ash. Maggie couldn't read her at all. Robbie couldn't have known he was going to have a heart attack. What happened three months ago that made him make new plans? And why wouldn't he have talked to Mom about it?

Mr. Bly continued. "Changing the will was a part of the larger bankruptcy filing."

Maggie felt like someone had poured ice down her back. "The what?"

Mr. Bly pulled out another file. "Robbie filed for Chapter 7 bankruptcy three months ago. It can take up to six months, but sometimes it goes through sooner. I expect a discharge of debts soon. You'll need to meet with the credit counselor then. I'll schedule that."

Maggie turned toward her mom. None of this made sense. "Did you know Dad filed for bankruptcy?"

"He had me sign papers. He didn't explain it to me. He said it was because of the recession. If we cut back on some spending, he told me we'd be fine. Robbie used the loans from Jules's tuition to get us through a rough spot. I didn't understand exactly that it was bankruptcy, though." Grace shook her head but it wasn't exactly a no. "But wouldn't the bankruptcy be thrown out or whatever because Robbie died?"

Mr. Bly looked almost pleased by the question. "I'm afraid joint debts are passed on. The process and case continue even after death. Creditors won't come after you, not yet anyway. They often look to the deceased debtor's estate and property to satisfy the debtor's obligations. Fortunately, the estate isn't worth much and we filed what we could as an exemption."

Maggie unclenched her fists from her lap and placed both hands on the table to steady herself. It was Tuesday. They'd closed the business Monday for the funeral, and payroll was due Friday. "How can everything we have not be worth much? This business is worth something. It's everything." At least it was to her and to their family's future.

"The business only has value if there is a buyer. The shares aren't liquid assets. They're on paper alone and not worth much right now,

Robbie borrowed against the business, using the building as collateral. He'd put the camp up for collateral too, on another loan he defaulted on. He missed last month's rent on the garage. You'll need to keep making minimum payments or else they can come after everything. Do you know how much is in your bank account, or do you have access to any other cash immediately?"

Maggie and Grace both shook their heads. Maggie wasn't on the company bank account. She'd need to go to the bank with her mom right after this to get it signed over. Everyone in town knew Robbie died. She had $1,100 in her own savings, but that wouldn't even pay the technicians for the week. Maybe the sales team would give her a break if she doubled their commission. She'd need to fire Jenn right away, but then who would manage the phones? Maggie's mind raced through all the possibilities to keep them afloat, but she came up with none. She needed a way to make money and fast. If the company bank account was empty, she couldn't even open their doors for business tomorrow morning. How could her dad have done this to them? She was pissed, and he wasn't even here to hear it.

Mr. Bly cleared his throat. "The easy stuff, of course, is what's not distributed in the will and doesn't go through probate because of joint custody."

"You mean the stuff we owned together?" Grace asked.

"Yes, but there was life insurance as well. As his wife, you are the beneficiary, of course."

"And the house. Though it's not worth much now." Maggie wondered how much value it had actually lost. They'd looked up their homes as an exercise in her Economics class and tracked them through the housing crisis. At the time the numbers didn't mean much; they hadn't thought to sell or get a loan. But now those numbers meant a lot.

Mr. Bly nodded. "And your cars. He has two listed here."

"I drive one of them," Maggie offered, but then she was embarrassed by how it sounded. Why hadn't she bought her own car yet? Her salary was embarrassingly low. She knew Robbie's was too. They both took cuts when the cash couldn't cover. Maggie had sent Jules money to help with her college books too.

"We have four cars," Grace clarified.

"Yes, but two of those are company cars. They aren't your personal assets."

"Oh. I'm afraid Robbie kept me in the dark about a lot. He paid the bills." Maggie knew that wasn't entirely true. She'd seen her mom check the accounts plenty when she was trying to stretch their prepping budget.

"That's often the case, ma'am. I believe the life insurance will provide for your immediate future, depending on how you use it. There was the prenuptial agreement, of course, for the business."

"The what?"

"You signed a prenuptial agreement, Mrs. Fehler. I have it right here. It says you relinquish all rights to Fehler Family Exterminating."

"I was eighteen years old. His father made me. I never even read it."

Mr. Bly patted Grace's hand. "You'll be taken care of. I'm sure his family did it to protect everyone. Family businesses are tricky. And you were about to be a mother, right? I'm sure they didn't want to worry you."

Grace blinked. "How do you know all these things?"

"I'm his lawyer."

"I'm his wife. He shared these things with his lawyer and not his wife?"

"May I continue? There is more to discuss. My job, ma'am, is to ensure Mr. Fehler's intentions are carried out."

Maggie kept listening but not really listening. The conversation seemed surreal. Like her dad was in his office and had set this all up as a big practical joke. Robbie would bust through the door any minute, sloshing coffee, and yell, "I got you all! I got you all good!" Grace would be mad and pout for a while. Then she'd hide in the cellar or her garden to punish him.

Mr. Bly shuffled some more papers, then stacked them neatly, straightening all four corners before he continued. "So, basically, each of your daughters will own an equal share of Fehler Family Exterminating."

"You mean, he cut me out of the company?" Grace asked. "But this very building we are sitting in belonged to *my* family."

"When it was gifted, it became property of Fehler Family Exterminating."

"But I'm a Fehler too." Her mom's voice sounded like an animal caught in a trap.

"I know this is a shock, ma'am. Robbie deemed twenty percent of the company would go to each of your daughters. For the time being. There are clauses for how they can buy each other's shares. For example, Jules may want to sell hers to continue her education. Tammy and Kate won't have ownership until they're eighteen, of course, but they can serve in advising capacities. I believe he was assuming, Maggie, that you may want a larger role."

"I do," she said weakly. This news stunned her more than his death. Her dad was still there, and he'd slapped her. It seemed cruel. He hadn't acknowledged her devotion at all. Equal? She'd been at the office with her dad since she was ten. Even when she attended community college, she worked full time at the office. She did inventory on the weekends. She could drive the trucks and run the routes. She knew every single part of this company except the money side, which Robbie had been tight-lipped about. Equal?

Her efforts had never been equal. She often thought she worked harder than her dad.

Jenn came in with mugs of coffee. She was using a shallow cardboard box as a serving tray. Maggie would have found it tender if she wasn't so numb. "Who likes cream or sugar?" Jenn asked.

Grace didn't restrain herself this time. "For heaven's sake, if you've been here one hour, you know Robbie made everyone drink his awful coffee black."

"Yes, but now . . ." Jenn didn't finish her sentence. She bit her bottom lip as she set the fresh pot, cream, sugar, and stirrers neatly on the table.

"I'll take cream and sugar," Mr. Bly said, patting Jenn's shoulder as he clouded and sweetened his coffee.

"Please don't touch our employees," Maggie heard herself say. Why had her dad bullied everyone about black coffee? And why did they allow it?

Mr. Bly's face was injured, as if a tiny rebuff was more than their grief. Jenn slammed the door too hard when she left, and Maggie saw her mother clutch her throat. She wasn't sure if she was startled or wanted to kill Jenn.

Then Grace said, "In case you haven't noticed, Mr. Bly, I have four daughters. My husband wanted a son, of course, but we don't always get what we want, do we? Your math doesn't add up."

"Actually, it does. The final share of the business goes to the only possible male heir, Bryan Schaler." He leaned over the table to fill his coffee cup and empty the creamer.

"What?" Maggie put her mug down hard. "What did you say?"

Mr. Bly read from his paperwork. "Your cousin, correct? Bryan Schaler. He will own twenty percent of Fehlers'."

"But why?"

"I'm not sure I can answer that, ma'am. My job is to convey the information and manage the estate. Once we hear back from probate, you may request the business value be accurately assessed if you're interested in making any offers. I do understand you'll probably want to continue running operations. But do remember that you'll need at least three shareholders to agree for any future business decisions. Robbie made an allowance for you to receive a raise for twelve months during the transition. I believe he thought it was generous, but after going over the cash flow, I can see it's modest. He couldn't have known how much worse the recession would get. I'm sure he didn't consider the stock market crash last month either. I'm sorry."

"Sorry?" Maggie's throat tightened. She wanted to scream at her dad. She wished she had the will to walk away, but where would she go? All the apologies meant nothing. Everyone was scared about the economy. Robbie was gone. The business had to go on, but how? How was she supposed to fix all this? Her dad had said not to trust the government. Ever. They'd bailed out all the banks and ignored the rest. The people like the Fehlers, who struggled, were all alone. Even their dad had left them. Maggie, who was tired of being known as cheerful and reliable, felt gutted and defeated.

"The most prudent thing now would be for a formal vote from the four shareholders present to appoint you, Maggie, acting general manager. That part should be easy enough."

Grace left her full cup of coffee on the conference room table and stood up. "What's a family business for, if not for the family? I'm going home to make lunch. Send your sisters home when you're done with them." She walked out.

Maggie was surprised she'd waited this long to leave. Her mom loved her, and she didn't blame her for wanting more than motherhood out of life, especially when getting cut out of the business was what she got in return. Why would her dad decide to do that now after all these years? It didn't make sense. Nothing added up.

Bryan wasn't even blood. Maggie's mom had reminded them often that he didn't carry the Fehler name. She'd told Maggie a lot more too, more than a kid should probably know. Aunt Charlene was Robbie's sister, but Bryan was her stepkid. Granted, he'd been in the family since he was three years old and Charlene had raised him alongside her own daughter, Missy, who was six months older. In fact, Aunt Charlene had met Bryan's dad, Jason, in the line for preschool drop-off. Jason let her cut in whenever he could. They'd flirted at Donuts with Dad day, which Charlene attended because her husband was in Iraq. He'd been deployed the day after Missy's first birthday. Missy hardly knew her father, only from the hurried visits twice a year when her father was mostly drunk. It didn't take long for Charlene to fall into Jason's outstretched arms. When she told her husband she wanted a divorce, he went on a bender but seemed mostly relieved, especially when she asked for only a small child support payment and agreed to leave his VA benefits alone. Bryan's mom had died from breast cancer the year before. Charlene and Jason married grief and desperation and came out stronger for it. They lived in a suburb of St. Louis now, but Maggie hadn't talked to Bryan or Missy in years, except for quick hugs at the funeral, which she barely remembered now.

Bryan wasn't a bad guy, but he knew nothing about the family business. One time, years ago, Charlene had brought the kids to the camp for the weekend. Bryan had caught spiders in the house by putting a mason jar on top of them and sliding a newspaper underneath so he could release them on the dock rather than stomp on them. He didn't even know how to bait his own hook and turned pale when Maggie shoved the sharp metal through the worm's guts.

"This is a lot to take in, I'm sure. Why don't you read over these and call me?" Mr. Bly slid the files and his business card across the table.

Maggie didn't reach for either. She scanned the room and thought of all the times over all the years she had begged her dad to invest in bed bugs and to consider their future, all the work she'd done to avoid exactly this. "Mr. Bly, before you go, let me make sure I understand. The business is part of the bankruptcy. The bank owns everything. We have nothing left. My dad is dead. Mom is broke. And I'm supposed to run Fehler Family Exterminating without money. Oh, and now my cousin is somehow involved because he's a boy." Her head hurt. Her stomach ached. She couldn't even pull her face together for her sisters.

Mr. Bly nodded. "There's one more thing, which may be easier since your mother left. Mr. Fehler left a note. You may want to read it with your sisters." He stood, fished an envelope out of his coat pocket, and said, "I know the way out. I am truly sorry for your loss, ma'am—Maggie."

Maggie didn't move. She stared at the envelope and swayed a bit. Mr. Bly laid it on the desk and then walked out. Jules, Tammy, and Kate appeared in the doorway. Tammy walked over, picked up the envelope, and handed it to Maggie. Kate wheeled her father's chair back in and curled up in it. Jules studied her fingernails, leaning against the wall. Maggie opened the letter and read it out loud.

Dear Daughters,

If you're reading this, I'm gone. I'm sorry because I can imagine how sad and confused you all are. Before I say anything else, know that being your dad was the greatest joy of my life. I love you all dearly. I never told you enough.

Next to our family, Fehler Family Exterminating has been my life. I'm not sure it is a path I would have chosen. I don't know. I was always told I'd be a bug guy. I didn't know much else. I want you to have a different choice. Go do something else with your life. Be successful somewhere else, somewhere where your last name doesn't get you a job. Go get hungry. You don't owe me or your mom anything. Then come back if you want to. Work it out together, as sisters. Take care of the hive.

Love,

Dad

What Maggie wanted—no *needed*—right now, more than any business decision or succession plan or valuing of assets, was to talk to her dad. She wanted to call him for advice. He'd tease her, of course—that's what Robbie did—but Maggie could always see through him. He was her dad. He was, she realized now, her best friend too. He was the one she spent her days with from morning coffee through the lunch sandwiches she packed for them both—Robbie's with extra pickles, of course—to a beer and fried mozzarella sticks at a local bar on their way home from work. She thought she knew his mind, until now.

10

Grace

Grace swore the room was thin on air. Her breaths were sharp and quick. Each inhale caught on a rib. A deep gulp brought shooting pain. She'd hyperventilate soon. Robbie had closed the windows in a fit about wasting heat after she'd opened the windows to air out their bedroom. It was a lifetime ago. It was yesterday. He'd locked the windows too, as if he was trying to trap something in, probably her. Grace flung the first one up and closed her eyes in relief at the rush of damp air. The fading light was low, but she could see slivers of a perfect pink midwestern sunset. Thunder growled a few miles south. Missouri was humid. The whole state was a wet blanket. Father Tom said to stop blaming herself and asking so many what-ifs. What if Robbie had lost weight and exercised? What if she'd cooked healthier food? What if she hadn't had an affair? It was all her fault, except the damn windows, and the blaming and guilt were safer emotions than the rest. An entire limb of their family had been hacked off. How would the rest of the body work? She was taking pills. Mostly to get her hands to stop shaking and to seem as if she could hold it all together for her daughters. Survival was solely on her shoulders, like she'd always suspected. Grace stood at the window and watched the rain roll in: a mist followed by fat, splattering drops, then a furious downpour. She worried that Robbie would get soaked from the storm. Graves don't need water or sunshine. They don't grow. They decay. How could she just leave Robbie there when she'd worked so hard for their survival?

The second window was stuck. A piece of folded cardboard had been jammed in tight to the sill. Grace tugged it out and ripped it to pieces. The cardboard shards stank of metallic fake florals, clearly a leftover box of company chemicals. Goddamn Robbie, pissing her off even in death. He'd abandoned her. She knew that wasn't true, but that's how the fresh grief landed. She put both trembling hands on the ledge and leaned in with her hip to pop up the pane, but then she saw the nest. A mourning dove: gray with ruffled brown feathers in muted colors. The dove looked at Grace with beady eyes and then fluffed out her wings, warning Grace with stiff neck movements. "She looks like a Nancy," Grace said out loud, deciding not to open the window. "Nancy Reagan, for sure." The dove cocked up one wing and revealed a white flash, a glimpse of milky eggs tucked safely beneath her, even as the rain pelted her feathers. Grace understood fierceness. She'd strut to protect her brood too. Nancy and she would get along fine. Then Grace made a mental note to cancel the gutter cleaning Robbie had scheduled with the neighbor boy. Surely his ten dollars could wait for the squabs to make their way into the world. Just as she decided to join forces with this mama, Grace closed the curtain and Nancy flew from her nest with a whistle.

The bedroom door swung open, and Nacho lunged from the bedside rug and barked. She expected it to be her husband, but their dog would never bark at Robbie. He was gone. Again. His absence caught in her throat every time. Travis tiptoed in, closed the door quietly, and plopped himself on the bed. "Jesus, Travis. The girls could have seen you come in. Nacho hates you. My husband slept right there. Get off the pillow."

"You said yourself he often slept in his chair."

"He had back problems. And he loved his La-Z-Boy. Don't judge me." Grace didn't kick him out, though.

"Brought you a present," Travis said, holding out a package. "Maybe it'll cheer you up."

"I'm a widow. I'm not supposed to be cheery." Grace opened the bag and discovered a Bible. Its cover was navy and sturdy, and each page was laminated for weather.

"It's waterproof. I got it from your favorite store, Self-Reliant Outfitters. Had to order the special edition to make it Catholic."

Grace was touched. The affair was mostly about making out and making plans for doomsday. She hadn't considered that Travis might be open to church too. Would Travis be willing to convert? That he'd considered weatherproofing meant a lot to her. Robbie wouldn't have thought of something like that.

"Let me draw you a bath," Travis offered, walking into the bathroom and pulling off the decorative towels from the bar. They'd hung there for years, and Grace wouldn't let Robbie touch them. Travis rifled through a cabinet and unwrapped a packaged loofah Grace had swiped at a hotel last summer and saved for a special occasion. Travis poured purple bubble bath into the faucet flow. One of her daughters had given her the fancy glass jar for Mother's Day, but Grace had never used it.

"Bubbles?" Grace shrugged. "Okay." She breathed an artificial lavender and didn't mind. It reminded her of the baths she had given the girls before bed when they were little. She could rarely squeeze all four of them into the same tub, but she tried. Hours of bubble games with plastic mermaids and pitchers for pouring over their long hair.

"At least Robbie won't have to see the election," Travis said. "Though I'm sure that's a small comfort at a time like this."

He sounded stiff, and his fumbling pleased Grace. She understood what Travis brought to her odds of survival, but she also knew she'd need to give him direction. At least she had a partner. At least he was still here. He was more valuable now than before. They'd survive together. It was a small relief in her cloud of worries and regret.

"Give me an update on supplies," she ordered as she undressed and climbed into the tub. Travis filled her in, listing recent procurements and future prepping for their mutual task. As he talked, he sunk his hands into Grace's hair and made suds. He reached for a cup on the side of the sink to rinse. Robbie had drunk from it the morning he died. Grace scooped water and brought it up to her nose to smell the floral suds. "The future is about water, Travis. Marlene was right last week at our meeting. Water. That's going to be the real struggle."

"You're right, baby. Absolutely right. I was waiting to talk to you about it, but there hasn't been a good time, and now, what with the funeral and all . . . Anyway, I want to go half on a Berkey. It's worth it for a water filtration system. Berkey is the best. All the preppers think so." Travis walked into the little toilet closet. He didn't shut the door.

Grace protested over the loud sound of his pee pinging against the porcelain. "But we already have those LifeStraws. The personal ones." She wasn't crazy about his new intimacy and willingness with bodily functions in front of her, but she assumed she'd have to get used to close quarters for survival.

Travis called back as he flushed, "Those are for amateurs. 'As Seen on TV' types. We're at another level now, Grace." He didn't wash his hands.

"That's a lot of money. We certainly need to store more, that's for sure."

Travis returned to the tub, scooped up some bubbles, and blew them into the air. "We need to be able to filter our own, to have our own source. I'm telling you, when it happens, it's not going to come down to ammo and guns or even food. It's going to be about water."

Grace frowned as the bubbles landed on the bathroom floor. They'd leave a slick spot. She might slip on it later. Or Nacho would lick it up. "Maybe you're right. But who can afford that?" There was no way now that she could even think about a Berkey. She hadn't told Travis about the bankruptcy or the will. She was still trying to make sense of it herself, but it didn't make any sense at all—unless, she realized, Robbie had known about the affair.

"It's an investment. That scout workshop I took last year—the one I told you about down near Springfield—taught me all about trapping and wilderness first aid. Cost five hundred for the week, but let me tell you, it was worth every penny for my skill set."

"Did that include food and lodging?" Grace asked, poking her toe at the faucet. Getting away for a bit sounded good right now, but was it even possible? She doubted it. The will. The business. The bankruptcy. The uncertainty. It made her want to be ready now more than ever. She hadn't prepared for the possibility of Robbie's death, and she owed it to her family now to help them all survive. She wondered what Robbie would think of her going away to one of those camps. She wondered when she'd stop wanting to tell Robbie the things that happened first.

"Camping is free," Travis said. "That's what I did. They said we shouldn't be on campus grounds because of their insurance, but they said it with a wink and a nod, you know? Stupid government regulations or something. Gave me more chances to put my outdoor gear to good use. The only thing missing was you. I was awful lonely, without you."

"What would I do at a camp like that?"

"Well, you're too advanced for basic survival school, but you might like the blacksmithing or wilderness first aid. There's one on medicinal plants too. The real way to go is the twenty-eight-day package. Everything is included. And they test you in a ten-K team at the end. Think about it, Grace. You and me. Alone. On our own. True prepping. The real deal. And the best part? We'd be together. And maybe even bring home prize money."

Grace was about to ask about cost. She'd been tallying up the resources he kept listing and wondered where he thought she was going to get that kind of money. Then Travis reached his hand through the suds and fished until he found the soft place between her thighs. She leaned way back and closed her eyes. His hands on her were a comfort and a release. Tears stung, but her body vibrated back to life. Then Travis stripped and slid into the tub behind her.

Afterward, she stood up quickly on wobbly legs, her sagging, weathered breasts and puckered butt cheeks flushed. She didn't even bother to suck in her sloshy belly. Travis handed her one towel for her hair and wrapped her body like a baby in a dry one. Grace couldn't imagine what Travis saw in her. She'd worried, after the funeral, that Travis might disappear, that maybe without the threat of Robbie the thrill might be gone, but he was steadier than she'd hoped.

"Go check on the eggs in the dove's nest, will you? On the windowsill. To the right."

"I don't see any eggs," Travis reported, "but I do see two fresh hatchlings."

Grace rushed to the window and caught a peek of the slimy feathers poking out beneath the dove's fluff. "Get away from the window before you scare Nancy."

"Nancy?"

"Yes. She was a fine woman, wasn't she?"

"She was. The best. Nancy was what a First Lady should be."

She exhaled with relief that she didn't have to mention Reagan for Travis to get her. Their shared wavelength was rare. His youth helped with prepping, and it didn't hurt in bed either. She regretted pushing Robbie's hands away so often, especially now that he'd never reach for her again. How could she have known?

"You know what?" Travis said, moving closer and holding her hand.

"What?" She dropped her towel to the floor and pulled her shoulders back for better posture.

"They look like Jeb and George, don't they?"

She took another pill with the water Travis had brought her and then could breathe again. She could do this. They'd be stronger for the struggle. Her daughters would be safe. Robbie was gone. He'd left her alone and unprotected. He'd bankrupted them and hadn't trusted her enough to even help. It would require a recalibration, but now she had Travis fully committed to her plan. It had to be enough for the nest.

"They do. They really do," Grace agreed.

11

Kate

In the garage, a few mornings after Robbie's funeral, Kate stared down at the beekeeper suit. It was still hanging on its hook where her father had left it the last time he went out to relocate a hive. The empty suit arms hung limp like a deflated phantom. It called to Kate when she couldn't sleep, which was every night since her dad died. She wanted to bring it to her bed, but her sisters would think that was weird, so she wrapped her body around Nacho instead and worried that one day he'd leave her too.

When her dad first got into the beekeeping part of pest control, he tried to educate the customers that they didn't need his services. Robbie said bees should be admired not feared, but a recent documentary of Africanized bees (a.k.a. "killer bees") was a boon for Fehlers' and they couldn't afford to turn away the business. Robbie found that chemicals on the hive did nothing. The bees buzzed louder but didn't die. He told Kate he hated to think of her mouthing a spoon of insecticide, which she found ironic considering the gallons they sprayed in Cape Girardeau homes. So instead of dousing the hives with a neonicotinoid, Robbie started bringing the hives home and reorienting them to the Fehler family yard, on the back fifty acres, where Grace reluctantly admitted they'd be useful for survival. The garden had tripled in size and harvest since the bees arrived. Bees pollinate more than one-third of the world's crops, but Kate wondered what crops would still be left when global warming destroyed them all. The loss of biodiversity was real too. She seemed to be the only one of the Fehlers who understood the science of their demise. Honey might help sustain them, but it wouldn't be enough.

"It'd be good for bartering," Grace agreed. "As long as the girls don't get stung."

"Bug girls know better," Robbie boasted.

Kate remembered her dad best in a bee suit. When she was younger, before Kate started worrying about fitting in at school and who liked who, and about Lila, she'd watched him one afternoon from the window of the passenger seat as he zipped up the white plastic jumper and masked his bearded face with the helmet netting. "Whatever you do, don't get out of the car," he said. "The bees will follow me. You stay put." But Kate didn't want to stay put. She wanted to dip her finger into the amber leaking from the comb. She wanted to lick it right off a bee's butt. Her sisters thought her the quiet one, but she was often plotting, strategizing, and collecting data, often on them. How else might she know their fears and decide which buttons to push and how best to defend the hive?

"But it's dark," Kate complained.

"Has to be," Robbie said. "If we move the hive during the day, all the bees will be out foraging and they'll come back without a house."

"Why'd we have to bring firewood?" She picked at the scrapes on her palms from carrying sticks.

"Your grandpa showed me that. If you put these branches at the front of the hive, the bees get a bit scrambled and have a reason to reorient."

Kate shrugged. It didn't make sense. "You want them confused?"

"Basically. So then we can move them and they'll figure out their new home. Bees are brilliant. Did you know nectar is almost eighty percent water? That's why they flap their wings all the time. They're removing moisture from the nectar."

"Then what?"

"Then they eat it and regurgitate the nectar into the combs. It's a chemical process actually. Bees have an enzyme in their stomach called glucose oxidase."

"I want to see them."

"You will soon. Just not today. One mile at a time. I have to move the hive bit by bit or they'll get lost. I'll be back in thirty minutes. Don't go roaming, you hear?" Kate rarely obeyed, but she was good at looking like she intended to. Robbie walked away. "Stay put, Kate," he called back over his shoulder.

Kate had tried to wait. First, she rolled the window up and down a few dozen times, but when her arm tired of the crank, she needed another task to occupy and distract her from how much she wanted to follow the buzz and her father's ghost costume behind the barn. She flipped through one of the two books in the car, *The Beekeeper's Bible.* The pictures made her hungry. Honey on toast. Honey on a banana. Sweet tea with honey. Honey on a spoon. She opened the car door, swinging it wide with a jab from her foot and letting its heaviness close itself. Then she did it again and saw how long she could stand to dangle her hand before pulling it back for the safety of her fingers. Kate adored bees, especially their danger. Honey smeared on crackers. Honey drizzled on raspberries. Robbie called her honey girl. She hoped it was because he thought she was so sweet, but Tammy had said it was because she was annoying. Jules said Tammy was the annoying one. Maggie told them to all cut it out. Grace, the queen, couldn't be bothered. Kate knew how to please, and she also knew how to get her share and then sneak back in line again for more.

Kate flipped *The Beekeeper's Bible* to the chapter Robbie had marked on moving hives and learned that bees listen to bees, at least when it matters. Successful foragers return from the field and give a little taste to other bees, through pheromones and nectar, of what's out waiting for them if they follow the same path. When the eager bees start paying attention, they start a little disco. Maggie said it looked more like little celebratory vibrations, thus the buzzing and boogie. Other bees circle the dancing one and reach out their antennae for directions and frequencies. Distance, nectar source, and angle to the sun are all communicated with a waggle. Kate would party for nectar too. "Bug girls must be self-reliant," Grace always said, and now they'd have to rely on each other even more. The bees were still teaching them.

When she grew even more bored, she thumbed through the dog-eared pages of the other book, Mark Twain's *What Is Man? And Other Essays* and read aloud from "The Bee," which her dad quoted when explaining work and order:

> The distribution of work in a hive is as cleverly and elaborately specialized as it is in a vast American machine-shop or factory. A bee that has been trained to one of the many and various industries of the concern doesn't know how to exercise any other, and would be offended if asked to take a hand in anything outside of her profession. . . . It is just as I say; there is much to be learned in these ways, without going to books. Books are very well, but books do not cover the whole domain of esthetic human culture. Pride of profession is one of the boniest bones of existence, if not the boniest. Without doubt it is so in the hive.

"It's the hive, Katie," Robbie would lecture. "The hive above all else must survive. You hear me?"

"Uh-huh," she'd nod. But she couldn't have known, not then, how much she'd one day wish she'd listened more and how sacred that time in the field with her dad seemed to her now when he had so suddenly disappeared from their structure. She read on:

> There are always a few royal heirs in stock and ready to take [the queen's] place—ready and more than anxious to do it, although she is their own mother. These girls are kept by themselves, and are regally fed and tended from birth. No other bees get such fine food as they get, or live such a high and luxurious life. By consequence they are larger and longer and sleeker than their working sisters. And they have a curved sting, shaped like a scimitar, while the others have a straight one.
>
> A common bee will sting any one or anybody, but a royalty stings royalties only.

"Are you a common bee?" Robbie asked her.

"Nope. I'm royalty," Kate said, to satisfy her dad. "Can we get a Happy Meal on our way home?" And Robbie took her and ordered himself a chocolate milkshake he pretended he couldn't possibly finish all on his own.

In the garage, Kate stepped closer to the suit as her belly complained, stomach acid juices churning on empty. She was dizzy and exhausted from not sleeping. The kitchen was stuffed with food condolences from neighbors and church friends, yet she couldn't bring herself to eat any of it. She didn't want to enjoy food without her dad being the one who provided it. Not like Jules, whose grief seemed to be contributing to her bad mood and appetite. Or Tammy, who said the smell of all the food was making her sick. Maggie labeled and put the casseroles in the Deepfreeze next to the bench with Robbie's tools. Boxes of canned foods and dried beans were stacked next to it waiting for Grace to unpack and organize. What did the prepping mean now? How could they keep preparing for a life without him? It had been only a few days, but Kate had to keep reminding herself that he wasn't out on a relocation mission. He wouldn't be finding his way home again, and no amount of strategy could make it so.

The beekeeper suit looked full, like her father's body might still fill it. She squeezed an empty arm, punched its gut, and felt it collapse without his weight. Her dad wouldn't bring her honey on a spoon ever again, teasing her like it was an airplane and she a toddler learning to use utensils. She unzipped its length and climbed in. The legs were too long, so she carefully rolled up the pants and tucked them in her boots. She did the same with the sleeves and placed a rubber band at each wrist before pulling on the gloves. When she ducked her head beneath the helmet netting, it smelled like her dad—sweat, sunshine, soap, and sour beer. She ripped it back off and threw it across the cement floor, so quick was her anger at his abandonment.

Kate was still a kid. It's not fair to lose your dad. Who would do all the dad things now? Kate wasn't only Grace's favorite; she was Robbie's littlest woman too. He'd told her so one night when she was ten and had woken up with a nightmare. Robbie tucked her back in and told her a story about the bees.

> Once upon a time there was a queen bee. Her name was Erma. She was a grouch. Technically, she was a Hymenoptera from the superfamily Apoidea. Erma didn't care that there were twenty thousand other types of bees. She knew that bumblebees were superior. And in her own hive, she had the longest life. Erma was going on four years old. She'd seen the infertile, inferior female

worker bees die quickly from their constant labor. Poor, weak things. Male drones weren't much stronger. They dropped dead directly after fertilization. Erma didn't see what else good they were for, so she didn't bother to get to know them at all. Erma would drop eggs in each cell and be off for her nap.

One day, Erma felt not quite right. Something had changed. That tree was different. The sun hit her behind from a different angle. The workers and drones buzzed and buzzed, flying in crazy eights, then buzzed louder. Erma couldn't get any peace at all, and she didn't feel like laying eggs. So Erma left her hive to figure it out. A dog named Nacho chased her back. A big white hand swung in her direction. She sent out some workers to sting it. Erma flew a few circles to get a lay of this new land. She liked the distant wheat fields and the sounds of little girl voices. She could hear other hives near but not so close that they'd come over and try to steal her honey. Erma decided she liked being a part of the Fehler family and settled herself back into her hive.

Kate had fallen asleep again promising she'd learn all the trees in their backyard the next day so she could find her way home.

When Kate threw the helmet, it landed near Robbie's favorite chair, his La-Z-Boy. The one with the fancy footrest Robbie could pop up with a side handle. "Watch this!" he'd say, making each daughter sit and marvel at the luxury of a leg lift. The threadbare plaid material was still rippled in the middle from his imprint. Her mom had already banished it to the garage, and Kate wondered if she could sneak out here at night and sleep in her dad's chair. She and Nacho could fit in it together.

Without the protective netting, Kate ran toward the hives, with Nacho barking at her back. He nipped at her shirt, trying to pull her back to safety, but nothing would ever be a shelter again.

Nothing would protect them from the Earth decaying, air pollution, bees disappearing, dads dying. She followed a trail of bees flexing their GPS location systems and imagined rounding a bend to see her father floating as a bee suit balloon in the field holding a sticky golden amber comb, waiting to feed her.

12

Maggie

Because her dad was the first person she saw every morning, Maggie had often told him her dreams. They'd sort them out on their drive to work or later at the coffeepot if Maggie had left the house early to race him to the office. Even as a child, she'd share the pieces of her night while he flipped pancakes and she cut strawberries for breakfast. Each of her memories led to one of his, and she knew she could get him telling stories about his own childhood or lecturing about bugs if she baited him enough.

"I dreamed about the bees again," Maggie had said on a rainy morning months before Robbie died. "They left the hive, and you were out trying to round them up."

"Why'd they leave?"

"Their queen died. They didn't know what to do without her."

"Bees are smarter than that," Robbie had assured her. "There is always a plan. They know how to survive. Did you know there is a bee in an amber fossil that is about eighty million years old? Not a lot of bee fossils because they're too smart to get caught. Ants, though, plenty of those. But bee DNA tells us bees are actually more like 130 million years old."

Maggie did know, but she didn't stop her dad from telling her again.

Maggie thought about last night's dream on her drive the next morning. The passenger seat was empty beside her. Even though it had been over a month since she lost him, it still looked haunted. One of her dad's tiny yellow legal pads was tucked into the door pocket. His notes from their visit to the Macon Products plant were waiting for Jenn to transcribe into their computer account so the next technician would have instructions. At a gas station, where she used a credit card she'd just opened and had already nearly maxed, she wrote her dream on the same pad, to both retrace her dad's path and to claim the story he was writing as her own.

> Bryan and I were kids again, in our backyard. It was during the week he stayed with us every summer. I pushed him on the swing, and he said it was too hard. Every time his feet swept the grass or dirt, he pulled them back, as if he didn't want to get dirty. Then he got stung by a wasp and made us take him to the ER while he whined. He made me carry his books and guard them in the waiting room.

Maggie realized now that even her dream summary was harsh. She was angry at her cousin. It wasn't his fault, but it felt wrong to be furious with her dead dad, so she blamed it on Bryan. He didn't even want a part in the business, did he? He'd never expressed any interest in bugs, never offered to help sweep the garage on the weekends as the rest of the girls were assigned. He didn't help count glue boards or fill chemical orders so that the technicians' trucks were stocked and ready for Monday morning. Bryan usually begged off with a book, and Grace didn't make him since he was their guest. He seemed delicate to Maggie in a way that nobody in business had time for.

Maggie would find out the extent of his interest soon enough. The will was still in probate, and they expected the bankruptcy ruling any day. The lawyer said they should prepare themselves to make decisions, so she'd asked Bryan to coffee. He said he'd be in Columbia giving at talk at the University of Missouri, so Maggie decided to make a trip of it and check on Jules too.

Without her dad, Maggie clung to her sisters. Jules had been the quietest since the funeral, and Maggie worried about her the most. Maybe it was too soon for her to go back, but Grace had practically shoved her out the door and Jules had run. Niko seemed like good people, but they'd been dating only a few months. He wasn't family.

There was also a garage with an apartment she was interested in renting for one of the routes. One of their best technicians lived halfway between Cape and Columbia, and she thought it was inefficient to have him waste the gas and miles to stock up. If she rented a space in town and offered to let him live there, the technician could exchange his travel time for sales and build up more business. Maybe they could expand their service area and use the garage as a northern base. It was the kind of plan that popped into Maggie's mind now that Robbie was gone. He'd never talk of investments, only expenses. Could you pay rent with a credit card? She'd have to find out.

"What kind of talk are you giving?" Maggie had asked Bryan on the phone. She knew he'd gone to college out east for a long time and that he studied something related to Mark Twain. She'd heard he was teaching history somewhere, but Grace said he'd lost his job because of the recession.

"It's about Jane Clemens's unpublished letters. You're probably not interested. Really, kind of only for Twainiacs," Bryan had said. "I'll meet you afterward." But Maggie looked up the talk anyway on the campus website and realized she could make it in time if she left right after the morning sales meeting. Grace warned her that they were expecting a few inches of snow, so she let her mom add a bag of salt to the trunk and a shovel in case she needed to dig the car out. She had looked up Jane Clemens and found out she was Mark Twain's mother. Then she looked up Bryan and learned that he'd recently published an article, "Lineage Helps and Hinders Creativity: Jane Clemens's Own Wit." Surely, a guy like that didn't want to go into the bug business.

Maggie found a seat easily. The auditorium was almost empty. Maybe it was because final exams were beginning. Maybe it was the time of day, 2:00 p.m. on a Tuesday. Or maybe Bryan wasn't the scholar he'd hoped he'd be. There were maybe a dozen students and two or three professors. They all looked bored except for one young man in the front row leaning forward in his seat and filling up his notebook.

On stage, Bryan paced behind a podium and clicked through slides of Jane Clemens: her official portrait, pictures of her children, houses she'd lived in. He finished her official biography—born 1803 in Kentucky, married John Marshall Clemens in 1823, died in Keokuk, Iowa, in 1890—and was moving on to his thesis.

"Mark Twain—or rather Samuel Clemens—wouldn't be Mark Twain without his mother. She was his model for Aunt Polly. It was her wit that makes it into his work so much. One time, when Sam was a kid, he got very sick. Later, he asked her if she'd been afraid he might die. She admitted that she was more scared he might *live*." A few audience members smiled, but the young man in the front row roared and slapped his knee. Maggie wondered if Bryan had planted him there or if he really was this big of a fan.

"Studying Jane helps us see where Mark Twain got his sharp tongue. He was a rascal, Jane knew, but she understood he couldn't be contained. He was often half drowning himself down in the

Mississippi River, on the banks of his boyhood home, Hannibal, Missouri. Twain claims that he had to be hauled out of the river on at least nine occasions. Of these near drownings, Jane remarked, 'I guess there wasn't much danger. People born to be hanged are safe in water.'"

Maggie was surprised to find Bryan's lecture interesting. She remembered how much she'd enjoyed her history classes at community college, even though she doubted she'd ever use them in the bug business. She wished she'd brought her highlighters so she could better read the program—the words didn't add up until they were color-coded, and the yellow one helped her track. Jane Clemens would definitely need a purple marker. She had energy and pluck. Maggie remembered that her marketing teacher had said, "Advertising is about telling stories. The consumer wants to be part of the tale." Bryan was a good storyteller, for sure. He could be decent at sales.

"I was passing through Hannibal recently," Bryan said, stepping to the center of the stage, "and visited her grave. She's buried at Mount Olivet Cemetery next to her husband and their son Henry." The young man in the front row shot his hand up.

"I'm happy to take questions at the end, but you seem pretty eager now." Bryan nodded for him to continue.

The young man cleared his throat. "I'm a student here and was born and raised in Hannibal. I wondered if Laura Hawkins, who Becky Thatcher was modeled after, ever gave us insight into Jane."

"What a thoughtful question. What's your name?"

"Bobby. Bobby Haymaker. I'm a sophomore. History major."

"Ah, well, Bobby. Mrs. Laura Hawkins Frazer was interviewed by the *New York Times* in 1928, and her account was published on February 5 that same year. It was written by Aretta L. Watts. In it, Hawkins described Jane as 'a great lover of fun' and one who 'preferred folks who were full of life, liked anything gay, and hated the solemn and morbid.' Hawkins also noted that red was Jane's favorite color but that because it wasn't proper for her to wear—because of her widowhood—her family discouraged her from fashioning herself in it."

"How did Jane handle Sam's mischief?"

"Mostly, with humor. He teased her a lot. Hawkins told of a time when Sam had written his mother a letter and marked it 'personal.' It turned out to be written in Chinese."

"And what of her relations with people of color in Hannibal?" Bobby asked as students started exiting one by one up the rows, passing Maggie. The lecture clearly wasn't over, but it had become more of a two-way conversation.

"You're practically rewriting my lecture, aren't you, Bobby? I'm flattered. You can imagine that most audiences want to hear about Twain."

"I was raised by a single mother. I know their influence." Maggie found this young man's oversharing endearing. He was sincere and unembarrassed by his interest. He seemed entirely at home with himself. Confident, even.

"Jane got along well with the people of color in Hannibal. She was very friendly with them, and they liked her. Hawkins said people of color called her 'Aunt Jane' or 'Miss Jane,'" Bryan explained, clicking through slides of Hannibal and Mark Twain's boyhood home. There was even one of the famous white picket fence, and Bryan was pretending to paint it with a brush wired to a wooden bucket bolted into the brick so no one would steal it. "Of course that's reporting from Hawkins's point of view. I'm sure the people of color felt differently about her station versus theirs. I do worry that their acceptance of Jane as kind implies their satisfaction with slavery in Hannibal. That's simply not true and—"

Another professor quickly joined Bryan on stage. "Just one more question, folks. And thank you, again, Dr. Schaler, for visiting us today and sharing your expertise. Anyone else have a question?" He looked around at the stragglers, but still only Bobby's hand was in the air.

"Did Mark Twain write much about his mother?"

Bryan smiled as he clicked forward to his final slide titled "Sam Clemens writes about Jane."

"We see her a lot in his work, for sure, but mostly in Twain's male protagonists. They're playful and cheerful, sometimes mischievous, more like Jane than his father, who was stern and serious. Sam wrote, 'She was of a sunshine disposition, and her long life was mainly a holiday for her. She always had the heart of a young girl. Through all of the family troubles she maintained a kind of perky stoicism which was lighted considerably by her love of gossip, gaudy spectacles like parades and funerals, bright colors, and animals.' Clemens shared that his mother couldn't hurt a kitten and she was always saving them from their drownings and assigned their care to him."

Bobby nodded his head in knowing. "I get that. I'm more of a cat person."

Bryan smiled. "Me too." Then he turned to the few remaining audience members, "Thank you for humoring me and my fascination with Jane Clemens. Remember there is more to every family than meets the eye. Success and creativity are fed from the home and often fueled by those we rarely hear from, like the mothers."

Maggie wondered if that was true. Grace had tolerated the business for what it provided them but treated it as an annoyance, a thing that took from them rather than gave. But surely Fehlers' wouldn't have survived without her steadiness. Robbie needed the pushes Grace gave him. Maggie had seen that plenty. Her dad could be a bit safe and simple, especially when it came to business risks. Her mom was often the one with the ideas, even the crazy prepper ones, but she made things happen.

After the lecture, Bryan joined her, and they walked to the bustling Starbucks on campus. Maggie thought he was nervous, but she wasn't entirely sure why. Maybe it was because she came to his lecture and he wasn't expecting it. Or maybe he was embarrassed by the low turnout and lower interest. Or maybe she was seeing her grown-up cousin with her own grown-up eyes. They hadn't talked at the funeral. There wasn't much then that they needed to say. It was still a blur for Maggie, and she was grateful that the business demanded so much from her right now. Busy was an easy place to hide grief.

She bought them both small black coffees and was outraged by the price. She could make five full pots of Folgers for the same amount. "It's the Most Wonderful Time of the Year" sang throughout the store. It seemed too early for holiday music, and the merriment was annoying. They pulled a pair of lounge chairs together beside a fake fire that flickered in a wall display. Bryan poured cream and three packets of sugar into his festive red cup. Maggie studied the stacked display of mugs and wondered what their profit margin was. She noted that the Starbucks logo was an understated ornament on this year's cup design with white trees and reindeer, not necessarily a declaration of secularism but rather a demure nod to Christmas.

"I should have told you sooner," Bryan said, adding an extra dash of cinnamon. "I'm moving to Cape next month."

"You're what?" Maggie stumbled. "But we haven't seen you in years."

"I need a fresh start."

"Why? What did you do?" Maggie could tell it hit a nerve in Bryan, but she wasn't sure which one.

"Nothing like that. I interviewed at SEMO about a month ago. Right after your dad's funeral. I should have told you I was in town again. I figured you were all busy, you know. I had to meet with your dad's lawyer, Mr. Bly, too. Didn't get the tenure job because of a hiring freeze but they offered me a term position. It's renewable." Maggie looked away from Bryan, trying to slow her breath. A mom and her two daughters sat at the table next to their chairs and began coloring postcards that Starbucks would mail to the troops overseas. Maggie sipped her coffee as the mom showed them how to write *Thank you for your service.*

"But why now? You have a life in St. Louis."

"It's an opportunity. A new town. A new job. A new challenge with the business. I loved visiting you all on the river when we were kids." Bryan waved at the girls coloring their postcards. He was trying to be friendly, but they scowled back at his stranger danger.

"Did you? I don't remember you being that comfortable with our way of life. Seemed to me you weren't a big fan of bugs."

"That's not necessarily true. I wasn't as accustomed to them as you all were. But I'd like to help, with meetings and planning, maybe." He paused. "I'm sure you aren't happy your dad included me. I wouldn't be if I were you."

Maggie didn't answer. She was angry and hurt, but she'd been raised to behave, to be polite. House manners, Grace called them.

"Truth be told, your dad meant a lot to me. He accepted me for who I am. Being at your house meant I could be me."

"Being at my house meant being a bug girl."

"I guess it's different from the outside."

"But, Bryan, you don't know anything about Fehlers'. Why not sell your share? Why not sell it to me? I don't have a lot, but the appraiser is taking a look now and I could pay you in installments." Maggie wasn't sure she could, but she'd figure it out if it meant getting more control over the business. They weren't rich people who bought up the market when it crashed in September. They weren't people with money in the market at all, but they still felt the panic and uncertainty. Surely, Bryan needed any measly money they could offer.

"I don't think I want to sell, Maggie. I know that's not what you want to hear. I don't know why your dad left it to me, but I'd like to find out."

It was true; it was exactly the opposite of what Maggie wanted to hear.

"He did it because you're a guy," Maggie said, not caring how it landed. "That's it. He didn't think a bunch of girls could run the business."

"That can't be true. I'm sure there's more."

"Best I can tell. It would be better if you sold it to me. Then I'd have enough say to invest in the bed bug rigs."

"The what?"

Maggie slid her business plan for bed bugs across the table to Bryan. She'd brought it in hopes of persuading him to sell his share. He thumbed through the pages and asked questions. He was more interested than her father had ever been.

"This looks completely sound to me. I mean, I don't study business, but the numbers add up. You've definitely done your research."

"I've been working on it for six months. Dad wouldn't even talk about it. But the truth is that the company won't make it for another six months without new business."

"You mean it would go bankrupt?"

"It already is. We barely make payroll every week. We can't afford the rent, and I don't know why Dad never bought property for the business. He could have even bought it himself and made the company pay him rent. He did things the way they'd always been done, and he wasn't interested in change."

"I'm all about change. Let me help."

"We've had a lot of account cancellations with the upcoming election too. Folks think Obama will be bad for the economy, so they're cutting corners. They don't realize pest control is an investment not a cost."

"I see that. I mean, I'll learn to see that."

Maggie checked the time on her phone. Jules was supposed to join them an hour ago. She'd texted instead: Can't make it. First-gen study session went long. Sorry, sis! And now Maggie had to leave. "I'm sorry to go, Bryan, but I have another appointment. There's a space I'm considering renting up here to store chemicals and one of our route trucks."

"Can I come along? I'd like to hear more of your thoughts. And soon we'll almost be neighbors, you know." Maggie thought he sounded too willing. Running a family business wasn't a game. You didn't try it out. You owed your community and your employees. Maggie felt the constant weight of it since her dad's heart attack. The business had mostly shelved her grief. Necessity ruled. But she wasn't hating Bryan's company, and he did own the same share as hers.

"Sure," she agreed. Maybe if she brought him along she could talk him into selling. "Can I ask why Jane?" she said, clearing their table of cups and napkins to toss on the way out. "I mean, everyone studies Mark Twain, right?"

Bryan's easy smile came back. He held the door open for her. "Because I want to understand someone who can't drown unwanted kittens. She made Sam take care of them, and he learned compassion. I don't think she gets enough credit for Sam Clemens becoming

Mark Twain. It's complicated with family, isn't it? I'm fascinated how women overcome what men do to them."

Maggie was about to agree when Bryan's biggest fan met them at the door.

"Oh, Dr. Schaler," Bobby said, holding the door for them. "Nice to see you again."

"Bobby, the budding Twainiac." Bryan shook his hand. Maggie thought Bobby's blush was adorable. She hadn't realized how tall he was before. And good-looking. He wore a plaid collared shirt and straight blue jeans that looked like they'd been ironed. His grin was open and earnest, but he kept ducking his blue eyes like he was embarrassed.

"I'm glad I ran into you again," Bryan said. "I meant to give you my card—in case you have more Jane Clemens questions." He reached into his bag for a card, and a bee landed on his arm. He waved his hand to shoo it away, but the bee scurried up and down his sleeve investigating the sugar still clinging from his coffee doctoring.

"Do you live here in Columbia?" Bobby asked.

Bryan flailed his arm again, but it seemed to only attract another bee. "Actually, I'm moving to Cape. I'll be teaching soon at SEMO."

"Oh, my aunt lives down there. She's a nurse in the ER."

At the mention of the ER, Maggie thought of her dad laying lifeless on the table where they'd tried to jump-start his heart. Robbie was already gone, but they still tried. And Maggie needed to know they'd tried to save their family this heartbreak, even if it was inevitable.

"Well, look me up when you're in town. We can have coffee and talk Twain." Bryan curled his thumb and forefinger like he might flick the bees, but Maggie intervened. She held his arm and gently blew on the bees until they flew away one by one.

"Thank you, sir," Bobby said. "That's a kind offer."

"Please, call me Bryan. And this is my cousin, Maggie."

Bobby shook Maggie's hand. "Pleased to meet you. Are you a professor too?"

"Business owner, actually. A bug girl," Maggie mumbled.

"A what?" Bobby asked, cocking his head to the side.

"Like an entomologist but with chemicals," Maggie said, using Robbie's line for the first time. She was surprised how well it fit.

13

Jules

Jules was relieved that it was Niko who found her passed out on the bathroom floor of her dorm. She'd avoided Maggie's calls and texts—begged off with bullshit about first-gen meetings and study sessions, as if any of that mattered now. She had vaguely heard Niko call her name before his arms were around her. "Jules? What happened?" he'd said, shaking her, and even then, woozy from the loss of blood, she thought he was overreacting.

If it had been her RA, Raven, then everyone would know—including Grace. Jules hated the dorm gossip, especially when it was about her. Since her dad's death, the girls on her floor lowered their eyes when they passed her in the hall. Nobody knew what to say. Raven had stopped by to check on her. Jules thought she had come to tell her to turn down her music again, but her RA stood in the doorway, twirling her black braids. "Sorry," she said. "I'm sorry about your dad. I'm here if you need anything."

"Like what?" Jules asked, because she was still Jules, even in grief.

"I mean someone to talk to. Or something like that. You know." Raven looked around the room and ignored the overflowing ash-tray. Her awkward kindness made Jules feel guilty. Everything was shitty, but she didn't have to be too.

“Thanks. Really, thanks for checking on me.”

She’d been thankful when her mom insisted she finish the semester. “Go,” Grace said, hugging her too hard. “Go on. Life goes on.” Maybe Grace swayed a bit. She might have renewed the prescription that had gotten her through the funeral. Her grief sent her to the basement where she was doubling down on her prepping. She seemed renewed by the increased responsibility. It was now her mission alone to save their family, though Jules thought the dangers were never specific enough. Most of what Jules feared came from inside her. So far, she was numb. Until she cut.

Jules had come into the bathroom to wash the wound. It was a tiny cut, but the bleeding, a bit of a gush, was a surprise—not an entirely unwelcome one. Niko could be a bit dramatic. “Lock the door,” she whispered.

“The door? I’m calling nine-one-one.” His voice was so loud. She wished he’d shut up so she could think. There was a lot of blood. More than she remembered.

Jules gestured toward his chest. “Give me your shirt.” She wrapped the plaid cloth tight around her wrist. “I wasn’t trying to . . . you know.”

“I know. But you need a doctor.”

“I want to sleep. I’m so tired. And cold. See? The blood stopped.” She used the shirt tails to wipe up the mess. She turned on the nearest shower nozzle to rinse away the rest. Jules wasn’t trying to hurt herself. She had just cut too deep. She couldn’t stop crying, and cutting calmed her. She wanted her feelings to stop. “I’m sorry, Niko,” she said and meant it.

“You don’t have to be sorry.”

“I’m fine. Just walk me to my bed. I’m tired.” And because he was Niko and genuinely seemed on her team, he did. He stayed, too, and made her drink chamomile tea and not smoke pot and take a few bites of a veggie burger even though he said beef would probably be better right now. Jules knew there had been more blood than usual, but she couldn't quite get deep enough for the lift. Cutting was a trance—a delicious type of stoning but with tools and soft tissue rather than drugs. She had passed out for only a few minutes, but it was enough time for it to look intentional. It was a slow dimming, and she had slid down the shower tile and rested against the cool slate rather than hit her head. But it wasn't on purpose. Not this deep anyway. That wasn't what it was at all.

"Promise me you won't tell," Jules said. She closed her eyes but tightened her grip on Niko's hand.

On Monday, Jules showed up at the university counseling center and signed in. She was only there because Niko had insisted. His mom believed in all the talk stuff. Niko had spent every second with her since he'd found her hurt. He wouldn't leave her alone. It was endearing and annoying all at the same time, but Jules had to admit, Niko stuck, even when things were hard. She adjusted her long-sleeve T-shirt over the bandage as she entered the counselor's office.

"So, tell me what happened," Pamela began, after all the intake forms. Jules had barely sat down when she ripped back her sleeve and revealed her injury, like a kid on the diving board who desperately needed an audience. "May I?" Pamela asked, holding out her hand to inspect Jules's arm. She was so tender, Jules had to close her eyes at the touch.

"It was nothing. A small cut. I guess I went too deep. I don't remember. I passed out. Niko—my boyfriend—found me."

"Why didn't he take you to the hospital?"

Jules's guard evaporated. She gushed, "They'd call my mom. Or Maggie, my oldest sister. They have enough to worry about. My dad just died. I didn't want to bother them. Doctors cost a lot, and we don't have a lot. It's no big deal. It's never happened before. It won't happen again. I made a mistake. But, seriously, no more cutting. I promised Niko."

The office smelled of lavender, and it made Jules sneeze. There was a tiny white noise machine in the corner that hummed nothingness. It made her want to nap. Her dad had told her once that the government hides recording devices in things like that, but she couldn't imagine why the government would care what she spilled to this old lady in counseling at college. Pamela. Her name was Pamela.

"That had to have been scary for him."

Jules flushed. She felt ashamed and mad at herself on his behalf.

"Cutting is hard to stop," Pamela said, folding her hands over her knee and leaning in like she had made a profound declaration.

"You don't think I know that?" Jules knew she was being rude. She was being impatient like her dad. She just hated the part where her old lady counselor repeated everything slowly back to her as if she didn't already know how she felt. Okay, validating, whatever. Move along. Give me answers. She got things quickly and lost her cool when it took other people so long to catch up.

Pamela waited. She was writing something down. Jules could only imagine how crazy this old lady thought she was and what her records might say. *First-year, first-gen student. Dad died. New boyfriend. Likes poetry but feels she must major in business. Cutter.* "Real change isn't possible if you do it only because you promised someone else. What if there comes a time when Niko is no longer in your life? Who have you promised then? My point is, Jules, you have to want to get better for you and no one else."

"I know," Jules snapped, but she didn't. "My dad just died, you know? I don't even understand it. Does this anxiousness ever go away?" She put her feet up on the coffee table and watched to see if Pamela would tell her to take them down, but she met her eyes and ignored Jules's combat boots.

"Not in my experience. You learn to manage it. You do the work every day. You get better at understanding it and avoiding the triggers. It's who you are. Do you want to change who you are?"

"Some parts, yeah. But I like who I'm becoming. It's cool to be with people who like poetry and art and music and not be embarrassed by how much I like those things too. My dad always said I was too sensitive. Mom says I poke at too many things."

Pamela smiled for the first time. Her short gray hair was cut in a sleek bob. She wore jeans and a black suit jacket. Jules had expected her to be stiff, but she was kind of relaxed like an old lady hippie. "That sensitivity is your strength. That curiosity can be fuel."

"I don't feel strong. I wish it hadn't happened."

"It did. Consider it an opportunity. If it hadn't happened, you wouldn't have had to confront your anxiety and the cutting. You wouldn't be here right now."

"Yeah, but it scared Niko." Jules studied the candle on the coffee table between them. The candle had never been lit. Probably a university policy or something stupid like that.

"And you, too, probably." Pamela scribbled in her notebook and nodded along in a way that made Jules wonder if she had practiced that move in her training. "Do you care about Niko?"

Jules nodded. "I do. A lot." She wanted to cry and punch things, but she wasn't sure which thing she would be reacting over: her dad, the stupid thing she had done, how she was nervous about Niko, her tuition bill, or worrying about her sisters and mom. Anxiety felt like a big cloak she wore that no one else could see. Or maybe they could. Maybe everyone else knew she was a mess too. But she wasn't. Not really. Not always. She struggled; that was true. But look where Jules had landed. Not too bad. She had shit to do.

"Have you heard of ANTs?"

"I grew up in a pest control business. I know ants."

"Of course you do. Not those kind, though. A. N. T. Automatic negative thoughts. Plural." Pamela picked up a plush gray anteater from her bookshelf and settled it by Jules's boots, like it was her new pet. "They aren't your fault. You can't control ANTs. They simply exist. What you can do is decide what to do with them."

"With the toy?"

"It's symbolic. You can stomp on ants. You can poison them. You can let your friend the anteater gobble them up. Redirect them. Reframe them. Ants exist. But you can manage them anyway you want."

"But the stuff that sucks isn't a negative thought. It's just stuff that sucks."

"True. Grief is real and changes and takes a long time. It creeps up sometimes when you least expect it. But you probably had an anxiety disorder before your dad died. The ANTs are more related to that. Your dad's death is making everything feel more acute."

Jules checked the time on her watch. Twelve more minutes. "I don't want the anteater."

"Then put it back on the bookshelf." Pamela gestured with her pen, like it was a dare. "Do it or don't. You decide."

"How am I supposed to sort what is an ANT from grief?" Grace said she asked too many questions, but Jules couldn't stop. She was curious about everything. Knowing seemed urgent sometimes.

"You probably won't be able to. The label doesn't matter. The question is, does this serve you? If it does, keep it. If it doesn't, don't. My point is, Jules, you have more control over the outcomes than you think."

Jules kicked the stuffed doll, and Pamela gave her a round of applause.

At lunch, Niko asked about her morning. He was in a mood, and Jules rarely saw him grumpy. "It was fine. You know. Pamela, that's my old lady counselor, totally fixed me. Whew." She picked at her lentil soup and wished it was Grace's chicken noodle—but secretly so no one would know she was a cheating vegetarian. "What's up your ass?"

Niko pushed his chair back from the cafeteria table like he was about to run. "You think everyone else has everything figured out? They don't. I don't. My mom called this morning to tell me she left my dad. He got a gig touring in Spain for the year, so he's leaving too. I go to college and they split up. Like they've raised me and now they're done. I asked you to lunch to tell you that. It totally sucks, but I wanted you to know. You're the one I want to tell stuff to. Why can't you see that, Jules? I'm in this."

"Pamela says that too, that I think I'm the only one suffering."

"Did you even hear me?"

"I did. I'm sorry. That totally sucks. Tell me what else your parents said." Jules nodded like Pamela had. It helped her feel maybe a little of what Niko was feeling. She liked that he was sensitive. She loved that life hurt him too—not that he was wounded, but that he didn't live on the surface or hide every time a problem popped up.

Niko sniffed like maybe he'd been crying. "My mom is working all the time. With the recession, her clients need her a lot. Everyone is scared. My dad got a break he's been waiting a long time for. He stayed home with me as a kid, so I know it was hard for him not to travel with the band and stuff. He's making up for a lot of lost time in his career. I get it, but that doesn't mean I like it."

"I get that. Everything at home has changed since my dad died too."

Niko shook his head. "That's exactly it. Like I need my head to be here and everything to be stable there, but it isn't." He took a deep breath and straightened his shoulders. "He said we could visit him in his apartment in Spain. He'll be on the road a lot, but it could be fun together, you know?"

Jules nodded. She didn't even have a passport. She'd been out of Missouri only one time in her whole life. But she didn't hesitate. "Yes. Absolutely yes."

"You are kind of a pain in the ass sometimes," Niko said. "But it'd be a blast. Both my parents really want to meet you."

"I'd like that too. I promise not to be a pain in the ass when I meet them." She moved her cafeteria tray to the side and held Niko's hand across the table. He ducked his head like her sudden affection embarrassed him; Jules knew better, though. "I have to drive home again tomorrow. Back to Cape for a few hours."

"Why? You just got back."

"My sister needs me. The business stuff. I'm going to try to help her get a loan to keep everything running."

"Maybe you can't save them, Jules," Niko said, kissing her fingers. "I can't fix my parents' marriage. That's for sure. Maybe you've got to save you."

Saving herself was a tempting idea, especially when what Jules wanted was simply out. She needed to sell her share of Fehlers' to Maggie, who couldn't afford it, so that Jules could earn the college education she couldn't afford either. It made perfect sense. About as much sense as trying to be a college student with a family that kept calling her home for every crisis. Other students complained about the same thing in their first-gen seminar. Niko said she'd never have any independence if she didn't take it for herself, but he hadn't taken her tuition bill crisis seriously. His bills were paid by a savings account his parents had started when he was born. His parents knew Niko would go to college before he'd even taken his first step, and they planned for it.

No one had planned for Jules, and she couldn't get the number on her last tuition bill off her mind.

"This can't be right," she had said, shoving her aging Dell laptop into Niko's face.

"Maybe it's a mistake, babe. Why don't you just make an appointment with Financial Aid. They'll help you straighten it out. Bills are wrong all the time, Jules." Niko was watching Obama at a press conference: stimulus bill, surge of violence in Afghanistan, pending global economic crisis, blah, blah, blah. It wouldn't matter anyway. She felt the fear of change grow every time she went home. They were terrified of the future, and Obama was the monster to blame it all on. The Fehlers and folks like them were ripening for a savior, someone who would reverse the order and bring back the good ole days that had been good only for them.

Jules stood in front of the TV screen. "It says I owe fourteen thousand dollars. That's just not possible. I have scholarships. Dad paid this bill. He promised."

"Can we just watch the rest? Obama's talking about the economy. Then we'll walk over together. It's not that big of a deal."

"It is, Niko. It is a big deal, especially to me. This just can't be right." Niko didn't have to pay his own bills. He'd probably never seen a tuition statement. He didn't check his debit card balance, as if it would just magically work every time he wanted a sandwich. Sometimes she really saw the distance between them. They came from different worlds and spoke different languages. She got tired of catching up. She got tired of having to adapt and to explain why she didn't know stuff in the first place. There was plenty Niko didn't know about her world, but she was living in his.

Jules hadn't waited. She'd sprinted across campus and ran up three flights of stairs to Financial Aid. It was 4:52 p.m. The sign on the door read Closed, but their hours of operation were clearly stated as 9:00 a.m. to 5:00 p.m. When you own your own business, there are no set hours—or at least no set hours anyone abides by. You're done when the job is done, and the job is never done. She knocked on the frosted glass door. No one answered. She knocked again and held up the bill on her screen as if someone could read it through the glass and solve the mystery. "Can I help you?" An older bald man with round glasses stared through the window.

She pointed to her screen. "I received this bill, and it's wrong. I need to talk to someone. You're supposed to be open until five."

"Our front office staff left early for a birthday party. I was on my way out too. Would you like to make an appointment? I could probably work you into the schedule with one of our financial aid officers late next week."

"Late next week? I need help now."

"We have fewer officers since the recession. Just one of many university cutbacks."

"But what do I do until then?"

"You wait, my dear. I know that's hard, but I assure you it will work out. This stuff usually does. It just takes more time than I can offer you to sort out a bill. Have you talked to your parents? About the bill, I mean?"

Of course she hadn't. Her mom wouldn't understand. Her dad was gone. Maggie was overwhelmed. Jules felt the weight of how much she'd had to grow up and how fast.

The following week, she went to the appointment and sat through a tedious explanation of the loans her father had apparently taken out instead of paying the bill up front. He probably needed the cash and saw a low-interest opportunity. But he'd paid the bill with a check from a credit card, which didn't go through for some reason. She was pissed that he was proud and desperate and dead. She wanted to call and cuss him out. She just wanted to call him. She'd tell him his American dream was a big fat lie. Work hard and you still lose. Not everyone starts in the same place. Equal opportunities were bullshit. She studied twice as hard as Niko, but he'd had a better high school education and his parents knew their way around college.

Robbie had said the liberal in "liberal arts" was political, even after Jules had patiently explained that in the history text Dr. Suda required, *A Brief History of the Western World* by Thomas Greer and Gavin Lewis, she'd looked it up in the index: liberalism. See also democracy. See also individualism. And then chapters on revolutions fought to free minds and the idea of equality and faith in reason and progress. These revolutions looked different in different places, of course, but the idea that education was dangerous had been born.

"Dad, *liberal* is Latin for *liberalis*, loosely translated as freedom. 'Liberal' education does not stand in contrast to conservatism. And the lowercase 'arts' refers to 'skill' or 'education.' It is not the same as the uppercase 'ARTS' that you hear politicians wanting to cut in budget deals. So 'liberal arts' leads to 'freethinking,' which conservatives like you should adore."

Robbie had dismissed her explanation. "Ok, college girl." Jules understood his coded sass well; she was fluent in the same deflection and avoidance, her old lady counselor called it. But it didn't take a college education to know that their family couldn't afford for her to go and that Jules's days at the university were done.

Maggie told Jules at breakfast the next morning she was hoping the banker, Mrs. Cooper, felt generous.

"If you need money so bad, let's sell the family camp," Grace offered. "The property has to be worth something."

"The camp?" Kate said as her mouth made an exaggerated *O*.

"Dad borrowed against it, remember? We probably couldn't get enough for it to even pay back what he owed. Mr. Bly said the court would absorb the cash as an asset. Besides, I have a plan," Maggie said. "We don't need to sell anything. We need to invest in bed bugs. Their comeback in this country is huge. While others are using baseboard sprays and bait, we'll have more success with heat. It's all in my business plan. I just need the money for the rig—and a majority vote." Maggie smoothed the pages of her plan and straightened the edges for the hundredth time.

"Mom may be right," Jules said, but the sisters glared at her. She was usually the outsider, mostly an intruder. Certainly she'd abandoned the hive.

"Where would we go if we didn't go to camp?" Kate asked. "Dad loved the camp."

"Yeah," Tammy said. "It's a Fehler family tradition."

Jules rolled her eyes at their traditions. So was slavery. And not letting women vote. Pamela said she didn't have to pick every single fight. "Maybe just let one go and see what happens," she'd said, and Jules promised to try even though she didn't intend to try at all. Jules believed that if people weren't pissed then they weren't paying attention. Most people just wanted to bury their heads in the sand. She found most people boring.

After rushing through Tuesday Mass, she and Maggie skipped out once communion ended. They parked Jules's car in the public lot in downtown Cape Girardeau and walked along the Mississippi River. The churning river created frothy caps for the ducks to float on. A bald eagle sailed above them and landed on a bed of cattails and shrubs. The air reeked of tangy barbecue mixed with foul fish. Jules stuck her nose in her sleeve and studied the flood-wall murals, which boasted portraits of Mark Twain, a self-proclaimed "border ruffian" with Missouri morals. Jules could imagine exactly what that meant. She felt torn too. Her loyalty to her family conflicted with her political views. Grace told her she thought too much, and Jules wished her mother would think a bit more. It was a battle neither could win. Her dad had been proud of her but he also teased her about being too good for them. Her reach was a rejection of him, even though that wasn't true at all. Robbie saw things in simple terms; every issue was black and white. Jules saw only shades of gray; every issue was complicated, and she had more questions than answers.

A three-story building hovered above them on the riverfront. It was bricked with an enormous sign advertising nickel Coca-Cola that would "relieve fatigue." Jules remembered eating lunch at the Port Girardeau Restaurant and Lounge for her dad's last birthday because he loved an all-you-can-eat Sunday buffet. "Eat up, girls," Robbie had said. "Let's get our nine dollars and ninety-nine cents worth. Who wants a waffle? Stuff yourself with bacon." Kate snuck bacon in a napkin to take home to Nacho. With their bellies busting, they walked the riverbank and counted the barges.

Jules was surprised when one of these dad memories hijacked her mood. Grief was a stalker, she'd learned. Jules put her back to the flood-wall mural and pressed into its stability. She watched the divided sky: a layer of heavy, steely clouds above crisp white fluff. A brewing storm with the sun trying so hard not to surrender. She closed her eyes and did Pamela's breathing exercise and was grateful her sister didn't comment. Maggie knew things. Sisters do. Then the rain came, like Grace had warned them it would, and they ran together for cover under the river walk pavilion.

Maggie said they should wear church dresses and mention that they'd been at Mass to seem more earnest and pious during the begging. Payroll was due, and they simply didn't have the cash. Jules knew Maggie hadn't taken her salary since their dad had died. She'd let Jenn go and hadn't rehired for route four, which covered what was left of the town of Cairo, when the technician gave his notice. Bryan was supposed to meet them at the bank, but Jules wasn't sure how it would help. She liked her cousin; they understood each other. But he was supporting cast, and this was a moment for a lead.

Bryan said he'd meet Jules and Maggie by the Mark Twain plaque on the river walk, but he was clearly running late. Maybe he'd never heard Robbie's lecture on how time was money. "'The Mississippi River will have its way. No engineering skill can persuade it to do otherwise.' Mark Twain said that," Maggie read. "Jules, name some other Missouri writers."

"Marianne Moore. Kate Chopin. Laura Ingalls Wilder. Maya Angelou. Mary Jo Bang. Do you want me to keep going? Or do we only honor dead White dudes?"

"Geez. Maybe put your gun down, sis. Not everything is political."

"Isn't it?" Usually, Jules would be interested in an argument about feminism, but she needed to be back to campus for a study group by 8:00 p.m. She'd read Maggie's bed bug business plan enough to know that it wasn't a good enough gamble, but as the only other Fehler sister of age, Maggie needed her signature on the loan. Either Bryan would have to reveal his gold or their mom would need to cosign. Neither seemed likely. Mr. Bly advised that the bed bug loan would be a stretch but that Maggie was in charge now. She could make bad financial decisions like her dad had; they'd all be paying for his for a long time.

Ten minutes later, Bryan sprinted toward them. "I'm so sorry. I had to teach a one o'clock class and let them out early."

At the bank, Mrs. Cooper ushered them all into her corner office. A fake fern sat sadly on the floor. Jules pretended to listen while Maggie desperately tried to sell her business plan. She felt sorry for her sister. The need was so critical. "You see, it's a thermal remediation trailer," Maggie plunged forward. "I mean, you must have a John Deere diesel generator with a block heater and fuel tank, right?"

Bryan and Mrs. Cooper nodded, as if both were huge John Deere fans.

"It's all included in this system: double axle trailer enclosure, high temperature fans, power cables, heater patch cables, infrared handheld thermometer. Even the extension cords and power distribution boxes. Tape and insulation too."

"I can see it's very comprehensive, Maggie. Tell me about the cost, dear."

"The whole rig is fifty-eight thousand dollars. That's a deal. A five-year term comes to twelve hundred per month."

"Tell her about the return on investment," Bryan nudged. "That's the most impressive part."

"The national average for a bed bug treatment is six hundred dollars. Of course, we're still in a recovery so maybe less here in Missouri. We have enough demand for at least ten treatments per month. And those are residential. There's a lot more in hotels and housing projects. So you can see that the potential profit margin is high."

"And a treatment takes an entire day? What about labor and training costs?"

Jules took a peppermint from the dish on Mrs. Cooper's desk to distract her, as in Mrs. Cooper—or herself, as in Jules? and unwrapped the plastic noisily, just like Robbie would have. It was a power move he pulled. The chemical smell of the candy caught in her throat. Her eyes stung. She swallowed and coughed to clear the emotion.

Maggie turned the pages on Mrs. Cooper's desk to the colored pie charts she'd created. Jules wished her sister would put away her stupid highlighters. It was like she hoped their cheerfulness would be persuasive, but all the jumping around from blue to pink to purple to yellow was annoying. The banker listened intently and followed her sister's finger, but she was clearly skeptical. "It seems like a good plan, honey. We've done business with your family for years. Fehlers' is a foundation in this community. I'm so sorry for your loss. Really, I am. But your financials are not in good enough shape to take on more debt."

"You're right, Mrs. Cooper," Maggie cut her off. "I was telling Bryan that you have to spend money to make money."

"But you have nothing for collateral. And I've run credit checks for all of you, and the bank doesn't feel it would be a good risk right now, especially after your own recent bankruptcy, Bryan."

Jules studied her sister's reaction to see if she had known. She clearly hadn't. Maybe that was another reason he'd moved to town. He needed a place to start over emotionally and financially. What a loser. A nice one, sure. But still.

"And your outstanding student loans are substantial, Ms. Fehler." She nodded at Jules, who took another peppermint and fingered the tight cuffs of her long-sleeve shirt that covered what needed to be covered. "Not to mention the jittery markets these days. Even the FDIC seems shaky. We can't take the risk on you right now. Your credit rating is extremely low, and the estate is still tied up in probate."

"Thank you for your time, ma'am." Jules pumped Mrs. Cooper's hand and pulled Maggie away before she made even more of a fool of herself.

The bed bug plan was not going to happen, and her sister needed to think about selling sooner rather than later. But who would want a failing family pest control business? The appraisal meant nothing without a buyer, and they didn't have any interest from the advertisement the lawyer had run. Jules owned a share with little value too. She probably wouldn't be able to register for classes in the spring. It was hard enough to pass her midterms and prepare for the finals for the one semester she might be able to complete, even with her debt and loans. She couldn't ask Maggie for a job, not one that paid anyway.

The sunlight bounced off the water and temporarily blinded them when they opened the double doors from the bank building's lobby. Maggie wiped her eyes and pulled at the dark circles her twenty-year-old face shouldn't have. She looked defeated. "It would have made Dad proud, you know? If the bed bug business succeeded. It's a good investment. I know it is." Maggie hung her head and said she was going to walk back to the office.

Bryan and Jules stopped by the river lookout together on their way to their cars. The water was in a hurry. The Mississippi River seemed to know where it was going and didn't care who it hurt in its path.

"I want to make him proud too, you know?" Jules said, throwing a rock into the curling current.

"Of course you do, Jules. We all do. Everything swirled around Robbie. I think you're all afraid to let him down."

"But he let us down." She didn't actually feel afraid. She felt a tightness in her throat. Either she was getting sick or coming home was strangling her again. "I want to draw. Did I ever tell you that?" She knew she hadn't, but maybe he'd remember that when they were kids she was often sketching. "Not like for a career or anything. Just for fun." It embarrassed her to say it out loud. She wasn't sure where she found the courage. Maybe it was Maggie's willingness to be vulnerable and to take a risk on her bed bug plan. "Sometimes I even illustrate my poems. Only in my journal."

"Take an art class. You probably have room in your schedule. Why not? Learning shouldn't hurt. You could even enjoy it."

"It's just . . . you know. A degree is supposed to get you a job.

That's what Dad always said. But there's this other stuff I want to know about and do. Music, poetry, art. But does it matter?"

"I get it. I see it all the time." He was only a decade older but acted like those years were a lifetime. "It's a first-gen problem. Our families mean well. But you and I are living in another world. We can go home, but home doesn't look the same. Our folks at home don't have a lot of access to our new world. How can they understand? That's not their fault. Take an art class." Bryan tried to throw a rock too, but it bounced on the muddy shore and settled.

They both turned to watch a family study a map of Cape. They were looking for the "cape," but it didn't exist anymore. Jules didn't have the heart to tell them that the only rock remains were up at Cape Rock Park. At least the view of the Mississippi was good from there. The way the father held his daughter's hand made her throat itchy again. She went back to watching the water and ignored them. "Dad figured out how much every single class cost us by the hour. He said if one of my professors canceled they were stealing money from our pocket."

"Learning is hard to quantify and difficult to measure." Bryan did sound like a professor. He was probably going to make a terrible bug guy. Maggie had told her about the lecture he'd given. He'd probably already researched whether Jane Clemens had bed bugs. Of course she did.

"Dad wouldn't agree."

"I know. You're right."

"Sometimes I'm still mad at Dad for dying. Is that weird?"

"It's not weird. Sounds like grief."

"It doesn't make sense, and he screwed everything up."

Bryan tilted his head to the side and looked like he had when they were kids. "Or it's terribly sad and we miss him and everyone has to find their own way now." She didn't like his answer. It sounded like something her old lady counselor would say. She'd always thought softness was a luxury she couldn't afford; but what if softness was a kind of strength instead?

Jules walked alone to the parking garage and thought about what the financial advisor called smart debt. He suggested she take out more loans. He said the investment in her future was worth it. There were graphs and charts like Maggie's of how much more college graduates make over their lifetime. But her family needed her more. The entire family business was up to the Fehler women now, and Jules was one of them, no matter the distance.

14

Grace

Grace thought Robbie's cell phone was in his radio room. When the ER nurse had handed her an envelope containing the pile from his pockets, she wasn't sure what to do with the contents: wallet, loose change, office and house keys, cell phone, belt clip, and receipts for things he'd bought that they clearly couldn't afford. Grace worried that if she opened the envelope, her guilt and secrets would spill out too. After that late hospital night, she'd left the envelope on the overflowing desk in the nook off the garage where he did his ham radio operations and shut the door tight. She hadn't opened it since.

The family was broke. They all realized the mess Robbie had left and the lengths he'd gone to to make them believe the business was fine. Nothing was fine, and he wasn't here to fix it or even be accountable for the hole he'd dug. She'd made a list of cost-cutting strategies, and canceling Robbie's cell service was an obvious task, but she'd have to go into his radio room to find the phone. What if there was cash in his wallet? It felt like a raid. In prepper meetings they'd practiced how to gather resources from abandoned homes. The key was to be quick and efficient without emotions—locate, assess, take. Travis offered to help, but that made her feel worse. She resented his kindness, even as she needed him more. She deserved this punishment. The task was Grace's to endure.

Just as she turned the knob on Robbie's radio room, Nacho barked to alert her that the barrier to their house had been breached. Grace rewarded him with a bacon-flavored biscuit. It was only Jerry, the mailman, whom she was avoiding because he insisted on saying he was sorry about Robbie with every delivery. Everyone was sorry. But none of their condolences could pay debts. Father Tom said she could be a bit softer in her grief for the sake of her daughters, but her softness wouldn't help them survive, that she was sure of.

She collected the mail after Jerry was gone. In the pile of grocery flyers and church bulletins, there were thick envelopes from the hospital, doctor's office, and medical facilities. She tore them open, recycling each envelope as Kate insisted, and smoothed the mound of bills on the kitchen table. She reached for her coffee and took a deep breath. She prided herself on staying calm in crises. Grace remembered that similar mail had arrived the day before and the day before that, and she had added these to the growing pile. Then she began her danger assessment.

Robbie's ER visit was more than $3,600 just for the hours in the hospital alone. The doctors who had tried to save his life billed separately as "independent contractors" at $900 and $1,250 each. The ambulance ride cost $2,200 because they were "out of network," as if you were supposed to call the insurance company when your spouse collapsed and then wait on hold through multiple transfers and operators to get a confirmation of approved ambulance companies before administering lifesaving efforts. The balance on the hospital bill was outstanding from two years prior when Robbie had his first heart attack and bypass surgery at a cost of $77,000, which included $11,400 for angioplasty, $3,100 for an echocardiogram, $5,978 for thrombolysis, $33,722 for the three-day hospital recovery, and $254 per month for one 75-milligram clopidogrel pill per day. Robbie rarely even took that pill, Grace knew. From the statement she could tell he'd been paying the hospital $5 per month for some reason, like that was going to ever make a dent in this disaster. He'd also been prescribed physical therapy, which he thought was a joke, and he certainly hadn't made any changes to his diet. Being a man too macho to go to the doctor had killed him. Maybe his tombstone should read "Died from Pride" rather than "Beloved Dad."

Even in death, Robbie had disappointed her. Grace wanted to shout, mostly at him and about him, but he'd gotten the final word. She imagined him pleased about that in heaven. She was so pissed that she ran out to the garden to weed. It was a kind of therapy that turned her anger into usefulness. Her tears mixed with sweat until she was spent in a pile of soil begging the vines to produce enough to sustain them. She waited for Robbie to bring her an iced tea—because sometimes he would, and it was so unexpectantly kind and loving that it melted her—but he didn't. Then Grace dusted herself off and returned to her duty for the day.

Scanning the kitchen table, Grace hoped these bills were mistakes. They had health insurance through the company. She'd heard Robbie grumble about high co-pays and rising deductibles, but this was outrageous. *It's too expensive to get sick*, Grace thought. How would they ever make a payment like that? The sum was insurmountable. Grace tallied up all the supplies they could stock for the cost of this bill. Robbie was gone, and now the family's survival was all that mattered. They certainly couldn't spend resources on a family member who couldn't even contribute. She said a quick Hail Mary that no one else in the family would need doctors anytime soon. They were already underwater on a sinking ship. For whatever it was worth, the insurance company hadn't canceled their policy. But these claims would surely make them reassess whether they wanted to offer their services to the company at all, rather than at a price Fehler Family Exterminating and their employees couldn't afford.

Leafing through the pages of bills, Grace dialed the office. Maggie answered. "Where's Jenn?" she asked.

"I let her go. We couldn't pay her anymore. Dad was worried about having her on the insurance anyway in case she got pregnant. Women do that."

"I did it four times, and I don't remember your father minding."

"Those were *yours* not *someone else's*. What's up, Mom?"

"The hospital bill came. It doesn't make any sense. It's more than one hundred thousand dollars. Can you imagine? They couldn't save your Dad, and now they're trying to kill us too."

"Maybe the insurance hasn't paid their portion yet. Did you call the insurance company?"

"I will. I wanted to call you first."

Maggie sighed. Grace was sorry she'd called. Maggie was doing her best to keep the company's doors open one more day. She couldn't help with this too. "I'm running a route myself today," Maggie said, typing something and shuffling papers. "I gotta go. I asked Tammy to come in after school to help with the phones."

"I'm glad," Grace said. "I mean, I'm glad you asked your sister to help. Might keep her out of trouble." Then there was silence on the line. Grace almost told her she loved her, but Maggie had already hung up. The feeling hung in the air and floated away.

Grace opened an almost expired Meal Ready-to-Eat labeled "Menu 22: Asian Beef Strips" and unpacked the main course, side dish of rice, and a cardboard-looking cookie. She sipped the Gatorade they'd included and stashed the Skittles for later. While taking stock last week, she pulled out the food that might lose its shelf life, like the MREs, and she'd been trying to convince the girls to eat them too. It was good practice, she figured, to get used to the flavors and textures. Between bites, she called the insurance company phone number listed at the top of each bill. She pushed the buttons through prerecorded operators and sat listening to classical music for twenty-seven minutes. Finally, a human answered. Grace told her everything.

"I'm sorry for your loss, Mrs. Fehler," the operator said with a heavy southern accent that made her monotone voice sound more sincere. "Can I place you on a brief hold while I review your claim?"

The hold wasn't brief. When she finally came back on the line, the operator read her the EOB, explanation of benefits, as if she was bored by Robbie's death. She informed Grace that they were denying coverage because Robbie had reported he was in good health when they took out the policy. They'd searched his medical records, knew his blood pressure was high, and found out that he'd once admitted to smoking cigarettes. That was true and more, Grace thought, but there was no reason to share that now. After more holds, more transfers, more operators, and more condolences, a supervisor in the benefits department finally told Grace, "You'll need to file an appeal. It takes ninety days to process."

"What am I supposed to do for ninety days?" Grace asked.

"I'd recommend you call the hospital's billing department. They might be able to negotiate the fee or help you apply for medical assistance. Again, we are sorry for your loss."

Like most things, Grace would have to do it herself. Monica from her prepper group did something in Billing at the hospital. Maybe she could help. Grace put the stack of papers in a file folder to make it look more official, changed her dirty gardening T-shirt, and drove to the hospital. In person was best, and she was exhausted from talking on the phone. Travis had called three times, and she'd ignored each ring. Grace assumed the government listened on the phones. This was none of their damn business.

Pulling into the hospital lot, she avoided parking in the same area she had on the evening Robbie died. She had to circle twice to find a place that didn't feel like she was returning to that night. She'd ridden in the ambulance with Robbie, but one of her girls must have driven their car because when they came out in the dark after it was all over, their car sat alone in the lot, illuminated by a single ray, as if God himself was guiding their way back home without Robbie.

Grace followed the signs away from the ER to the billing department. The floor color changed from a serviceable gray to a soft, sparking white. Cubicles lined the office in a pleasant pattern, and there was a low hum, phone calls, and keyboard typing. Grace was surprised by its cheeriness. All these workers happily overcharging sick people and their families because they were unlucky enough to need a doctor.

She wandered around until she found Monica in a windowless corner. Monica looked shocked. They'd never seen each other outside of the prepping meetings.

"Is this it? Did something happen?" she asked, her eyes excited and wide.

"I'm not here about prepping, Monica," Grace said, wheeling over an empty office chair. She joined her in the cubicle and put the stack of Robbie's bills on her desk. "I need your help with these."

The ordinariness of Grace's request seemed to disappoint Monica, but she flipped through the bills one by one, neatly restacking them after she'd read each. "Did you get an EOB?" she asked.

"It's coming. They told me over the phone that they were denying coverage. Much of the care was 'out of network' and Robbie lied on the application. Is it true that I have to pay what they won't cover?"

"Uh-huh. Then you start negotiating."

"How? With who?"

"The doctors. Each office. Tell them Robbie died."

"I have to call each of these providers separately and ask them to give me a break? Will they do that?"

Monica shuffled the papers again into a tidy stack and slid the file back to Grace. "Sometimes. Not all will, but it don't hurt to ask. I'll submit a request on your behalf for a reduced rate on the ER bill. They'll usually approve that because of your . . . financial need." She looked embarrassed. Grace was too. She worried that Monica might not take her seriously as a survivalist now. If she couldn't manage this life, how would she survive in the next one? Then Monica whispered, "Tell them up front that Robbie died and that you're a widow with four kids. It may sway them a bit." Then she patted Grace's knee.

Back at home, Grace marched straight to Robbie's radio room. She didn't hesitate this time. She was on a mission. She flipped the wall switch, and the radio equipment hummed. Red lights flashed. Green lights danced. The nook came alive. On the wall was the Ham's Code framed: "The ham is friendly. Slow and patient sending when requested, friendly advice and counsel to the beginner, kindly assistant, cooperation and consideration for the interests of others; these are the marks of the ham spirit." Beside it was Robbie's American Radio Relay League license, his certificate for Amateur Radio Emergency Service member, and a foil stamped entry-level FCC license. When Robbie had told Grace that the classes and exam fees would help them be the first to know about local emergencies and extreme weather, she enthusiastically agreed. He'd even bought expensive carry-in-car handsets to broadcast from the scene. "We're more reliable as reporters because it's from the community. We're usually the first ones at a disaster, and you can trust us." He'd printed a post from the newly organized Tea Party Command Center Blogger Spot and read it to Grace in bed in an official sounding voice, "I highly recommend all Tea Party and Patriot groups have someone with a ham radio license. We need to upgrade our communication capabilities and connect first locally, then statewide, then across the country ASAP. For when the grid goes down."

At least the radio equipment worked, she thought, though she didn't have any idea how. Without Robbie, when the grid went down, they'd be cut off from civilization. Maybe they could still listen to emergency calls and hear local distress signals, but no one in the family was licensed to operate. Maybe Jules could take a college class in this or something, or she could buy Tammy a manual. Kate wouldn't be interested and Maggie's hands were plenty full.

On the desk, Maggie's copy of the bed bug business plan was open to page twelve like Robbie had actually been reading it, and a few pages were dog-eared and marked with question marks. Grace rifled through the rest of the papers. There was an application for something called a "Hamvention," but Robbie hadn't filled it out yet. Then she saw the hospital envelope and ripped it open. She found the dead cell phone and took the forty-two dollars from Robbie's wallet. It would buy groceries that week. She opened drawers and found his handguns. She could sell them both. In the bottom drawer, in the back, she found a lockbox with a code. She punched in their anniversary date, and it clicked open. There were silver coins in a plastic sleeve and one hundred dollars in cash. Robbie had done a bit of his own prepping it seemed, and Grace was relieved. This was exactly what they'd have to do after the end of the world when they went into abandoned houses to replenish their own supplies.

She thought of her neighbors. Who would be most useful to them in the apocalypse? The Matthews had a garden. The Wilsons drank a lot, so maybe they had a wine cellar or stocked bar. She'd seen Mr. Wilson in the bushes late at night sneaking cigarettes too. He could be an asset, but she probably couldn't trust him. Bonnie, the single mom on the corner, was a hunter. She'd definitely have ammunition but also the guns to defend it. She might have a freezer full of venison.

As Grace was making her mental list, a message popped up on Robbie's computer screen. She must have accidentally hit the keyboard and woken the thing up.

Bug Guy, you there?

Grace froze. She stared at the equipment. He had seventy-two other unread messages. She scanned the messages, but she didn't recognize the names and most were in Ham code.

Bug Guy, this is War Room One, please copy. She wondered whether War Room One was a fellow prepper. The name seemed a bit on the nose. *We await your confirmation. Operation Take Back instructions will be sent through secure source. We've valued your participation and the front lines need you now more than ever. Please respond asap, Bug Guy. Over.*

She'd heard rumblings and gossip about a new civil war, but it seemed like boys and their toys wanting to play battle. Grace studied his books: *An Inconvenient Book* by Glenn Beck, *American Conservatism* edited by Bruce Frohnen, Jeremy Beer, Jeffrey O. Nelson, *To Renew America* by Newt Gingrich, *The Way Things Ought to Be* by Rush Limbaugh, and *Freedom Under Siege* by Ron Paul. Had Robbie been in on something? Surely he would have told her. What Robbie did or didn't do wasn't relevant to their prep plan now, was it? Besides, who was she to judge?

Grace's guilt about all that she hadn't shared with him hung in the air like someone had cut onions. It made her eyes sting. She stomped on the power strip, and the equipment went dark. Grace grabbed the guns and locked the door behind her.

15

Kate

Nacho listened to Kate the most—probably because they were often left home together and left out of family discussions and decisions. Except for when he got the dog zoomies and sprinted around the coffee table knocking off iced sodas with his tail, Nacho was watchful, like Kate. Robbie had called him a stalker when Kate reported that Nacho had figured out their agenda based on Grace's shoes. If their mom pulled on sneakers, Nacho might get a walk and he emptied his water bowl in anticipation of the relief; boots meant she was driving somewhere and he might be invited for a car ride, so he waited by the door; but flip-flops in the summer or slippers in the winter meant she'd be prepping in the basement and Nacho sulked in Kate's bedroom on her lime green carpet.

Kate didn't need to use a leash anymore. She simply told Nacho to stay outside the public library and he sat in the same spot, panting, until she opened the double doors and released a burst of conditioned air. She felt safe knowing he was waiting and parked her skateboard at his feet. Sometimes she went inside for only a few minutes to pick up a book she'd put on hold, but if she got immersed in an anthology of ants, Nacho never minded.

Because Maggie went on and on about bed bugs and they were often in the news—usually in a fancy New York City apartment—Kate decided they'd make a good topic for her dumb biology project. Her teacher shuddered when Kate announced her topic, and that encouraged her. Her dad would be proud that she didn't even flinch watching bug videos on YouTube. They seemed as harmless as lice, just harder to get rid of. But still, Kate wished she could ask her dad questions. He'd tell her more than she needed to know. He'd ramble and get off topic and repeat himself, but she'd put up with it all to hear his voice again, to know she could call her dad with questions. Robbie had an answer, even when he didn't know the topic at all.

After twenty minutes of searching, Kate had three books and dozens of articles—plenty for the stupid summary paper. She'd learned about nests, mating, feeding, and fear. Five hundred words would not be a problem, and she didn't think her teacher read any of her work anyway. Just gave her B+ or A- for being Maggie's littlest sister and forgave her for not having Jules's brain; at least she wasn't as dim as Tammy. On her way out, Kate could see Nacho through the glass doors, and his perked ears revealed he'd sensed her already. He'd probably been using her skateboard as a headrest during his snooze. She hoped he'd have to get used to the smallness of her Penny board soon. Kate thought she heard Nacho whimper, but she stopped to read a yellow flyer on the community bulletin board:

Scent Detection Dog Training
$50 per hour
Call Valerie 573-386-3571
(Tarot and Teller too)

Kate thought fifty dollars an hour was incredible. Who *would* pay that? Who *could* pay that? And what were the dogs trained to find? One of her books had a picture of a dog flipping a pillow on its side to reveal a nest of bed bugs. Could this be like that? Kate flipped open her sister's hand-me-down phone and dialed the number. She readied her best customer service voice, but the answering machine clicked on. Just as Kate was about to hang up, a low voice answered, "Yeah? This is Val."

"What kind of things do you train dogs to find?"

"Who is this?"

"My name is Kate. My dad owns—used to own before he died—a pest control company. I was wondering if you do bed bugs—you know, train dogs to find them. I saw something like that on the news."

"You sound like a kid. You watch the news?"

Kate was annoyed. Fifty dollars an hour for this? Val needed to work on her customer service. Robbie wouldn't put up with them talking to customers like that. He could, of course, but everyone else needed to be sincere and demure. Nacho scratched his backside with his hind leg and yawned.

Kate didn't know what to say to Val's bluntness. In the Fehler family, folks rarely said what they were thinking and never meant what they said. Whatever the thing was, Maggie talked around it, Jules hit it with a big stick, Tammy flashed something to distract it, and her mom avoided it. Kate usually waited to see what happened to it. Her dad used to say, "Sometimes doing nothing is doing a lot." But Kate wanted a plan, an answer, to know if she'd be okay. She heard dogs bark in the background through the phone and wondered what kinds they were and if they were friendly. She'd like to find out.

"I'll tell you what," Val said, breaking the silence. "Bring your dog by, and I'll meet him. No charge. It's the blue house on the corner by the bait shop. I'll be in the backyard. Oh, and kid, I'm sorry about your dad." Then she hung up.

The walk was three blocks and nobody at home was missing her, so Kate headed in that direction. She figured she could peek over the back fence and bolt if this Val lady seemed even weirder than she did on the phone. She was curious and bored, and this seemed a bit of adventure in a town that mostly made her sad since her dad died.

As she got closer, Nacho sprinted ahead. A pack of dogs met him to bark through the chain link at each other. Clipped on the fence was a small wooden sign:

Dog Whisperer
Tarot Reader & Medium

A red-headed woman with long braids held up one hand. "Shh." The dogs assembled at her feet, and Nacho sniffed the ground.

"I'm Kate," Kate said through the fence.

"I know," Val said. "You sound the same."

Kate pointed at the sign. "What's a medium?"

Val tucked her hands into the pocket of her overalls. "People come to me when they want answers. Sometimes the questions are about dogs or about the future or about their loved ones who have passed."

Kate felt it in her chest first. The reminder of the absence. The heat that flushed her body and made her clench her fists. She wondered if she'd always react strongly at the mention of people dying.

Val watched her struggle. "What's your dog's name?"

"Nacho."

The corners of Val's lips perked up from their wrinkles. "Nice to meet you, Kate. Come on in." She unlatched the back gate and swung her arm wide in welcome. The dogs leaned forward to smell the newcomer but stayed at attention.

"Where's his leash?"

Kate felt like returning Val's earlier phone rudeness. It was like she wanted to punish someone for her dad dying. Anyone would do. "He don't need a leash. He stays with me."

Val handed her a well-worn black leash. "In here he does. Put it on him. He needs to know you're the boss."

Kate obeyed, relieved to have someone else in charge, clipping the leash to Nacho's collar and pulling him back to heel. Val nodded and the dogs circled him for a proper welcoming smell. Nacho held his head high and endured their nose invasion. Only when the shepherd got too close to his chin did Nacho jerk away.

Val explained some of the training while the dogs got acquainted. She mostly ignored the dogs, but they gave her a wide path whenever she gestured. Kate felt her power; she wanted to please Val too, but she couldn't help but interrupt her explanations with questions. "How do I know if Nacho finds bed bugs or a tasty pretzel under the couch?"

"Trust me, he wants to work. He gets a treat only when he finds the bugs. Otherwise, he'll go hungry."

"He's a mutt, you know."

"Mutts are best. They're smarter. Live longer. And are more motivated." Robbie used to say the same thing.

"Do you have a bathroom I could use?" Kate should have gone at the library, but she thought she'd be back home by now.

"Sure. Inside on the right. Nacho is fine here. He's a good boy." Nacho seemed hypnotized by the sound of her voice and ignored Kate.

On Val's coffee table was a *Pest Control* magazine Kate recognized from her own house. An article was circled with a black marker: "Are bed bug dogs up to snuff?"

After she finished in the bathroom, Kate heard Val talking to someone on the phone, so she skimmed the article and waited.

Apparently, human noses can't find bed bugs but dogs can be trained to detect them. Entomologists say the bugs smell sticky and sweet and dogs like that. And since 9/11, dogs were being trained in explosives, drugs, and bed bugs more and more. Handlers could even get a special certification and train dogs for pest control companies. To pass the test, the dogs must sniff out vials of five to twenty bud bugs hidden among dozens of hotel rooms. A dog that's certified can sell for ten thousand dollars. Kate would never sell Nacho, but could she train him and train other dogs? The certification of a few free dogs from the shelter would fund half of Maggie's bed bug plan.

Just as Kate was cross-checking one of the references against the book in her bag, Val and Nacho came through the screen door.

"How do you know it works?" Kate said. "I mean, the book I got at the library says that dogs do great in the laboratory but less well in the field."

"That's true. There is no guarantee. That frustrates a lot of people. They'll put up with a few roaches, but a single smear of bed bug feces and they're dragging the mattress to the curb. If they can afford to lose it, that is."

"What makes them so scared?"

"What makes everyone scared? Fear of the unknown. Fear that they can't control the end. Isn't that what everyone is afraid of?"

Kate didn't know. She didn't know what to say either. Val had a way of talking about big stuff that Kate didn't think anyone had answers to. Jules was afraid a lot. She worried about stuff her other sisters didn't even consider. When Kate was little, Jules's fears scared her. She was often waiting for her sister to snap, and so she learned to stay quiet and not set her off.

"Having bed bugs makes people crazy. Like grief. First, they deny that they're infested. Then they panic and purge," Val said.

"Purge what?"

"Everything. Anything they think might have bed bugs. I knew someone who sprayed their whole body and bed with insect repellent every single night. He'd obsessively point out pieces of lint and thought every speck was a bug. He became terrified of sleeping and almost overdosed on antihistamines as a nightcap."

"Are you certified? Like trained and everything?" she asked, looking around the sparse living room for diplomas that Val might have boasted on her walls.

Val huffed. "Trained? I train the trainers. I'm the best." As if to confirm, Nacho sat down behind Val and rested his head on her cowgirl boot.

Kate jerked her head to the side, as if to signal him. She clicked her tongue. Finally, she snapped her fingers, but Nacho wouldn't budge. He'd already chosen Val. "How long does it take?"

"Three months if he's any good. Six months if he ain't."

"I can't pay you."

Val leaned down to pet Nacho, who rolled on his back and bicycled his paws in the air in complete submission. "Can you clean out kennels and brush the dogs? Fill water bowls and pick off ticks? We could work out a trade."

"I can do that." Kate could see she'd be useful, and she settled into that as an answer. "And what about the tarot and teller part? Can I work for that too?"

Val put a teakettle on the burner. "I don't need to read your future, kid. Your dad has already told me you'll be fine."

Katherine Francis Fehler
Mrs. Salvos
Honors Biology

Bed Bugs: The Resistance

Bed bugs do not care about class. They make their homes as comfortably in a New York City penthouse as they do on a farm in rural Missouri. Mobility is a luxury bed bugs can afford. The more money to travel, the better your chances of inviting bed bugs into your life. They'll hitch a ride anywhere and happily with the promise of an equal opportunity blood bite as reward. It's their lack of prejudice that makes bed bugs prolific. They bring shame to the richest mogul and the proudest factory worker, if they can endure the attack.

An adult bed bug bite lasts a glorious eight minutes. Your blood plumps the bug body three times bigger. They aren't just taking out either. Bed bugs send saliva packed with forty-six proteins into your body. These include anticoagulants (to prevent clotting), antibacterial juices, vasodilators (to widen blood vessels), anesthetics, and lubricants. A bed bug bite is . . . complicated. After a feast, they scurry back to their nests and send text messaging pheromones to their peers.

With their bed bug bellies ready to bust, sex—otherwise known as traumatic insemination—follows. It is exactly what it sounds like. Male bed bugs rape. Females have had to evolve to survive the act. They've learned to guide the penis for less violent, injury-producing probing. They've evolved to store sperm that can later inseminate eggs once they've recovered from the assault. Because of female ingenuity, the bed bug population thrives. Even when we assault bed bugs with harsh chemicals, like DDT, that hurt us more than them, they adapt and survive.

No one really knows how DDT works. We just know it does. Basically, a bug walks through the chemical concoction and it makes its way into the nervous system when the unsuspecting bug cleans itself or nestles in its nest. DDT zaps the bed bugs nerves and causes convulsions that lead to death. Blame WWII. Roosevelt signed and Big Science invested in anything that would boost national defense. Infectious diseases prosper in combat quarters. Typhus, lice, and mosquitos thrived, and DDT dust controlled their outbreak. It was a short-term solution with long-term consequences few considered. A few tons of DDT and decades later, bed bugs seemed eradicated. Was the price too high? No one asked. Baby boomers grew up without them. Bed bugs were a thing of childhood nursery rhymes. Their parents sang out "Nighty night. Don't let the bed bugs bite." Bed bugs became a quaint relic of the past.

But bed bugs missed us. They long for humans most. Scientists exploited their weaknesses in war. Lice, ticks, and fleas couldn't pass their test, but bed bugs triumphed over even DDT. It wasn't glamorous, but their evolution was glorious. Resistant bed bugs emerged in the bunks of Pearl Harbor and the barracks of French Guiana. Other insects admired the bed bug fruition and followed their fight.

A revolution in pesticides was inevitable. Bed bugs were the first soldiers. Rachel Carson was their commander. Her battle began in 1962 on the pages of the *New Yorker*, where she wrote a three-part series that would become *Silent Spring*. She rained on the entomologists' parade, and the modern environmental movement was born. DDT was found in our human nervous systems too. It clung to fat tissue, especially in breasts that produced milk. A decade after Carson first spoke up, the United States banned DDT, and the bed bug population applauded.

Works Cited

Cooper, R. 2007. "Are bed bug dogs up to snuff?" *Pest Control* 75: 49Ð51.

Tharpe, Val. Personal Interview.

16

Jules

Jules had promised her dad she wouldn't vote for Obama. It was her first election as an eligible voter, and Robbie had threatened not to pay her bills if she cast her ballot in the wrong box. Wrong to her dad meant any liberal-minded candidate. "Obama wasn't even born here!" Robbie had yelled at the TV a few weeks before his heart attack. Jules had come home for a quick visit but had decided twelve hours later that she needed to get back early to study—to see Niko, who hadn't traveled because his West Coast home was too far for a weekend. His parents wanted him to stay on campus because they worried about his safety in rural communities. When he'd told her there were still "sundown towns" in Missouri, she felt ashamed to have always traveled so freely in the state and never considered that kind of danger.

"Obama was born in Hawaii, Dad. Chill," Jules had said, picking out the kernels from the popcorn bowl.

Her professor in Intro to American Politics had lectured extensively about the Birther Movement and Donald Trump's "erroneous and obnoxious" accusations about Obama's ineligibility to run. *If facts are so easy to come by,* Jules had written in her response paper, *why are voters still swayed by fiction?* She thought it was super clever, but her professor had given it a B- and said it was merely a summary of everything he'd lectured and suggested she "construct her own argument to her own thoughtful question," whatever that meant. It was new to her even if it wasn't new. Every time she realized her classmates already understood something that blew her mind, she itched a little more. Heat flushed her cheeks, armpits, and thighs. She stopped herself from sprinting around the block.

Jules held the almost empty popcorn bowl up for Maggie, who was clearly on her way to the kitchen. She thought her dad was smart, a bit bullyish in his teasing, but mostly harmless. She was starting to see him differently though. Being away had opened her eyes, and home didn't look the same. It wasn't their fault. But why would her dad believe and repeat something so incorrect? Why did he fall for every conspiracy theory? There were plenty of evidence-based reasons to object to Obama. She preferred to blame everything she was beginning to disagree with her parents about on Rush Limbaugh, who droned on from every radio in Cape. The town seemed prouder of him than all the well-known writers, politicians, and athletes it had also born and raised. For her dad's birthday one year, they'd taken a self-guided driving tour past Rush's boyhood home, the hospital where he'd been born, the barber shop where he'd first worked shining shoes, and the radio station that broadcast his first show. The Limbaughs had been called Cape Girardeau's first family, but the more Jules learned, the less honor she felt. It wasn't just Rush; it was FOX News blaring in every house and restaurant. FOX fear was eating her family. In the months since she'd been gone, Grace and Robbie had been learning a language of conservative platitudes. They often repeated all the talking points to each other. McCain will defund Planned Parenthood and repeal *Roe v. Wade*, therefore he's a Good Christian. The recession is all talk. Obama will steal from the elderly with his plan to stimulate the economy. Tax cuts for all. McCain will support judges who strictly interpret the Constitution as God intended. Jules believed in equality and self-reliance; she also thought those things should be applied to her own body and her ability to make choices for herself. How could the same values of independence her parents had taught her not also be useful to her?

"I want to know what he'll do with the economy," Maggie had said, accepting the bowl as she passed. "It's your dishes night, Jules."

Jules shook her head. "No way. College means I'm out of the rotation. Can we watch something besides FOX News? Something, maybe, with actual news? Obama says he's going to end the recession, fix Wall Street, and do something about health care, but I don't see that on the likes of FOX. His economic plan is clear, even if you don't like it." She looked from her dad to her sisters for a response, but it seemed that no one had heard her at all.

"If you ate, you're in the dish rotation," Tammy insisted. "Tell her, Dad." Jules thought her sister was being lazy. She looked plump and glowing, like a pretty pink queen who couldn't be bothered.

"I read he wants to eliminate the capital gains tax for small businesses," Maggie offered. "That sounds reasonable, but I still wouldn't vote for him."

Jules stood with her hands on her hip. "Because he's Black?"

"I barely notice the color of someone's skin. Not everyone who disagrees with Obama is a racist," Maggie said. Maggie couldn't imagine a world where their dad was anything but right, it seemed to Jules. Robbie refused to acknowledge racism. He wasn't sexist either, he said—he had four daughters. Sure he wanted them to have opportunities. He'd explained many times that men and women were different and it wasn't good for anyone when women acted like men just to be equal. The more Jules thought about it, the less sense it made. And she knew how insulting it was to say, "I don't see color." It dismissed the whole existence and the struggle that came with it. Mags should know better, but how would she learn if she was never exposed to another way of being, another way of thinking. Bubbles work to keep people in and out. Jules had been raised in that bubble and knew that they didn't mean to be racist. She struggled with the language to counteract something she was only beginning to get.

"Jules," Robbie had said, "your vote matters. Certainly to me. Obama is a liar, and he wasn't even born here. He's from Africa and he's a Muslim. Don't do anything stupid, you hear me?" Then Robbie nudged Tammy up from the couch. "Go clean up the kitchen. Your sister needs to study for her exams." Jules couldn't remember when her dad had ever taken her side against her sisters. It felt wrong and so deliciously right.

When Jules stood in the ballot box six weeks after her dad's death, she wanted to keep her promise but absolutely couldn't. Of course she voted for Obama. It felt like a vote for her and her future, maybe with Niko in it. On election night, Katie Couric's nasally voice droned from the TV and made it hard for Jules to focus on the back rub Niko was giving her. She turned her head away from the half-packed suitcases. Niko kept trying to unpack them and insisting they could work it out together. But saying so didn't make it so, and Jules knew she'd be gone in a month. What would happen with her and Niko? Maybe she could still drive up on the weekends and visit, but that wouldn't last. She didn't want to think about it anymore tonight. Jules was naked from the waist up, facedown on her dorm bed. Niko's wide hands worked the knots at her neck, and Jules relaxed from the release.

But her thoughts kept returning to her dad. She hadn't even gotten to hug him at Maggie's ceremony because it all happened so fast. The last time they'd spoken was when she'd wave goodbye and halfheartedly apologized for cutting her weekend visit short.

Back on campus, life churned. Election night parties were planned. The Young Democrats canvased every dorm room, even though most of the campus had already declared their support for Obama, and the Young Republicans focused on the neighborhoods around Columbia where the McCain message was more welcome. Once the dean's office had been notified of Robbie's death, Jules's advisor had emailed her teachers on her behalf for extensions on her essays and more leeway on her final exam schedule. They'd put a hold on her unpaid bill until second semester, but Jules knew there wouldn't be a second semester. She'd take her finals, finish in good standing, even with the debt, and move back home to work in the family business. She had A's in every class and only needed to coast through exams. Maybe she'd come back to college one day, but they needed her home now.

Jules was back in a space that Robbie had never occupied. It was like he was still at home, in the garage, with his bees, at the office, fishing on the camp dock. Anywhere but in the ground and gone. Jules felt the luxury of distance from her family. The funeral had exhausted them all, but grief was only beginning to grow. Jules found that her dad's voice was in her head: when she pumped gas and her father had taught her to top it off even though she'd read in a brochure that it was bad for the environment; when she checked the Sunday Mass schedule and decided she'd never attend again to avoid the empty space at the end of the pew where Robbie had always sat; when she accepted a free peppermint candy from the server with her takeout bill and remembered her dad's "there's no free lunch" speech. Her email inbox that once contained daily forwards of false political analogies, conspiracy theories, and chain mail hoaxes from Robbie was now empty. The absence made her furious—the hole he left that she'd never be big enough to fill. Bluster isn't the same as courage, the old lady at the counseling center had said, and that had pissed Jules off more.

Niko's hands brushed the side of her breast as he massaged. He kissed the back of her head and bent to lay his chest on her back while his muscled arms covered her fleshy ones. Jules's emotions were raw, and they were both listening for Katie Couric to call it. The polls in California were still open.

"The fat lady isn't singing yet," Couric said, "but we can hear her clearing her throat."

Thirty minutes later, Couric declared Obama the forty-fourth president and declared it "momentous." Jules wasn't that surprised by the outcome, but she was surprised by her own numbness and ambivalence.

"Don't you know what this means?" Niko yelled, leaping from the bed and doing a version of the running man on the carpet next to her. He was wearing his favorite silky black basketball shorts, and Jules hoped he'd let her borrow them when she left. She wanted every piece of him she could pack. Jules rested her head on the side of her arm, spent and sleepy, and flipped through the news channels to see who else had declared Obama the winner.

"An African American has broken the barrier as old as the republic," NBC News anchor Brian Williams said. "An astonishing candidate, an astonishing campaign, a seismic shift in American politics."

"Barack Obama will be the forty-fourth president of the United States," ABC News anchor Charles Gibson said.

Since handing Missouri to Obama an hour earlier, even FOX News relented. "Unless something miraculous happens in one of these nonbattleground states, McCain's situation is looking pretty dire," FOX News anchor Brit Hume admitted, pursing his lips.

The one thing Jules was certain of was how tired she was of watching all these old White guys tell her how she was supposed to think.

Niko cocked his head to the side and tensed his pectoral muscles. First one, then the other. She giggled, so he did it again. "It means everything, Jules."

Jules pulled on an "Obama Hope" T-shirt. "That sounds a bit optimistic." She tossed a popcorn pack in the microwave, opened a bottle of water, and handed one to Niko.

"Yeah, but there's the hope of it. Let's do something to celebrate!"

The kernels began popping, and Jules fished around in her desk for a bag of M&M's. She kept the peanut kind stocked because they were Niko's favorite.

"No, I'm serious. There are parties everywhere! But let's, let's . . . drive to Chicago. Let's go right now. Jules, let's do it. We could be there by midnight. The party in Grant Park is supposed to be huge. We could see Obama!"

"But I have class tomorrow. So do you."

Niko reached into the popcorn bag too, because she offered and insisted. "Nope. Mine was canceled. And your professors aren't expecting you back so soon. Jules, let's go."

Jules and Niko traded childhood stories most of the 385-mile drive, except for a long nap she took around Springfield. Niko played her a CD of his dad's music and told her the history of each track and corresponding books he'd read that influenced the beats. She could see why he loved literature so much. He got all excited just talking about authors, or maybe he was just trying to stay awake for the drive. When they stopped for french fries near Jacksonville, Jules thought about texting Maggie, to let someone know where she was. Their dad dying made time more urgent, and she missed her sisters.

The anonymity and freedom of the road trip was refreshing. Jules wanted this moment to last, to sustain her through the inevitable move back home and drudgery of what her days would become at Fehler Family Exterminating. She dipped each fry into the miniature paper cup of ketchup and fed them one by one to Niko while he drove. He'd bought her a candy ring pop at the last gas station, and Jules admired it on her hand as if it were a diamond. Would she ever want a ring from Niko? She'd recently read an article on how damaging Americans' lust for stones was to parts of Africa, and it made her think of the whole wedding business as fabricated. Maybe a candy ring pop was all she needed.

On the radio, they listened to the live broadcast as the Grant Park crowd grew to more than two hundred thousand people. The host interviewed people who described the night as "electric" and "surreal." One grandmother said, "It's like going to the best concert you ever dreamed of but couldn't believe was actually happening." She'd brought all seven of her teen grandkids to watch history be made. "And you better believe they're still going to school tomorrow," she said. "Michelle Obama would want them to."

Jules and Niko ditched the car six blocks away minutes before 1:00 a.m. and sprinted with the crowd. They could hear Brooks & Dunn jamming with "Only in America" before Stevie Wonder crooned "Signed, Sealed, Delivered I'm Yours." The chants of "Yes, We Can! Yes, We Can!" almost drowned out the music.

When they reached the edge of the crowd, they realized they couldn't push any closer and settled by a group of moms pushing sleeping babies in strollers near the Jumbotrons. Jules was relieved anyway not to feel the crush of other bodies too close. She squeezed Niko's hand. "This is good enough. Close enough for me." She took a deep breath, closed her eyes, and counted to ten, like the old lady counselor had told her to. On stage, an empty lectern waited.

The air was dusty from fireworks, and Niko rubbed his eyes. Jules couldn't tell if it was the lack of sleep, the contagious emotion of the crowd, or actual tears of joy.

The guy to their left, dressed in a loose plaid shirt over an Obama T-shirt, rubbed his beard and leaned into Niko. "Obama may be Black but I don't think he has a color, you know? Like, he doesn't see it that way. Me neither."

Niko rolled his eyes. Jules knew he'd heard worse. She saw the looks people gave them when they realized they were a couple. Folks didn't know how to sort Niko's not-White-enough or not-Black-enough brownness. He'd told her that growing up biracial meant always being aware of moving through White spaces. Would he date a Black girl once Jules left? She hated to think of him with anyone else. It caused the pit in her belly to explode. She didn't know what it was like to be Niko, but she certainly wouldn't deny that his skin color was part of his daily living, especially in a White state like Missouri. Jules hadn't really noticed how White it was until now.

At 1:12 a.m., Obama emerged behind two sheets of bulletproof glass. Niko told Jules they'd studied the lectern in his Criminology class: ten feet high and fifteen feet long on each side to deflect any shots that might be fired. Only police helicopters were in the air, and thousands of extra army and Secret Service personnel were brought in.

The crowd roared for ten minutes without pause. Obama kept holding up his hands, but it made them cheer more. Niko punched the air and high-fived the plaid-shirted guy.

"Tonight, because of what we did on this day, in this election, at this defining moment, change has come to America," Obama began. A young woman Maggie's age reached out to hold Jules's hand as strangers hugged and slid their arms through each other's.

Jules had never felt more connected in her whole life, like she belonged here in this moment more than anywhere else. She fit, and that was foreign to her.

"The road ahead will be long; our climb will be steep. We may not get there in one year, or even in one term—but America, I have never been more hopeful than I am tonight that we will get there."

Even the police officers had stopped weaving through the masses and were watching the screens. An older officer, who looked a lot like Robbie, was wiping tears off his cheeks and crossing his arms over his chest like he was holding himself, again and again.

"Let us remember that, if this financial crisis taught us anything, it's that we cannot have a thriving Wall Street while Main Street suffers." *Maggie would like that*, Jules thought. Small businesses like Fehlers' might do well under Obama's policies.

"As Lincoln said to a nation far more divided than ours, 'We are not enemies but friends. Though passion may have strained, it must not break our bonds of affection.'"

As Jules listened to Obama quote Lincoln, she wondered what her mom was doing. She probably went to bed once she realized watching wasn't going to change the outcome. Jules felt a pang of pity. Grace had lost her husband and probably any hope she had left.

"This is our time, to put our people back to work and open doors of opportunity for our kids; to restore prosperity and promote the cause of peace; to reclaim the American dream and reaffirm that fundamental truth, that out of many, we are one; that while we breathe, we hope. And where we are met with cynicism and doubts and those who tell us that we can't, we will respond with that timeless creed that sums up the spirit of a people: Yes, we can."

On stage, Obama addressed his daughters. "Sasha and Malia, I love you both more than you can imagine. And you have earned the new puppy that's coming with us to the White House." Jules remembered when her dad had brought Nacho home when he was a puppy. He'd put a red bow around the puppy's neck and sent him into the room on Christmas morning. The sisters had fallen on him instantly and began debating names while Grace kissed Robbie on the cheek. It was only a moment, but her parents were happy to be together and Jules could tell. She felt that rush right now with Niko. Like the world had stopped and that tiny slice of time was all that mattered.

When Obama mentioned his grandma had died, Jules felt lightheaded. She wasn't sure if she was going to throw up or faint, but she leaned heavily into Niko, who put one arm around her waist and the other tightly on her shoulder.

"I got you," he said, "for as long as you want. I mean it, Jules," he continued, his eyes on her rather than Obama. He moved her hair away from her face and kissed her. "This isn't some fling for me. I think I love you."

She pulled Niko in and slid her hands up under his shirt so she could feel his bare skin. The chill from her hands met his hot back. "At least Dad will never know," Jules whispered into Niko's neck, "who I voted for."

17

Tammy

Tammy didn't think the chocolate-covered crickets looked bad at all. With the baby kicking, her appetite was back. Wade said it had doubled. Yesterday she'd eaten two bean burritos at Taco Bell with an entire side of nachos. Wade complained that the nachos weren't on the dollar menu. "I'm eating for two," Tammy said, slathering on hot sauce and sour cream. A dollop fell on her swollen chest, and she wiped it with her pinkie and stuffed it in her mouth. "The baby loves dairy."

"Does that baby still love me?" Wade asked and gave Tammy his puppy dog eyes.

Tammy thought he looked kind of pathetic, but he was the father of her baby—the baby they still hadn't told anyone about—and she was glad he was sticking. She decided to see what puppy dog eyes could get her. "You know what's good after nachos?"

"Sure do. Least we can't get pregnant." Wade had worn out the line, Tammy thought. Her indigestion and heartburn weren't sexy. She also may have what she'd learned online was a hemorrhoid and wanted to keep it to herself.

"Cinnamon twists," Tammy said. "Two orders, please."

"That's my girl." Wade nodded. "The dollar menu!"

This morning at the Show Me Southeast Missouri District Fair, Tammy poured the bag of chocolate crickets into a glass bowl Maggie had brought from home. "Should we label them or something? The bag says they're gluten free."

"Probably," Grace answered. "You know how liberals are with their gluten-free religion and peanut-free everything. I'll make a sign."

"Everyone has a right to their own opinion," Maggie said diplomatically. "And the right for their allergic kid to go to a trade show." One of the biggest family fights Tammy remembered was over an Obama monkey doll one of Robbie's ham operator buddies had mailed him. He said it was funny and that Tammy was being too sensitive. Maggie said it was offensive and bad for business. Jules said it was racist. Grace agreed with Jules, for once, that it was in poor taste. "We welcome all customers. Besides, aren't crickets naturally gluten free? Why would you even need to say that?"

Tammy could still hear her dad's sad apology, *I'm sorry you're offended*, which wasn't an apology at all. Whenever she thought of his faults now, she felt guilt piled on her frustrated grief and heartache. The baby gave her a swift kick in the rib cage, and her mind raced off elsewhere, mostly back to the nachos.

Maggie unpacked brochures and Fehler Family Exterminating pins, swag she'd bought now that she didn't have to get approval from her dad. Tammy complimented them all. Robbie had believed trade shows and community events were a waste of time. Sure, he'd give fifty dollars for T-ball uniforms for the Little League Mudders and sold his fair share of tickets to the annual Chamber of Commerce pancake breakfast, but a booth was for show-offs. Robbie had always said, "Good enough is good enough. Work hard and don't get too big for your britches." Tammy knew Maggie saw Fehler Family Exterminating's potential, but her dad wouldn't put up the $200 booth fee. Months after his death, with the will still in probate and the bankruptcy court verdict outstanding, their future remained uncertain and Maggie told Tammy it was time to take some risks. She'd ordered a professional booth display, the crickets, and BBQ roasted mealworms to draw in the crowd. She put it all on the credit card she was living off of and told Tammy it was an investment in their future. Of course they'd be grossed out at first, Maggie had told them at dinner, but then she knew the crowds wouldn't be able to resist. She was serving the crickets and worms next to the cages of hissing cockroaches and Hairy. The spider seemed to be molting, as if even he was missing Robbie.

"Don't eat them all before the customers arrive," Maggie said, pulling the bowl out of Tammy's hands. "You're getting chipmunk cheeks as it is." Father Tom had said that grief comes in many forms, but Maggie still teased Tammy about her extra pounds. Tammy wanted to shut her sister up, but not at the expense of telling her about the baby. She'd have to suffer folks thinking she was getting fat.

"How can I tell people how yummy they are if I haven't sampled them myself?" Tammy opened the BBQ roasted mealworms, crunched a handful, and declared the crickets the gourmet winner. She asked Wade if he wanted a taste. He was piecing together the booth display while the sisters set up the table. She'd begged Maggie to hire Wade to clean the garage and help repair the sprayers. He was working for next to nothing and only a few hours a week but saving every penny for their future. He'd offered to work the trade show for free. Every time he held up a stabilizer, Tammy appreciated his strong arms. She wondered who the baby would resemble more. They were both good-looking—everyone told them so—but Tammy hoped the baby had his chin. Her eyes and smarts, of course, but maybe Wade's eyebrow shape.

Maggie was giving orders and reading the instructions for the booth.

"You sound like your dad," Wade said. Then, quickly, "Sorry."

"No, it's fine. I'm being bossy because I'm basically the boss now. It's a compliment." Maggie waved it all off, like nothing bothered her when Tammy knew it did.

"We'll do it," Tammy said, taking the instructions from her sister. "Wade and I got this."

Maggie looked relieved. "Ok, good. Then I'll walk around and talk to the other business owners. Pass out cards and such. Follow up on sales calls we made last week." She picked some Nacho hair off her sweater and pulled her shoulders back like she was readying herself. Then she tucked a new pen in her clipboard and marched off.

The fair loudspeaker crackled: "Folks, we're going to open the doors in about fifteen minutes. It's a bit earlier than planned, but as you probably know, there is a winter storm warning for southeast Missouri and we want to get the crowds to you and on their way before the snow hits. So finish up your last-minute fixin's and let's do this!"

Maggie swung around halfway down the aisle and headed back to the booth, but Tammy waved her off. "Seriously, sis. It will be easier to do without you sweating all over us. Go. Mingle. Be our family business face. We have enough hands here to get everything ready."

"She's right, Mags," Grace said. "For once, listen to your sister. Look, Kate and Wade almost have the booth built."

An instrumental version of Lee Greenwood's "Proud to Be an American" kicked on after the announcer, and Grace put her hand over her heart and looked up toward the rafters. Tammy bit her lip. Before her dad's death, she would have made fun of her mother's patriotism in this moment, but everything felt softer now. Even Wade swayed a bit to the music, and Tammy wondered when her family might ever be normal again. But maybe that was it. Without Robbie, they'd have to figure out a new normal. She pushed the thought aside and tidied the tablecloths and panels while keeping her eye on Maggie, who was shaking hands and mingling near a table with tethered handguns on display. A little boy in a Cub Scout uniform was aiming a gun at his foot, and it made Tammy nervous. She'd grown up with guns, but seeing a kid with one suddenly made her queasy.

One enormous plastic Christmas tree sat in the center of the convention hall. A skinny Santa—Tammy was sure it was Mr. Coleman, their elementary PE teacher—sat on a folding chair. His teenager elf, who'd remembered to plug in the tree but couldn't do much about half the lights that were burned out, distributed tropical fruit-flavored candy canes—the ones usually on sale because nobody liked the flavor. Santa kept saying, "Ho ho ho" and telling each passerby to cheer up. She knew that was going to piss her mom off if she heard it. She'd said one of the worst parts of grieving was how much advice everyone gave: "Everything happens for a reason." No, it doesn't. "At least he's in a better place." We'd kind of like him in this place, thank you. "God doesn't give you more than you can manage." Seems like he did this time.

Tammy imagined that if her dad was here, he'd be wearing his ridiculous Santa hat, the one he put on at work for what he called "Company Christmas." Each year at the beginning of December, Robbie would hang stockings on the front desk counter for each employee. He'd buy everyone a Christmas ham and happily accept the free one the store gave him as a bonus.

This year, Maggie was getting each employee a gift certificate. Tammy had helped her write "Happy Holidays" on all the cards while they watched *90210*, her favorite new show. "Wouldn't Dad have wanted us to write 'Merry Christmas'?" Tammy asked.

"Probably," Maggie said. "But two of our employees are Jewish and one of them doesn't celebrate at all."

"Did Dad know that?" Tammy added curly loops to the *y*'s, which seemed to mean more now.

"He did. But you know how he was with the War on Christmas stuff. Whatever Rush Limbaugh said that morning, Dad repeated that afternoon. It was a stupid fight. I'm declaring a truce." Tammy thought that sounded diplomatic, like something Miss Cape Girardeau might say.

Three hours later, the fair was packed and the same announcer was reading the paid advertisements. He finally got to the Fehlers: "Stop by booth 302 to learn how to get rid of your bugs and to eat some bugs too! Oh, Fehler Family Exterminating is serving up tasty chocolate crickets and barbecued worms. Delicious! The Fehlers are a fourth-generation family-owned and -operated business here in the Cape, and they know how to keep your home and workplace safe from pests. Booth 302 is where you'll find the Fehler family little women!"

"Did he just say that?" Maggie asked. "That is not the script I paid for. Little women? What's that supposed to mean?"

"You paid for that?" Wade asked. Tammy punched him playfully in the chest. He pulled her in for a cuddle.

"Obviously not that, Wade. He was supposed to remind folks that though flying insects might hibernate in winter, mice, cockroaches, and spiders like to hide in your home." Maggie raised her voice, "And how monthly preventative treatments are more effective and cheaper!"

Wade teased, "Sounded like a bunch of girls were running the show now."

Grace cleared her throat. "A bunch of tough girls, as far as I can see."

"A bunch of girls can run the business just fine. Shut up, Wade," Tammy said. Maggie greeted a new group of kids and their parents to the booth to taste the bugs. She stirred the display pot over a fake fire so it looked like she was cooking up the bugs fresh. She handed out brochures and shook hands. Tammy wondered if she'd learned how to be so professional in 4-H or at community college. She already looked more in charge than their dad ever had. His jokester approach worked sometimes, but mostly just with older White guys like him.

Her mother stayed behind the table straightening pens and restocking brochures. There was an extra bowl of edible bugs by her elbow.

"We're sure sorry for your loss, Grace," Mr. Owen said, tipping his cowboy hat and popping a cricket into his mouth. "You too, girls." He nodded in Maggie, Kate, and Tammy's direction like they were all the same person.

"Thank you, Mr. Owen. We appreciate that." Grace folded her arms over her chest and leaned against the booth table. "Seems the right time to stick together, doesn't it?"

Mr. Owen moved the toothpick around in his mouth. The readjustment seemed to be giving him time to think. "Well, business is still business, ma'am."

"And Fehlers' has been taking care of yours for thirty years. Our kids went to school together." Grace moved the bowl back from the front of the table, out of his reach. "We've lost Robbie, not our business."

"Truth be told," Mr. Owen said, "folks think you won't be able to keep the business running for much longer. I heard you needed a loan and couldn't get it."

"Mom, don't do this now. Please," Maggie said, joining her mom at the front of the table. "Thanks for stopping by, Mr. Owen. We wish you the best. Merry Christmas. And keep us in mind for your future pest control needs."

He reached for the bowl and brushed Grace's arm in the process. "We've reevaluated lately. It's not personal. We're looking to make some changes. Hell, everyone is tightening their belts since the election. I'm sure you understand."

Grace shook her head. Then she squinted like she was trying to find something very tiny on the floor. "You know, I actually don't. I don't understand."

Mr. Owen stared like a cat caught with a mouse in its mouth. Tammy wasn't sure if he wanted to run or to offer it as a present to her mom. She remembered riding her bike by him and his brother when she was twelve, while they stood outside the ice cream store. One of them said, "By God, that one's almost legal. Did you see those tits?" Tammy was used to the attention, but she also wanted to tell the likes of Mr. Owen that she existed in the world for more than his viewing pleasure.

"I don't understand," Grace went on. "Everyone keeps telling me how I should think and how I should feel and why I should be okay with this or that or Robbie's death or your cowardice, but I don't. It doesn't make sense to me. Why a business as old and as established as Fehlers' is questioned because of a rough patch. We're struggling. It's true. But your disloyalty and dismissal of our family doesn't make sense. Your belief that my daughter can't run the business as well if not better than her dad doesn't make sense. And I'm real tired of being told it should." She took the bowl from the table and cradled it in her lap like she was going to eat the whole cricket batch herself.

Grace's face reddened with both fury and tears. Tammy reached out her hand to her, but just as her mom squeezed back, something ripped inside Tammy and she hunkered down in her own pain. She felt the clawing from inside and heard her mom from outside, "I know it happened to him, but I can't stop feeling that it's something that happened to me." Maybe it was her mother's grief and self-pity splitting Tammy in two. Maybe it was this moment because they'd all been waiting for Grace to crack.

Suddenly Wade was at her side. "What's wrong? Did you trip? What are you doing down there?"

Tammy reached from her squat and swatted at his hand. "No, just a cramp. Feels better bending somehow."

Mr. Owen bowed his head and mumbled, "Sorry for your loss," before turning his back.

Tammy wasn't embarrassed by her mother's outburst; she was relieved. They were in this together, even if this stupid town judged them. And if the pain in her gut would pause, she might even reach out and hug her mom.

Grace stared at the bowl of crickets until Maggie lifted them out of her lap and set them back on the table. Kate returned with Styrofoam cups of steaming black coffee and passed them around. "To Dad," Maggie said, lifting her cup. She took the lid off her mom's cup and set it in front of her like a child.

Wade leaned into Tammy's ear. "If it's the baby, we have to tell someone. Something could be wrong."

"It's a cramp. The baby is fine." Tammy winced and slid her hand under her bulky holiday sweater to lift some of the weight off her uterus. It helped a little. But then, the baby moved again, like a front head roll, and landed with a punch in her ribs. "Shit, that hurts." She closed her eyes and took a few deep breaths like she'd seen pregnant women do in the movies.

"What are we waiting for, Tammy?"

"I just can't. Will you please be quiet for once?"

Wade's face in hers was more than she could manage right now. He had BBQ breath from the crickets, and it was grossing her out. She wanted to be left alone, and she wanted the jumping jacks on her organs to stop. "But you need to go see a doctor. What if something is wrong with the baby?"

Tammy stomped off toward the bathroom. Of course Wade was worried. She'd be pissed if he wasn't concerned. But she didn't like to make a scene, especially not one about the baby. The baby was fine. She couldn't explain how she knew, but she did. She was also sure it was a girl, even though Wade probably wanted a boy.

She kept waiting for the right time to tell her mom, but since the funeral nothing felt certain. With her dad gone, everything was falling apart. She didn't want her mom to have to worry about this too, and Tammy knew she was going to be furious at her and Wade. How much did having a baby even cost? They were broke, and this wouldn't help. Maybe there was a crib still in the attic. Maybe she could get diapers for free from the church.

She needed to get back to the booth before they came looking for her.

Kate was leaning against the bathroom sink when Tammy came in. Her hands rested where her hips would one day be, and she gave her sister the side-eye.

"What?" Tammy said, washing her hands. She leaned over the sink to hide her belly.

"I know," Kate said.

"Know what?"

"Oh, come off it. You've been weird for months. Throwing up, getting fat, eating everything in sight. It doesn't take a genius."

Tammy knew she'd fooled everyone else, but little Kate was

always watching. Such a stalker and a pest. "I have no idea what you're talking about." Tammy smeared on some lip gloss like she didn't have a care in the world. "It's cramps. You'll know one day."

"I know cramps."

"You do? Has little Katie gotten her period?" Tammy teased, trying to distract her.

"You're pregnant, and I'm telling Mom. You should go to a doctor and stuff. Are you taking vitamins?"

Tammy rolled her eyes in the mirror. "This is none of your business."

"We learned about prenatal vitamins in health class. You need to take folic acid every day. We also learned about birth control."

"You think I need a lecture right now? From my baby sister?"

"I think you need help. We should ask Maggie."

"You can't tell Maggie. You can't tell anyone. Promise me, Kate?" Tammy grabbed her shoulders and squeezed. "I made a mistake. Wade and I are going to figure out what to do. But you keep your mouth shut, or I'll tell Mom you have a crush on Lila."

"I do not!"

"And I'm not pregnant!" The silence and their gaping mouths proved them both right. "I need a pretzel. You want a pretzel?" She walked out without waiting for an answer, making a beeline for the concession stand, her sister trailing behind her.

"Does the baby want a pretzel?"

"Stop it, Kate," Tammy said, handing over the cash to the vendor with one hand and sharing the warm baked salted dough with her baby sister with the other. "You promised."

"No, I didn't. You have until Christmas. Then I'm telling." Kate followed Tammy back to the booth where a small crowd was gathering. Maggie was cooking up another batch of bugs. Just as the sisters rounded the corner, a blast echoed through the convention center.

It sounded like fireworks, but then there was another staccato pop and people rushed the doors.

It's Mom, Tammy thought. *She's finally let loose and has her gun.* "Duck! Hide!" she shouted at Kate, tucking her under a table selling hot dogs. Then she used both hands to cover her belly and ran toward the table, where Grace stood aiming her gun at Santa.

18

Kate

The Fehler family always made it to midnight Mass. They rarely arrived early, but most Christmas Eves their pew was empty and waiting. There was the one year, though, that they ended up huddled in the crowded balcony because some out-of-towners took their seats. Jules had spiked a fever on the drive over—Kate hadn't been born yet, but she'd heard the story plenty of times—and the family had to stop at the drugstore for ibuprofen. Grace usually kept the first aid kit in the car well stocked, but Robbie had used all the stuff in it and didn't fill it back up. Grace had dipped her handkerchief in holy water and rubbed it on Jules's forehead to cool her down while she waited for the medicine to kick in, which it finally did during the offering.

There was also the year that Maggie busted open the stitches on her kneecap when she kneeled for the Eucharist. Kate remembered that year best because she got in trouble for shouting, "Maggie is bleeding like Jesus!" during a moment of silent prayer. Robbie cracked up, and Grace elbowed him out of the pew to get some paper towels. But the year all four girls had strep throat everyone agreed never to talk about again. Kate could still feel the broken glass in her throat, and she vowed never to share a straw with a sister again. Besides, plastic straws were ruining the oceans.

Kate liked the smells at Blessed Family Catholic Church; incense, poinsettia, pine, and too much cologne swirled together and made her sleepy. There was an organ playing "Silent Night," and the pipes reached toward the rafters.

But this year, Grace had said no. No, they weren't going to midnight Mass. No, she wasn't going to watch everyone clutch their purse like she was a criminal. Like no one in this congregation had ever fired a gun unintentionally. Like she was a terrorist or something, or a crazy prepper. No, they weren't decorating the tree and torturing themselves with the moment Robbie usually put up the star and pretended—same joke every year—to pull down their newly tinseled tree, heavy with years of elementary school homemade ornaments. They'd all outgrown Santa anyway.

Most midnight Masses when she was little, Robbie carried Kate to the car, her dangling legs in white tights, a red-and-green velvet hand-me-down dress with oversized bows bunched up so that her mom had to tug at it for decency before Kate accidentally flashed the congregation. It was a point of pride among the dads to carry the kids—hopped up on candy canes, frantic for Santa's visit, stuffed with Christmas ham—who inevitably dozed before the three wise men even made it up the aisle bearing their gifts to the plastic baby Jesus asleep in the manger.

Though Kate had been too big to carry for a few years, last year at midnight Mass she'd still rested her head on Robbie's shoulder. If she'd known it would be their last Christmas together, she wouldn't have pulled away when he tried to hug her. She wondered what her sisters regretted. Did Tammy wish she'd told him about the baby? Would Maggie have made a better plan for the business? Would Jules have held her tongue about the election? Would her mom have gone a little lighter on her dad?

Now she wondered how much it all affected how Grace

responded to the Santa at the trade show. Mr. Bly, their family attorney, had argued that Grace screaming at the Santa, "I will NOT have a happy holiday! Stop telling me what to do!" was a separate incident than the unlawful discharge of her firearm. The judge agreed she was still grieving and decided it wasn't technically negligent discharge. Grace was told to pay her fine and get some counseling. It helped that Robbie had known the judge through Kiwanis. Maybe it was better, the judge had argued, not to have a gun handy when you're angry and unstable. Grace had called the judge a hypocrite, but Mr. Bly said it was best for his clients to listen and to not speak in the courtroom.

"I want to watch the Mississippi River on Christmas morning," Grace said when they got home from the courthouse, "instead of the congregation at Mass sizing up how we're doing without your dad. Let's do it different this year. Let's go out to the camp. The weather looks cold and clear. We never even got around to closing it up for the winter."

"We'll freeze," Tammy had complained.

"I'll bring the space heaters from the office," Maggie offered. "It's a great idea, Mom."

"Can we ice skate?" Jules asked.

"Probably on the pond by the bend. Should be frozen. I'll bring hot chocolate and marshmallows." Grace opened kitchen cabinets and began packing. "Ice skating sounds much better than faking a bunch of 'Merry Christmas' wishes I don't mean or walking on eggshells around that 'Happy Holidays' crowd."

Kate disagreed. "But you're wearing a sweatshirt that says, 'Jesus Is the Reason for the Season.'"

"I think we're not feeling very merry is all," Maggie said. Then she whispered, "How about we cut Mom some slack, okay?"

"Actually, one of my professors published a paper on how 'Happy

Holidays' was printed commonly in the nineteenth century to include Christmas, Hanukkah, Solstice, et cetera. It's a dumb debate, if you ask me." It surprised Kate to hear a full sentence from Jules. Since she'd moved all of her stuff home from her dorm and quit college, she'd mostly lain in bed, sulked, and texted Niko. When Kate saw the mess, she wanted to pout too, but Jules was so sad and pale that she didn't blame her.

Grace's stare said no one had asked Jules nor cared about her lecture. "And I'll get some holy water from Father Tom, and we'll have our own little blessing. Kate, pack the manger—and don't forget baby Jesus."

Jules called back, "One of my professors also said Jesus was a radical," on her way to the basement for their skates.

Kate sat at the kitchen table and wondered if anyone remembered how much she still wanted that Penny board. There had just been too much going on to bring it up since her dad's death, and Kate knew her mom couldn't afford it anymore. Val was the only one still interested in hearing about her skating plans. Last week after Nacho's training session, Kate found a newspaper with the headline "Local Widow Threatens Santa at Trade Show." She hadn't told Val her last name, but she'd know the Fehlers, especially since she was in the bug industry. Just what Kate needed right now was someone else in this town thinking their family had gone crazy since their dad died.

Kate just wanted them all to stop talking about it at school. Like everyone didn't have guns that sometimes went off when they weren't supposed to. Like their parents didn't lose their temper. It was just a bad mix. Christmas was a welcome break.

Maggie was quiet through most of Christmas morning. Grace made donuts and cheesy scrambled eggs. Jules set the table, but they all ended up eating off paper plates on their laps and staring at the sad little pine tree top Kate had dragged in and strung with the lights she'd packed in their holiday bin. She hadn't remembered to test the light strands—as her dad would have—and only one of the three strings she brought worked.

"I know! Let's make popcorn and string it for the tree!" Tammy said.

"Absolutely," Grace nodded, through her own tears. "Let's do that. Then we'll open our presents."

Kate helped her mother unpack the presents they'd shoved into plastic garbage bags. Their mom had said it was like practicing to Bug Out, and they should get quickly out of the house and away from Robbie's memories. The truth was that Robbie was on every surface of family camp. A framed picture of the first fish he'd caught as a boy hung next to a clock in the tiny galley kitchen. His camp clothes still hung on the hooks in the bathroom and smelled like him: sweat, beer, river water, catfish bait, Dial soap. If the house at home felt like he'd abandoned them, the camp felt like he'd simply stepped out for a boat ride. Kate expected to hear the troll of his bass boat pulling up to the dock any minute. She'd run out to meet him, and they'd catch each other up on the bees they'd seen and the goings-on of the hives. But every passing boat reminded Kate of the truth. The silence afterward was loud. Her dad was gone.

Maggie bought them all festive red scarves, even herself. They unwrapped them first and put them on, tying the scarves on each other's necks and admitting that they brightened the room a bit. Kate adjusted hers so it trailed down her back like a superhero. Jules distributed Mizzou Tigers swag: a bumper sticker for Maggie, a key chain for Tammy, a plastic coffee tumbler for Grace, and a hat for Kate, which she immediately molded to her head and hid under. Tammy gave them each their own plastic popcorn bowls on which she'd puffy painted their names. She stuffed them with a microwave popcorn packet and their favorite movie candy: Twizzlers for Maggie, peanut M&M's for Jules, gummy bears for Kate, and a Butterfinger for Grace. Kate gave out tiny gift bags of travel size lotions with sample lip balms, and the room was scented with artificial strawberries. Then Grace passed out four identical packages. The sisters knew the first present was usually something lame and useful, like the year she'd given everyone their own thermal blankets and embroidered each with their names. The blankets were better than the year she stuffed their stockings wit h emergency food ration blocks, which Jules had immediately started munching and declared "not terrible" and Maggie claimed tasted like a cinnamon-coconut cracker. "You're supposed to save them," their mother had complained when they decided to experiment by adding ketchup, mustard, and pickles. Robbie had stuffed his in the truck glove compartment and in the Christmas spirit thanked Grace for thinking ahead.

Kate unwrapped a black solar hand crank radio, which she didn't immediately hate. "It'll charge your phone too," her mother pointed out.

"It's very thoughtful, Mom," Maggie said diplomatically.

"Handy in a dorm room, for sure," Jules added, which Kate thought was charitable for her. "If I ever get to go back."

Tammy played with the crank and tuned hers to Christmas carols. Mariah Carey sang "Joy to the World," but Kate thought it sounded corny.

Grace gave the older sisters gift cards to the mall for their annual after-Christmas shopping date—they usually circled the sale ads for weeks in anticipation—though the amount was small this year. Then her mom pushed a big box to Kate's feet. She ripped it open knowing it was her Penny board and that her father had probably bought it months before he died, when it was on sale, which made it both better and worse. It was the classic lime green one they'd tried out together and her dad had approved of because of its "made in USA" sticker. Kate hoped they'd go home the next morning so she could hit some pavement and round up her friends, including Lila, of course.

"Here, Mom," Tammy said, bringing a tiny package to her mom's lap. "This one is from all of us. Nothing fancy, just something we knew you wanted."

"Oh, you didn't have to, girls," Grace said, carefully untaping each end so she could reuse the paper. "Firestarter rods! How fancy. I've been wanting a pair of these!" She opened the packaging and inspected the rod and metal striker. "Look, there's even an emergency whistle and a waterproof storage compartment for some tinder. Very smart. Thank you, girls." She went around the room and kissed each of them on the head before sinking back into the couch, as if the energy of gratitude exhausted her.

Maggie collected trash into the same plastic bags they'd used for packing.

"When you girls were little, your dad would stay up all night Christmas Eve putting together your toys. We'd practically sleep through the opening because we were so tired," Grace said, smiling a little, like she wasn't actually talking to anyone in particular. "Then you'd play and play. Remember that year we bought you all the big plastic kitchen? You insisted on making everyone fake food for breakfast, Maggie, and we all had to pretend to eat it, even baby Kate."

Tammy joined their mom on the couch. Grace sipped her coffee. Kate wondered if it was spiked. Tammy looked like she was about to say something but laid her head down in Grace's lap instead. Her mom seemed surprised by the sudden affection but pulled an afghan off the back of the couch to cover Tammy's legs. "What's up?" she asked.

"I have to tell you something, and you're going to kill me."

Grace took a long swig. "I once said exactly that to my own mother. Did you know that?"

Maggie snapped off Dolly Parton's "I'll Be Home for Christmas," which was much too cheerful for the occasion, and the room became quiet. An owl hooted nearby, and the trailer was still enough that they all listened. Kate watched the window for snowflakes.

"I was only a year older than you," Grace continued. "Grandma said, 'I'll probably kill him instead' and lunged for your dad."

"I'm pregnant."

"What?" Maggie and Jules yelled together.

Grace smoothed the hair away from Tammy's face. "I was afraid that's what you were about to say."

Kate nodded as each sister looked to the other and realized who had known and who hadn't. Lines were drawn. Alliances threatened. Everything shifted.

"You don't have to have it," Jules said abruptly, as if it had just occurred to her.

Grace rubbed her temples. "Jesus, Mary, and Joseph, what did you say?"

"Tammy has a right to choose what she does with her body."

Kate thought Tammy had clearly already decided what to do with her body.

"You don't mean an abortion, do you?" Maggie asked.

Jules shook her head slowly, then stopped and nodded.

Grace rubbed Tammy's back. "That is not an option, Jules."

"It is an option. It is always an option."

Maggie brought in the plate of donuts and set them on the milk crates they used as a coffee table. "Who's hungry? Look, it's snowing!"

"You have no idea what you are even saying." Grace glared at Jules like she didn't know her at all. "No daughter of mine is going to kill her baby."

Jules took a deep breath and looked around the room as if for an ally. Kate hoped she was realizing she'd gone too far. "I'm not saying she should. I'm saying it's her choice."

"Kate, have a donut," Maggie said, licking powdered sugar off her fingers. Kate didn't want a donut. She wanted her dad there to settle them all down. He'd make a joke about their little women hysteria, which might give Jules an out from the corner she'd backed herself into. But then she didn't want her dad there because he'd flip out over Tammy's news.

"I don't want to have an abortion," Tammy said. "I thought about it. Jules is right. But I don't want to do it."

"It's your choice," Jules said.

"I know," Tammy nodded. "I even looked for a Planned Parenthood, but there's none nearby. Wade and I have talked a lot about it and decided to keep the baby. I'm five months along."

Tammy had told Kate she loved, loved Wade, for whatever that meant. She believed her.

"Months?" Maggie asked. "I thought you were getting fat. You know, missing Dad and all."

"I am missing Dad. That's part of why I decided to have this baby. It feels right. I mean, wrong, of course, but then right. I'm due on Easter."

Kate burst out with, "What about the Miss Cape pageant?"

Grace put her fingers to her lips to shush them all like she did when they were little.

"I can still do it," Tammy insisted. "I'm already registered, and I'll have ten weeks to get back in shape. I can be Miss Cape. And if I win the scholarship, well, I'll take the baby with me to class. It will be like another backpack. Wade is paying for what I need for the pageant from his Fehlers' check."

Grace frowned. "We'll have to talk to Father Tom immediately and get you to a doctor for checkups. We are certainly prepared for whatever comes our way, even a baby. You prepare for the worst and hope for the best. The life insurance check came last week. It will tide us over for a few months, and we'll just have to put our heads together after that. Maggie, we'll need to expect the health premiums to go up and hope they don't cancel us. Maybe you can ask Wade's family to help, Tammy. Have you talked to Wade's parents? I assume you'll want to get married soon."

Tammy burst out crying, and the sisters came to her side with hugs and hands to hold. Kate didn't think it was all that bad. At least they loved each other. Her parents had made it work. Why couldn't they? They were young to get married, but what else would you do? She was sure Jules had different answers, but Jules lived in a different world.

"Mom, where's Nacho?" Kate asked suddenly, scanning the scatter rugs. Her bag with training supplies—two vials sealed tight with bed bugs, two empty ones, and treats—was sitting where she left it last night, but Nacho wasn't sniffing around it like usual.

Grace looked around the room, like Nacho might be napping under some wrapping paper. "Did anyone let him back in last night? Surely he would have barked. It's too cold to stay out all night." Kate had fallen asleep on the couch with Tammy. They were watching an old VHS tape of *Christmas Vacation*, their dad's favorite. It was all her fault. If something happened to Nacho, she'd never forgive herself. Surely Robbie had brought him home knowing she'd one day need the comfort. Her dad, more than anyone else, understood her affection for life, especially the simpler forms like dogs and bees.

When it became clear that Nacho wasn't in the house, the sisters pulled on their winter coats and boots to go look for him. Grace said she'd stay behind in case he came home while they were out in the woods.

"Let's stay together in pairs," Maggie said. "Jules, you take Kate. Tammy, you're with me. Use your whistle if you see him to let the rest of us know."

They spent the whole afternoon searching without success, meeting back at the trailer at sunset.

"He's okay. We'll find him," Maggie said, rubbing Kate's shoulder.

Tammy went to lie down, and Jules flipped on the television while Maggie helped Grace fix dinner. Kate was just setting the table when the door suddenly swung open. The women might have expected—for the second before each remembered—Robbie. But it was Nacho, covered in sand and burs, wagging his tail so hard it whacked the side of the door with thuds. Kate plunged her face into his river-rotted fur. Then she saw another dog, scrawny with a spotted white mutt patch on a slick coat of black. The dog ran through the door, hopped up on the couch, and buried her face in Grace's lap. The sisters swarmed the newcomer.

"Can we keep her?" Kate asked. "She doesn't have a collar."

"Looks like a stray, but we'll knock on some doors up the road to be sure," her mother said, giving in and stroking the adorable black ears.

"I've seen her around, Mom. She lives in the woods," Maggie said, grabbing an old beach towel to wipe her clean. "Poor thing. She's so skinny."

Kate knew that her dad would have said she needed a burger. Once a month, he used to run them all through the Wendy's drive-through and pretend he had no idea how there was an extra cheeseburger and then pass it along to Nacho.

Nacho barked as if to make introductions, and the new dog—Kate had already named her Cheese—exposed her belly for the rubbing.

PART III

Winter Cluster

No animal is so insignificant that it might not reward our attention with great discoveries.

—Karl von Frisch
Ten Little Housemates

19

Grace

Grace knew her daughters could take care of themselves. She'd raised them that way. Robbie had once given her a Mother's Day card that said mothering was about teaching kids to have "wings to show you what you can become and roots to remind you where you're from." He'd forgotten to sign the card, but it was a sweet gesture. She scribbled his name on it just like she did for all the family cards he got credit for but never saw. Grace had cut out the quote and tucked it into her bedroom mirror next to her laminated Nicene Creed.

Her girls were even more independent these days. Their roots were heavy with missing their dad. And though they were certainly too old for it, she still worried about who would do their hair while she was gone. Maggie had been the first to demand pigtails in hopes of containing her curls. Grace would try to separate the ringlets with a plastic pick, then section her toddler head into "piggies" so that Maggie could meet Robbie at the door and oink. Her dad would snort back and chase her to the couch for tickling. "You know why you shouldn't wrestle a pig?" he'd say. "You both get dirty, and the pig likes it." Jules wore her hair long and straight but would settle for a simple braid if Grace insisted that she pull it back from her face. "I wish I was a boy," Jules would complain. "Boys don't have to have pretty hair." Tammy's hair was glorious: blonde and luscious. Tammy's hair couldn't be managed, but Grace tried. Every morning she brushed it out and then puffed it with a steaming hot curling iron and coiffed it into a Dolly Parton style. Kate pulled on a hat to escape her mom's comb, but sometimes she'd ask Grace for a high pony or beg Maggie to do a French braid.

Since Robbie's death, Maggie clipped her hair tight at the base of her neck with a severe metal barrette like she was trying to hold everything in its place. Grace thought about leaving extra brushes, hair spray, and headbands just in case. Even with extras, though, there was usually yelling about hair supplies. One Christmas Kate used her label maker to add each sister's name to their respective hairbrushes and Robbie praised her, saying it was their best bet to end the morning "hair wars." But only Kate actually paid attention to the names. Robbie had also called Grace a genius when she'd bought ten pairs of pink matching stretch gloves and dumped them all in a basket by the front door. That worked, ending the bickering over who had the black pair, the polka-dot red left glove, and the cream-stripe gloves that they each coveted. Mismatched gloves and socks were the new style. One day she might tackle the black leggings battle, but not today. That the girls were little women now continued to swell her with pride and gut her a bit. *Parenting adults is precarious*, Grace thought, and then she felt guilty and relieved to be stepping out of the role for a bit.

"You're bringing all that?" Travis asked when he swung by after work in his truck. He assessed the three suitcases, four duffel bags, and two tents. "Seems to me if we're preparing to live with less we should go in with only our BOBs. You do pack a mean BOB, Grace."

"We're prepping to live with fewer people which means we need gear. What's the point of having all this stuff if we don't try it out?

I'll bet you don't even know how to use some of it. You'd be the only joker trying to read the instructions on a cooking stove during a nuclear fallout. God, Travis." Grace was feeling cruel and impatient. She knew deep down that the end—to this world and maybe this relationship—was near. And Robbie wouldn't be around to help her at all, bless his soul.

Travis was fit. Younger and more willing to do the heavy lifting. They were a team. She was definitely the brains. Her conscience twisted a little. Sure, there was a tiny crack in her grieved heart. But mostly she was tired. Tired of worrying about her daughters and wondering about where they'd get the money. Tired of dodging Mr. Bly's phone calls because the judge wanted to know about her every expense. Tired of doing what she thought she should, like march them all to Mass on Sunday waiting for the Epiphany, when she didn't want to, and looking away from the usher when she couldn't spare twenty dollars for the collection plate. Surely, Jesus would forgive her missing one of his baptisms. He'd had plenty. She'd gone to each in the past, except that one when Tammy had been born, but that had to be overlooked. She'd go to confession next week and ask Father Tom for forgiveness. She might even slip in a hint of her affair. Could she insinuate it and not say it? Receive the forgiveness without fully admitting to the sin? Grace doubted it. She knew she'd sinned, but so had others. How was hers worse, and who was measuring anyway?

At the doctor's visit last week, Tammy had asked why Grace needed to travel now. "Dad's been gone three months, Mom. I need you here for the baby." The social worker who introduced herself at that moment saved Grace from having to answer. The woman helped them fill out prequalification forms for government assistance, and she and Tammy had both been embarrassed.

"Why can't we use our insurance like we normally do?" Tammy whispered.

Grace stared at the floor. "Because we don't have coverage anymore." Robbie's hospital bills had doubled their insurance premiums, and Maggie had canceled it for all Fehlers' employees. The company's policy was now "don't get sick" and pray hard if you do.

Mr. Bly had assured them that because of the pregnancy, medical bankruptcy, and ongoing probate, they would now likely qualify for programs like WIC, SNAP, and TANF. It sounded like a handout, and Grace thought that the acronyms were meant to make them all look stupid. Regardless, they meant checkups for Tammy, food for the baby, and a hospital delivery that wouldn't sink them any more than they'd already been sunk. Still, it was humiliating to need help when she was usually the one who offered it. All of it had made her even more sure that the end of the world was near and being prepared was their only option. A new baby brought new threats, but Grace was a survivor.

"I'll be gone only three days," Grace told Tammy on the way home from the hospital. "It's work, not a vacation. I'm doing this for us. Prep U is the final step in sharpening my survival skills. You should be grateful. When the time comes, I'll be the one saving you and your baby, Tammy. Trust me, the likes of Wade won't know what to do."

She made the girls promise to keep their Bug Out Bags with them at all times while she was away, and she led them through one final drill to see how long it took to secure the basement. If they were all home when it happened, they could lock down in three minutes and twenty-two seconds. Not bad, but they could shave off a full minute if Kate didn't run outside to grab her Penny board. Grace had wanted to recreate the Lights Out drill from last year, when she and Robbie shut down the main breaker and practiced how they'd live without power. But now she figured Maggie would just flip it back on and go about her business. Her eldest daughter was the least imaginative, and she worried it would hurt her in a true emergency. Maggie couldn't see what was coming; she was too much like her dad.

Travis would not shut up on the drive, no matter how many times Grace flipped through the country stations. Every channel was reporting on the stimulus bill Obama was shoving down their throats. More spending, just like the Democrats. And where would they get the money? Not from the fancy banks that caused all this—the ones Congress had bailed out. They'd raise taxes. They'd make families like theirs suffer more. Clearly, she wanted to listen to music and not to the voices of Obama or Travis.

"Total immersion, baby!" he said, slapping the steering wheel. "This is what we've been looking for. This is the next level. I'm so glad you talked me into this." He slipped his arm around her shoulder and tried to pull her closer on the truck's bench seat.

"I think I'm coming down with something," Grace lied, sniffing a bit for good measure.

Travis patted her thigh. "You're tough. You'll be fine," he said, as if sickness was a weakness.

Prep U was the ultimate experience, and Sara Beth—the one who hosted their weekly meetings—had signed people up for a 50 percent discount. She said Prep U was as close as they could get to the real thing. Prep U wasn't for hobbyists; it was for survivalists, folks like them who took the end seriously and seriously prepared. And because of the deal, three days in Lake of the Ozarks was only one hundred dollars. Grace knew Robbie would have wanted her to use some of the life insurance money exactly this way. That must have been why he left it.

It wasn't the official Prepper Camp or Prepper Con, but it was a good place to start. They couldn't afford the fancy, commercial camps anyway. Maybe next year they'd be ready for those leagues—if there was a next year.

"Did you print out the list of classes?" Grace asked. It was one of the tasks she'd assigned Travis after their prepper meeting last month when they'd decided to finally do it.

"Yep. Already planned my schedule for the first day." He patted the thick envelope on the dashboard. "Our event tickets and a vendor map are in there too."

She pulled out the contents, finding his schedule on top.

07:00	Registration	
08:00	Ammunition	Big Tent
09:00	Food Storage	North Tent
10:30	Firearms	Big Tent
12:30	Lunch	
14:00	Solar Energy	South Tent
15:00	Combat 101	North Tent
16:30	Threat Analysis	Big Tent
18:00	Dinner	

"There's a beekeeping class, but I figured you already knew all that stuff."

Grace nodded as she scanned his schedule and scribbled in the weather forecast next to each time. She'd bet Travis hadn't even considered the winter storm watch. Kate, as their resident beekeeper, had. She'd asked for a ride before Grace left so that they could check on the hives they were in the process of moving to their property. She still had Robbie's map marked with GPS locations and dates. The winter weather slowed the business calls, but Maggie had asked Kate to work bees for the upcoming spring and summer and promised her a commission on each job. Truly, it was Jules who had been putting in the extra hours at the office, applying for small business loans and doing the books. Even Bryan was coming in on the weekends and managing the chemical storage and orders. Maggie seemed grateful. If the Fehler women worked for free, the business could stay in the family a bit longer.

Grace turned next to the list of classes. "Canning," she read. "I got that down. And I know all about butchering. Maybe I'll do more first aid, especially with all those bees around. What's Spy Craft?"

"Strategy stuff. Like if you're bunkered down but your neighbors didn't prepare and you need to know their next move. High level work, I hear."

Grace realized he'd made that up and didn't know what Spy Craft was at all. Why can't men say they don't know sometimes? It was exhausting sorting through their layers of bullshit.

She missed Robbie's straight shooting. He meant what he said, even when what he said was second-guessing her. A conversation with Robbie felt like a big mind game. "Where should we eat? Are you sure that's what you want for dinner? Why don't we try something new? I mean, if you think that's what you want, sure, we can give them another shot. But remember last time your steak was cold. Maybe you were right the first time. Or not." He couldn't imagine she had any idea of her own desires. Of course she needed steering; Robbie believed women needed that from men. Jules would call it gaslighting or something about the patriarchy. Grace liked knowing what she wanted, and she felt liberated from not having her every decision doubted.

She studied the brochure. "Raising Rabbits and Secret Livestock might be useful."

Travis pulled into a gas station. A full tank was something they agreed on, and it turned Grace on that she hadn't had to remind him.

"Why is there an awards ceremony and keynote?" Grace asked. "Sounds showy. Maybe we'll skip that for some extra tent time."

"How about I fill up and then we take a little dirt road detour? Why wait for tent time?" Travis leaned in, kissed Grace's neck, and then he nibbled behind her ear. She slid her hand down the front of his pants, curious, then relieved by how quickly and how often Travis could perform.

Truck sex made Grace feel like a teenager again. She'd felt so old since Robbie's death, so tired and withered, but here she was like a kid, not giving a damn and excited about maybe getting caught. She wondered if it was a midlife crisis and Travis was only a fling to get her through it. But she cared about him, more than she wanted to, and they had a real connection, even if it was mostly physical.

An hour later, after circling several fingers of the big lake, they found a placard sign on a stick in the median that read "Preppers" with an arrow pointing to the right.

"Huh. Looks like summer camp," Grace said, assessing the rows of white tents in the open valley.

A man dressed in full camouflage with a clipboard and an assault rifle strapped to his back approached their truck. "I'm Captain Jake. Welcome to Prep U!" he said.

"Howdy," Travis said. "We're the Fehlers."

Grace choked on her own spit when he used her name, as if he'd suddenly joined the family. Maybe it was because she'd made the reservation and written the check. But still.

"Here's your updated itinerary. We had to switch a few locations around. Oh, and it looks like you, ma'am, are registered for the Entrepreneur Prepper Showcase tomorrow morning."

"The what?" Travis asked.

"It's where our inventors and entrepreneurs like you show us your prepped stuff. New products and such," Captain Jake said.

"That's how we got the big discount, honey. I told you about it." Grace took the legal paperwork from Captain Jake. "We'll read through this and bring it back later."

Travis rolled up his window and followed the dirt road toward the campground signs. She looked over the competition registration and imagined the money she could make and what that could mean for her daughters.

"Remember the Little Women Survival Tote I made for Charlene? Every BOB needs that stuff. Just a little extra for the women." Her sister-in-law had laughed at the menstrual cup and body wash. She even tried out the feminine urination device in her own backyard and declared it a success. In addition to the fifty-two mini essential survival items, Grace had tucked into the BOB's side pocket lip gloss, hand lotion, and a miniature bottle of Moscato wine, Charlene's favorite. "She would have nothing prepared if I hadn't sent it, though. Not even a seventy-two-hour supply. Some people need others to prep for them."

"It's a genius idea, Grace. It really is. I just didn't know you wanted to be in business."

Grace flipped through the pages of lawyer talk. "I do know a little about running a business. See, they have this competition for new prepper products. It's a ten thousand dollar prize for the rights. You pitch them your product idea. I read about it on their website, and it seemed worth the try."

Travis nodded slowly. "I'll help with the sales stuff. I'm the highest-ranking salesman at Fehlers', you know? You'll see."

"Uh-huh," she agreed, already imagining how the BOBs for Ladies could make her a fortune. It was a fantastic idea, and it was hers.

She pulled out her cell phone to call and let the girls know she'd arrived, just to check in, but found there was no signal. Made sense; the camp was remote. She was sure the girls were fine. Their skill set was strong.

On their second morning, Grace realized she hadn't slept this well since Robbie's death. She woke to fresh air and finally cut the tags off her all-weather clothes. She hadn't needed a pill since she arrived. She was bored by the campfire parties with their stuffed coolers of beer and lunch meat. Travis said they should make friends to build a community for the end, but Grace wasn't interested. She didn't want to be social like the rest of the preppers. She preferred the silence and the solitude of her walk along the lake. It reminded her of the moments after the girls had left for school and the house was quiet after their morning tornado of lunch boxes, backpacks, and homework location. The front door would slam as the girls rushed for the bus, and Grace would get a fresh cup of coffee and watch the birds out the window while she sipped it. She could finally hear herself think.

The lake view was a constant calm, especially the first morning when it glistened with frost before the sun came out and warmed the ground. It reminded her of the river view at the fish camp and how their cove protected them from the current. She even dropped in on a yoga strength training class and didn't hate it. When she closed her eyes on the mat, the birdsong settled Grace. It seemed useful to resume exercise, which she hadn't done since the funeral. They'd been coming off a frigid cold front the day they arrived but now the weather had turned unseasonably warm, with a high of sixty degrees by noon, and the sun was blindingly bright. Most of the tents had generators anyway, which sounded a lot like the bass boats from her dock. It looked more like what Tammy called "glamping" than what Grace was expecting.

"Stupid liberals would probably say it's global warming," Travis joked, spreading out the ashes from their campfire to cool. "Can't teach stupid. Anyone who has studied history knows it's only a correction. A natural cycle of the Earth. But you can't tell them anything. Those folks need your BOBs for sure. Maybe they'll make it twenty-four hours to know how wrong they'd been—about everything." Grace didn't respond. Kate went on and on about the science of global warning, and Grace was persuaded there was something to it. Certainly the bees acted different these days. She'd noticed Travis talked a lot more now. He told her about everything he learned in his class immediately after he learned it.

Travis turned out to be as good at sales as he'd bragged. After three rounds of judging, Grace's Little Women Survival Tote was being sought after, although there was an ongoing debate about whether to call them BOBs for Ladies or Ladies' BOBs. Two of the judges had told her they'd fund it themselves if she didn't win the overall competition. One judge wanted more urban dweller items, like Survival Playing Cards and earplugs to drown out city chaos. "Maybe a small bug spray too, since those kinds of people aren't used to roughing it," one judge offered. "Won't do much good, but they won't know that."

"The truth is," Travis said, unpacking each item from the BOB slowly, "some who don't want to do their own prepping could be victims of their own laziness. They'll crowd the shelters when the time comes." He held up each item with a flourish. "We all know that a shelter is the last place you want to be. Shared resources are for the weak. We are survivalists not socialists." The menstrual cup made some judges look away, but it was the urination funnel that won folks over. Travis would bring Grace up at that point in the presentation and make her demonstrate by pretending to hold it between her legs, as if everyone hadn't already gotten the idea.

"Liberal preppers are good for all of us. They are weak and nonviolent. They'll be easy to steal from when the time comes, right?"

"But why Little Women?" one judge asked.

"Have you read the novel?" Grace asked. "It is about the March sisters during the Civil War. They're a self-sufficient bunch. They know how to make do, and they're skilled too—first aid, fire building, homeschooling, rustic cooking. They are the perfect heroines for survivalism, and this bag will help all Little Women survive those crucial first seventy-two hours." At the end of this part, Travis would toss a paperback copy of the book in the tote and tell them they could read it or use it for toilet paper, and the crowd would break into applause.

By the third morning, Grace had even grown accustomed to the near constant gunfire that carried through the valley from the outdoor targets. Once she reframed her thinking that the gunfire was not an assault but a defense, it was comforting. She was surprised by how at ease she was. She and Travis were a couple here without any questioning. They were together and it fit well, even though they crossed paths only in the Big Tent and took different Prep U classes to maximize their skill set. But mostly it was the shortcut in each conversation that helped Grace relax. She didn't have to explain her fears; they were shared. She didn't have to say "prepper" three times because the other person didn't know what that was; prepper was their instant bond. She even liked to try out her newly acquired lingo: FEMA for Foolishly Expecting Meaningful Aid, and WROL meant Without Rule of Law. She noticed Travis was flexing his new fluency too. At Prep U, Grace could be herself, or at least this version of herself that felt true. *If only the girls could see this*, she thought, *they'd understand that all my efforts to provide and to protect them aren't in vain*. The end of something was imminent, and she'd be ready.

Grace had chosen "Surviving Obama" for her first class of the day and found a support group in session. Ten folding chairs were placed in a circle with an easel that listed five "action items for the resistance." It seemed more of a therapy session than useful strategies, but she related to how scared others were about the new administration. It was clear that their assault on small businesses was calculated. There would be more regulations, higher taxes, and skyrocketing insurance premiums.

Family businesses like theirs were the backbone of America, but Robbie had always said they also took the hardest hits from the economy and the corrupt cronies in Washington. Now that Grace saw their finances, though, she was surprised by how little they paid in taxes compared to how much her husband had always complained about them. She'd watched her own parents do the same and barely scrape by. Grace knew poor people didn't choose to be poor, but she also believed that poverty was a shameful sin. At least you could have the decency to hide it, like her own dad had with his drinking. Her own mama had always said, "A head in the sand is a safe head." Grace was raised to fend for herself and to not put her dirty laundry in the street, but the threats to their way of life had grown. It was harder for her daughters to survive. The world had changed, but much of their way of life hadn't. Grace didn't feel nostalgic; she just needed to figure out a new way, and the business had to adapt. The family needed to also.

"Hey, are you the lady who invented that Little Women's BOB?" a bearded man asked once Grace had introduced herself. "I want to send some of those to my aunts. I'll sleep better knowing they have a fighting chance."

"I am," she admitted, but it made her feel suddenly shy to say so. She wasn't raised to bring that kind of attention on herself. Men were successful, and women propped them up. But maybe it didn't have to be that way. Grace was ready to take the risk, especially if it meant money for her family and running her own business. "Here's my email address. We can work something out." Was that her first deal? It didn't feel half bad. She was proud of her idea and her skills. Why wouldn't others find Grace's product valuable? She'd spent a lot of time researching and figuring out how to survive. She liked the idea of helping others do the same.

As the panel organizer was summarizing why the president kept jacking up gas prices, which Jules had said Obama didn't even have the power to do, the loudspeaker interrupted. The bearded man put his hand to his heart as if the alarm was too much to handle. Grace thought he'd be the first casualty in an actual crisis with his dramatic flair.

Ladies and gentlemen, may I have your attention. Your attention, please. We've been informed that the time has come. Our radio operators have confirmed some disturbing news that requires our immediate action. A catastrophic event has occurred in Washington, DC, and New York City. Our sources report that both cities have been eliminated. I repeat. The magnitude of the attack—we believe it is foreign terror-ism—has wiped out much of the East Coast of our United States of America.

People in the next tent cheered, and it took Grace a second to realize they were celebrating the East Coast's demise, maybe even Obama's assassination. Then someone else shushed them so they could hear the rest of the announcement.

We do not know what is next, but we know you are well prepared with your new skills from Prep U. We'll have more details soon, but you are safe here. In fact, this is the best place on God's Earth you could be right now. Please return to your campsites in an orderly fashion. You've been training for this. You're ready. We'll have more details soon. You know what to do. May God be with us all.

"Is this a drill?" Grace asked. The bearded man was weeping into his hands and wiping snot on his flannel shirt.

"I don't think so," the tent organizer said. "I think they would have told those of us in positions of authority."

She needed to call the girls. She needed to hear that they were okay and had their BOB bags and would wait in their basement for her instructions. But when she checked her phone, there was still no service. As she exited the tent, Travis took her by the elbow and updated her that his phone couldn't get a signal either. They'd cut CB service for their protection.

"Let's calm down," Travis yelled, even though Grace felt fine. She just needed to know her daughters were safe.

"You need to drive me to a phone. I need to reach the girls. Now."

"The camp is on lockdown. There is no way in or out." Travis bit his bottom lip. "They've secured the perimeter ten miles out."

"They're holding us captive? Hell no." Grace pushed his arms away and reached in his front pocket for the truck keys.

"The keys are back at camp. I forgot them."

"Jesus, Travis. What good are you? How can you survive when you're not even ready to escape in a loaded truck?" Grace meant it. He was unprepared in the exact moment she needed him to be prepared. If she couldn't rely on him, she'd rather be alone.

This thing with Travis definitely wouldn't last. It wasn't his fault. He seemed suddenly like a kid to her, not the solid partner she wanted. She'd mothered plenty and wasn't looking for more people to take care of. She needed a man like Robbie, not a boy like Travis, and it choked her to realize this too late.

As Grace stormed back to the tent, five guys in the camp next to theirs formed a circle, shooting their guns in the air. So stupid. Bullets come back down. Why would anyone waste their ammo like that? She hurried past three moms passing around a bottle of homemade wine. Their kids were running too close to their campfires, and Grace had to resist the urge to pull them back. Finally, she saw a group of men who seemed to be in control, huddled over a map. When she got closer, she heard their plans to raid another camp. This wasn't survivalism; it was chaos and greed.

Grace began packing. She needed to get home. She needed to get to her girls. She'd enjoyed being off the grid at first, until this crisis. She rifled through the pockets of Travis's clothes but couldn't find keys. "Are you hiding them?" she screamed. "Are you trying to trap me?"

"I swear they were in my coat. Honey, you know I'm on your side," Travis said, putting his hands on her shoulders, trying to slow her down. "Let's wait a bit. Reassess. Use our checklist."

Folks, we have an update. We will open the perimeter in twenty-four hours. The first team to reach the border will win a cash prize and be allowed to leave. You must arrive on foot with only the contents of your BOB. I repeat. Driving vehicles is forbidden. This is about your wilderness skills. We'll expect the rest to survive here until we know more about the situation out there. Cooperate, of course, but consider your team. Think about your best interest first. God bless us, one and all.

"See?" Travis said. "Everyone is cooperating. This is the safest place to be."

But Grace didn't see. According to the Prep U officials, the end of civilization was beginning and they were holding a survival contest? No way. This was a drill. A dumb, scary one. Grace was furious. These people were the terrorists. Their fear justified their withdrawal from folks they didn't want to protect. Why not use their skills to prevent disaster instead? The world outside looked suddenly much safer.

"But, Robbie, I didn't want this. I wanted to be prepared for this."

"What did you say? You called me Robbie."

"These people want the war. We may have lost half of this country, and they're happy. This is not what I signed up for, Robbie."

"You just did it again."

"I'm sure I didn't." Grace wiped her eyes with her sleeve. "Here's the thing. Most of them wanted this to be real. You can see it in their eyes. They aren't preppers. They want a civil war. Maybe Robbie wanted one too. It's not about flexing their skills. It's a justification for who they've decided is the enemy. And if you're the enemy—if you believe they threaten your survival—you can hate them all you want and do anything necessary in return. That is certainly not the message of Jesus Christ."

Travis cleared his throat and spit into the dirt. "When did you get all religious?"

Grace stared as he became a stranger. "You don't know me at all, do you? Today is the Epiphany." She pulled out her pistol and aimed it at his feet, then raised the barrel to his crotch. It was the second gun she'd pulled on a guy who pissed her off, and it felt powerful. The Santa thing was sort of an accident, but she had no regret. "Epiphany means manifestation, as in let me show you something. The Pope says wise men—the magi—recognized Jesus as Messiah, Son of God, Savior of the World. I just got it. I see this thing for what it really is. We're through, Travis."

She didn't even have to cock her gun before he reached into his BOB and held out the keys.

"You don't get any of this, do you?" Grace said as she swiped them from his hand. She was taking his truck and leaving him behind. "I'm going home to my girls, where I belong. I already have what I need to survive."

20

Jules

Jules was sitting at the front desk at Fehler Family Exterminating when a familiar truck sped around the corner. It stirred up dust, and now a cloud hung in the air. She'd cleared the front window view by throwing out all the dried flower arrangements covered in cobwebs. She'd even hung her dorm posters in the communal bathroom so the technicians had to read her feminist views while they peed. She wasn't happy about being home. She missed Niko. But Jules was good at the books and waded through collecting on years of customers who hadn't paid. With Bryan's help, they'd found a new supplier and cut their costs in half. When the bank froze their assets because of the bankruptcy, she discovered Robbie had leased their vehicles and at an obnoxiously high rate. Jules had gone herself to see Mrs. Cooper and renegotiate the terms. Maggie didn't even know yet that they'd applied for loans and tax breaks from Obama's stimulus package, which promised to bolster small businesses like theirs out of the recession. Jules was fighting the patriarchy by staying afloat. She wondered what Pamela would say about her progress.

Out her window, the sun was hiding behind the bluff and the white oak trees around the office glowed from the light. When the earth settled around the truck, her mom got out of the driver's seat, disheveled, and leaned against the door. She was either praying or pulling herself together, and Jules went out to the parking lot to find out which. Grace caught her in a long hug.

"Mom, what's wrong?" Jules asked, trying to pull away from Grace's grip. She was running her fingers through her hair like Jules was little again and refused the curling iron. "Are you okay?"

"They said it was the end of the world. They wanted us to think people were dead."

"Who did? That doesn't make sense. Slow down. What happened?"

"I can't lose Robbie and you all too."

"I'm home now. It's kind of hard to get lost here."

"I don't know what I'd do if something happened to you, Jules. Or your sisters."

"We're fine, Mom, but you look awful. Let's get you something to eat." Grace nodded, but she wouldn't let go of Jules's hand. "Whose truck is this?"

"You don't want to know, honey."

Jules drove them to Country Kitchen and ordered piles of waffles with strawberries and actual whipped cream. She added a side of vegetarian sausage. Her mom didn't complain. A crisis called for breakfast for dinner. The time away from home, Robbie's death, falling in love with Niko, quitting college. Pamela had accessed something in Jules, and she felt vulnerable and raw. She didn't like it at all.

"Mom, can I ask you something?"

Grace added creamer to her coffee. "You're probably going to anyway."

"Did you go with Travis?"

"That's my business." She scooped her whipped cream onto Jules's plate.

"In a family business, the family's business is everyone's business, or something like that, Dad used to say." When the waitress stopped by to check on them, Jules ordered another round of coffee because her mom liked coffee.

Grace took a sip and smiled. "Your dad was wrong about a lot of things, God rest his soul."

"I miss him, Mom."

"I do too, Jules."

"When I go back to college, I'm not majoring in business."

Grace put down her fork. "We need you here now, Jules."

"I am here now. But . . ."

"What's your plan?"

"I don't know yet. Literature or history. I want to take some art classes too. Drawing and painting. I want to study abroad. In Spain . . . with Niko." Jules imagined an apartment with Niko somewhere in a city where they could pick up takeout on their way home from their fancy jobs and have sex anytime they wanted. She could make it work. She needed to help her family get back on their feet, but if she stayed too long, they'd fold her back in for good. Pamela had insisted it was an opportunity to learn to balance her family with her future. She called it a silver lining in the darkness of her dad's death, but Jules wasn't ready to be grateful. She'd settle for being okay enough not to want to cut again.

Grace covered her mouth, laughing. "I always thought you were your father's daughter, but you have plenty of me in you too. I see that now." It wasn't a dig. It felt like her mom was proud of her for the first time, or maybe she'd just missed the other times. Jules's anger protected her, but it pierced her too. "You've got guts, kid. I think you'll survive us all somehow."

"I've been seeing a counselor. She thinks I should consider medicine."

"For what?"

Jules cut up the last waffle and smothered it in whipped cream. Then she held out a fork to Grace. "For my anxiety, Mom."

"Just because it's been a hard time doesn't mean you have a condition."

"I do though. I have an anxiety disorder, and I can't manage it on my own."

"If you say so. I'll make you an appointment at the clinic."

Jules nodded. "Thank you. I mean it. I want to feel better."

"Me too," Grace said, reaching across the table for Jules's hand again. Something had definitely shifted in her mom. She was clingy and soft, and it unsettled Jules a bit. Once Grace had told her about what happened at Prep U, she didn't mentioned prepping again. She talked only about the family and how to take care of each other. She seemed to be actually listening to Jules and taking her plans seriously.

After breakfast, Jules drove her mom home in the truck and helped her unpack. The BOBs were lined up and labeled. Jules smiled when she saw there was an extra one marked "Niko."

When Jules pulled back into the lot at Fehlers', Travis was leaning against the car she shared with Maggie.

"Get away from my car," she said, clicking her key toggle so the car's alarm blasted. Travis held up his hands like he was surrendering, and he moved three feet from the car door. Jules turned off the alarm but tucked her keys in her palm and brought a single key through her fingers like a knife if she needed it. Tammy had shown her how, and Maggie had taught Tammy, like sisters do.

"You're driving my truck." He smiled like they were old friends. He looked hungover and smelled like piss.

"Is that so? What do you want? I'm in a hurry."

"What I want is what's mine. See, your mom owes me money. I

tried to talk to her like an honest man would, but she didn't respond like an honest woman. She even left me without a ride, and I had to hitch here. I figured I'd settle up with you, on your mom's behalf, seeing as how she's grieving and all."

"What's your name again? Tim? Tony?"

"Travis. You know my name. I've been a guest at your house plenty. Mostly at your mom's invitation, if you know what I mean."

Jules feared she did. She hoped none of her sisters knew Mom's little prepper vacation included him.

"That's right," Jules nodded. "Travis. Now I remember. You're the one who stole this company truck from us."

He took two steps in her direction and pointed his finger. "I never took a goddamn thing from your business. In fact, I made you all plenty and wasn't paid what I'm worth."

"Really? Because this truck is leased to Fehlers' and you've been driving it all over town like it was yours. Even charging your gas to our company. I have the receipts with your signature. Last month you filled up at Lake of the Ozarks. Was that for work?"

"Your dad gave me that truck so I could make sales calls. It's mine."

"It's Fehlers'. This truck belongs to my family. You won't be making sales calls anymore."

"You can't fire me, stupid bitch. You're not Robbie. You're just the uppity sister who left."

"Damn it. I was going to offer you a ride somewhere, but now you'll have to walk."

Travis scuffed his boots in the gravel and sniffed. He watched the horizon and huffed.

Jules tried to stare him down, but the bastard didn't have the courage to meet her eyes. "You'll stay away, or I'll have Maggie call the sheriff and file a report. I'll personally call your references and any future employers and tell them you're a thief. If you come near my mom again or any of my sisters, I'll hurt you myself." Then she raised her knee to his nuts, and he flinched like all men do when you threaten their precious package.

She climbed back into the truck and peeled out of the parking lot—tires squealing with smoke, just like her dad had taught her.

21

Kate

The hive's main job in winter is to take care of the queen," Kate explained to Sister Ruth Ann and her class. "Bees are cold blooded. The workers form a cluster to keep her safe and warm." She clicked to the next slide on her PowerPoint presentation. Becky sat in the front row and rested her chin on her fist in a clear sign of boredom. Kate pretended she couldn't see her and paused to look past her, as she'd seen Val do when a dog didn't obey. "The beekeeper makes sure the honey supply stays full so the bees sustain enough energy to keep shivering to move their wing muscles and produce heat."

Becky held up her hand. Kate ignored her. Val had told her that alphas aren't easily bothered and they know they are in charge.

"I think Becky has a question," Sister Ruth Ann nodded.

Kate scanned the room like she had no idea who Becky was. Lila smiled and gave her a thumbs-up. Then she wiggled her body like she was a bee shivering and shook her adorable wing arms. Kate felt light-headed.

"Anyway, in the Fehler family we practice what's called the rose hive method. It's based on the idea of colony cooperation, and all the parts of the hive are interchangeable. We work with the bees rather than against their nature so bees can do what bees do best."

"So last year, when you did the same presentation," Becky said, dropping her hand and interrupting, "you said you were a beekeeper or whatever. You said you and your dad had a bunch of bees or whatever. Do you still?"

Surely Becky wasn't asking because her dad had died? Like the Fehlers would just kill all the bees or something? Or as if the family couldn't possibly raise them without Robbie? Kate continued as if she hadn't heard the question, but it cut her confidence. "Rose hives are often taller and stronger. The method requires closer work with bees by giving them the space they need. The structure of the queen excluder isn't necessary because we allow an unlimited brood nest. That way the queen can lay eggs wherever she wants." When she'd practiced her presentation at home, Jules had told her to just breathe through the bumps. "Colder weather and more threat make the bees cluster more compactly. Some studies show a hive consumes thirty pounds of stored honey per winter—even more in the Midwest."

"How much more?" Lila called out.

Kate's face was hot and happy. "One winter I think it was fifty pounds."

"Wow!" Lila said, nodding and leading her row in agreement. "That's a lot!"

Kate moved through three more slides with pictures of her hives and her altered bee suit. She'd cut the lengths of her dad's suit's arms and legs to fit her; Tammy had helped her mend them. "To produce one pound of honey, bees must visit two million flowers. Finally, honey never spoils." Then she passed out plastic spoons and walked up and down the aisles squirting honey from the Fehler family's own hives for her classmates to try. She gave Lila two spoons.

"Thank you, Kate," Sister Ruth Ann said, and everyone clapped except Becky.

An hour later, the class was boarding the school vans for a field trip to the Trail of Tears State Park when Kate heard Tammy's name called on the intercom. Their mom hadn't said anything about a dentist or doctor appointment, and she rarely let them miss school, even with colds. "I have to pee before the trip, Sister. Can I please have a pass?" Sister Ruth Ann frowned, probably at her use of "pee," but she wrote the permission slip anyway. Kate had noticed that Sister Ruth Ann rejected 50 percent of the requests for bathroom breaks from girls but wrote a pass every time one of the boys said the word "pee."

Tammy was coming down the hall just as Kate rounded the corner. They saw each other and shrugged in a silent sister conversation of "What's up?" "Nothing." "Who knows?" "You okay?" "Yeah, you?"

Kate held the office door for her. As Tammy passed, Kate asked, "You in trouble?"

"Probably. I told James Thompson where he could stick it when he tried to read a note Wade passed to me."

They sat together in the front office waiting for Father Tom to call Tammy in. Kate told Mary, the school nurse, that her stomach hurt and if she went on the field trip, she'd puke. The nurse frowned, probably at her use of "puke," but she called her class and told Sister Ruth Ann she'd keep Kate in the infirmary. Kate heard her whisper in the phone, "She's probably missing her dad. Poor thing." Mary had taken care of the Fehler sisters for years. Kate suspected she knew all their tricks. Jules had told her that reporting your period to Mary got you a Tylenol and a cup of lukewarm water, but any mention of throwing up and you were rewarded free range.

"You don't have a fever," Mary said, feeling her forehead with the back of her hand, "but I'll call your mom anyway."

"You can't. She's not home. Call Maggie or Jules at the office."

"I thought Jules was away at college," Mary said.

"She was. Now she's back. Here, I'll call them." Kate dialed and then shared with Jules a list of her vague, fake symptoms. "I'll lay down until you get here and will try not to vomit all over the nurse." Tammy hid her face in her sleeve to stop from laughing. Then she pretended to cough to cover it up when Father Tom called her in. "Must be contagious."

Ten minutes later, Tammy slammed Father Tom's office door open, startling Kate and Mary, who'd given her a cool washcloth for her forehead. Tammy's face was fury, and Kate ran after her to the bathroom. Tammy tended to be emotional, it was true, but what had hurt her this much? It had to be bad. Where was Maggie, who steered them all straight, and Jules, who was great in your corner when you needed courage?

"They're kicking me out. Father Tom knows about the baby. My baggy sweatshirts aren't hiding anything. Stupid small town. They're such jerks! I wish Jules were here. She'd tell them all to go to hell. Don't use birth control. No wait, don't get rid of babies."

"Mom is going to kill you." Kate knew that wasn't helpful. It slipped out. She wasn't good at consoling her sisters.

"How is this my fault?" Tammy said, pulling off toilet paper and blowing her nose. "Well, this is, maybe." She patted her belly. "But I was hoping to finish the school year and then take my GED or something. This is going to impress the pageant judges. I had it all worked out. I've even figured out how quickly I can lose the weight and still fit into my swimsuit. I signed up for a Zumba class at the YMCA."

"What about Wade?" This didn't just *seem* unfair; it was unfair.

"What about him? He certainly gets to finish the school year. He's not an embarrassment to the congregation. He gets to do whatever he wants. In fact, the other guys are probably congratulating him for making it all the way with me. I hate this place! They're all hypocrites."

Maggie opened the bathroom door, and Kate was relieved. Tammy filled her in, and she listened, calmly, as Mags always did. You could count on her. She never overreacted.

"I guess we'll save on your tuition," Maggie said. "You're not sick are you, Kate?" She put her palm on Kate's cheek to feel for fever.

"Sick for my sister counts." Kate sniffed like she'd just developed a cold. She might miss the lemon antiseptic smell of the school bathroom, which was sparkling compared to her sisters' hairspray and makeup mess at home.

"There's more to be sick over. Wade broke up with me." Tammy let out a wail. She pulled more toilet paper off the roll and handed it out among them.

Maggie turned on the sink and indicated they should all wash their snotty hands. When she was extra calm, Kate knew she was extra pissed. "He can't do that."

"That's what was in the note that James tried to take. He broke up with me in a note. Said he wasn't sure he was ready for all this—as if I have a choice."

Kate snatched the note Tammy held out, and she and Maggie leaned in to read it.

Tammy,
You know how I feel about you,
but this is all to much for me. I'm sorry.
I can't be a daddy right now.
I need some time too think. Don't be mad.
You'll always be my girl.
—Wade

The sisters each stood at a sink, splashed water on their faces, and eyed each other from their mirrors.

"Dad would not want to see this," Maggie said. "I'm almost glad he's not here." Kate thought that wasn't true at all. He'd make Wade do the right thing, and Wade would never have written such a cowardly note if their dad was around to threaten him.

"This is as bad as it can get, right?" Tammy said, and Kate hoped so. "How does he not know which 'to' to use? My baby does not need a dumb daddy anyway." Maggie held Tammy in a side hug. "Besides, Wade wouldn't be able to support us anyway. But now what's going to happen to my baby?"

Maggie watched their reflections in the mirror, as if she couldn't face her sisters when she spoke. "We will take care of each other. Somehow. We will make it work. Dad knew that."

Kate leaned against the tiled wall and felt its sturdiness. She wondered how many sisters and nuns had stood in this very bathroom sorting out life and their options and all that went wrong along the way. There was so much you couldn't control, no matter how prepared you were.

They left the school and headed toward the parking lot. Kate had an urge to check on the hives as soon as she got home. If she closed her eyes, she could almost hear their buzzing siren. When she'd told Lila that bees headbutt each other when danger is near, Lila had gently nuzzled her blonde curls into her neck, as if she was a bee warning her. "Like this?" she'd said. Kate had felt warm and safe smelling her scent. She couldn't help how much she thought about Lila, and maybe Lila liked her too.

Kate climbed into the back seat of the car. Maggie started the engine but then left the car idling and just sat staring out the windshield. The look on her face made Kate's thoughts of Lila fall away.

"I have bad news too," Maggie said. "Since we didn't get the bank loan and we don't have enough money for rent and payroll, we need to sell Fehlers' . . . if there are any buyers, that is."

"Sell Fehlers'?" Kate said, as if it was the first she'd heard of it. "But I've been training Nacho to find bed bugs. It could work."

"It won't save the family business, kiddo, even if Nacho and Cheese are both trained. But thanks for trying. I tried too. And Jules did as much as she could. We all did."

They sat in weary silence. Finally Maggie shifted into gear and started driving toward home.

"I know what we should do," Kate said to Maggie and Tammy once they'd left the school parking lot. "We should talk to Dad."

Maggie looked in the rearview mirror. "That sounds nice, Kate. I wish that were possible too, honey."

"No, I mean it. We can talk to Dad. Trust me, okay?" Kate had an answer, one that might make everyone happy, at least for a little bit. "Just this once, follow me. But first swing by the office and get Jules. We have to all be together for this."

Kate didn't bother knocking at Val's house anymore. She spent almost as much time there as her own home. She'd gone from thinking of the piles of papers in Val's living room as messy to cozy. Sometimes she dragged the trash cans in from the curb if she noticed they'd been there for days. Val's door was usually open; the dogs kept track of visitors, and there were a lot. TV crews, reporters, clients, and strangers who stumbled in like Kate looking for answers. Val's skills were sought after. Kate didn't mind cleaning out the dog runs and scooping up pup poop. She liked having them play around her while she worked, and Nacho had practically joined their pack. She'd brought Cheese a few times too, but Cheese had bonded so tight to Grace that she whined any time she couldn't be with her, clawing at doors that blocked her from Grace's lap. Nacho was catching on to the bed bug training though. Last week he'd found three vials of fresh bed bugs completely on his own, and Kate had hidden them well in places that would have made her mom scream.

She wasn't so sure what her sisters would think of Val's brashness. She reminded her of an older Jules in how she didn't seem to care what others thought of her. She was the absolute opposite of Maggie and Tammy, but they seemed curious when Kate brought up the idea during a moment of weakness.

"There seems to be many of you today," Val said when she found Kate, Maggie, Jules, and Tammy around her kitchen table.

"We brought coffee and donuts," Maggie said, extending her hand in greeting.

"Good Catholics, I see, with the coffee and donuts." Val ignored her hand and stuffed a powdered jelly into her mouth. Kate handed her a kitchen towel to wipe off the powder from her chin, but Val stared at it like she had no idea what it might be for.

Kate hadn't noticed the smell of the house before, but it was definitely musty with animal scent. She hoped the good smells they brought in might mask the rest. "This is Maggie, Val, my oldest sister. Tammy and Jules, my other sisters."

"Should I get some mugs?" Maggie offered.

"Coffee sounds great," Val said. "Kate has told me all about you. Nacho shared some secrets too."

"I don't have many anymore," Tammy said.

"Nacho told me that too." Val nodded and slurped from the mug Maggie handed her. "You want something. I can tell."

After Kate had asked and Tammy and Maggie had apologized for her asking and Val had listened, she said, "Alright. We'll do this. But you each get only one question and you may not question the answer, understood? This stuff exhausts me, and I need my energy. Got it?"

"Got it," the sisters said in unison.

"Well, it ain't fancy," Val said, joining their circle, "but here is good." She sat at the kitchen table and held out her hands. "Go ahead. Grab each other. We need the flow." Val closed her eyes, so Kate did the same. The dogs fell silent, as if they, too, knew something sacred and beyond this world was about to happen.

"Okay, he's here," Val said. "Maggie, you're the oldest, right? You go first."

Maggie was quiet for a while. Val waited. Finally, Mags whispered through a cracked voice, "If you're here, Dad, please tell me what to do at work. I don't know how to fix it."

In a voice that was clearly Val's but a bit tired, she said, "If anyone can, it's you, Mags. Keep trying. Don't sell. There is an answer. Wait for it."

"But—" Maggie began.

"But nothing," Val said. "I told you. You can't question the answer. Next."

Jules didn't hesitate. "I'm next, and is this bullshit?"

Val laughed. "Only one way to find out."

"I want to go back to college. Can I leave again?"

"Yes, you can always leave, and you can always come home again too."

Jules shrugged. "Which is it?"

"Both. Next."

Tammy cleared her throat. "I don't know how to ask this because I don't want him to know." She rubbed her belly and nodded toward it.

"He doesn't," Val said. "It's feelings not facts. My job is to give you access to him, but it doesn't work both ways."

"Okay. Fine. Should I try to make up with and marry Wade, and will I win the pageant?"

"That's two questions. Also, he doesn't know the future. That's not how this works."

"Fine. Ask him about Wade."

"He thinks you should do what your mom says is best."

"But—" Tammy began. Val put her finger to her mouth to shush her.

Kate didn't hesitate. "Can you tell him the hive is fine? I don't have a question. I just want him to know that." Then she closed her eyes.

It was peaceful and quiet again. Kate didn't mind the wait, but then it became a while. When Kate opened her eyes, it was Val who was weeping. Her face was broken and tender; it alarmed the dogs. They had gathered around her and were licking at her cheeks and her hands. She leaned down into their fur and let them.

"Kate," she finally said, "everything is going to be okay. That's your answer. He wants you to know that he understands. I'm not sure what that means." Kate nodded. She couldn't talk yet. She needed time to think. Surely he couldn't have known what she was only beginning to know about herself.

On the drive home, Maggie said, "We're not telling Mom, right?"

Tammy turned off the radio. "I think we have to tell her some of it."

"What Mom doesn't know won't hurt her," Jules said. "She has secrets too."

Maggie nodded as she drove. Fresh snow was falling. "She needs to know about school and probably Val, just maybe . . . maybe not Dad."

"Sisters' secret?" Kate asked. It was childish, she knew, but she wanted to be the baby again, for a little bit.

"Sisters' secret."

22

Grace

When Grace returned from the grocery store an hour later, Nacho and Cheese sprinted around the kitchen cabinet corner, tails thwacking in rhythm, and took turns sniffing her hands. Nacho rushed her, as dogs do, but she nudged her knee into his broad pit snout. Cheese sat on her haunches waiting for permission. She had turned out to be a well-mannered lady aimed at pleasing. She understood her place and moved away from her own food bowl if Grace entered the room. Cheese spent a lot of time curled at Grace's feet and sometimes snuggled in her bed too. All four daughters were at the kitchen island, spreading honey on toast, at a time of day when they should all be elsewhere and not invading the peace and sanctity of Grace's hours.

Maggie licked the honey from the knife and passed it to Jules for reloading.

Grace set down a bag piled high with apples. "Did my girls forget how to unload the groceries?" She looked at her daughters' faces and saw the signs: dark circles, puffiness, creases, red splotches. Grief. Life. This morning. Just getting through a day felt like wading through, well, honey—except bitter not sweet. Each move since Robbie's death was a tepid new normal. The past with their dad was a continent slowly drifting from the shore while they flailed for a floating stick to hold on to.

Grace narrowed her brow at them, and Kate gushed. "Tammy got kicked out of school. I'm not going back either. Wade broke up with her. Maggie says we have to sell Fehlers' because we can't afford to run it. Jules hates being home. She misses Niko." Kate couldn't keep secrets. Even the ones she thought she tucked safe inside seeped out.

Grace stopped unpacking the eggs. "What? Why didn't the school call me?"

Maggie popped more slices into the toaster. "They said they tried but that none of the calls went through. Maybe your phone was off."

Grace had turned her phone off; it was true. Travis wouldn't stop texting her harassing messages. At first, he'd begged. *i miss you. can we talk? come on, baby.* But when she ignored him, it pissed him off and he showed himself. *ur fake. when SHTF, you die first. ur a weak bitch.* She powered her phone back up and blocked Travis for good.

"I'll call Father Tom," she said, patting Tammy's hand. "I'm sure it's a misunderstanding."

"It's because I'm showing," Tammy said. "Can't hide this." She palmed the back of her hips and made her belly stick out even more.

Kate nudged the tightness of her sister's stretched stomach, and the baby kicked back at the heat of her hand. "I felt it!"

"It's a her," Tammy clarified.

Jules nodded. "Definitely a girl."

"Is it?" Maggie asked. "How do you know?"

Tammy sat down heavily on the stool. "Like we'd have a boy. Wade wants a boy. He's not getting one."

Grace put both hands on Tammy's belly and felt the life. She remembered each girl kicking inside her. Jules was the feistiest, of course. Like Grace, she trafficked in action not empathy. "I'll fix this. I'll fix all of this," she said, grabbing her rosary off the crucifix that hung above the kitchen sink. "Girls, unpack those groceries. Add some ham to that honey toast so it counts as lunch, and somebody feed those dogs. They keep sniffing for food in the couch cushions, and they better not find any there."

"They're looking for bed bugs, Mom. Not food," Kate said.

Maggie blushed. "We do not have bed bugs. I would know."

"Of course we don't. They're in these little glass tubes. I've been training the dogs to find them. Cheese isn't getting it, but Val says Nacho is a natural."

"Who's Val?" Grace asked, watching Tammy poke back at the places on her belly where the baby was forming lumps. Grace suddenly remembered that when she was pregnant with her, Tammy liked to kick a knee into her rib cage as she was finally drifting off to sleep.

Jules cleared her throat. "Val is a famous dog trainer. She flies all over the country with her bed bug dogs. They hunt them. According to my research, it's not a terrible idea. Maybe even lucrative."

"I've heard of it," Maggie said. "It's big in the cities, like St. Louis and Kansas City."

Kate nodded. "She lives in Cape now, but if she doesn't find another job soon—something with benefits, she said—she's going back to Chicago. She said integrated pest management is the future."

Grace noticed not one of them was looking at her. Something was up with them, more than what they'd already spilled, or the worries of their future were too much.

"I'll figure this out, girls. Get to the groceries while I'm gone. Those bags need to feed us for a week." She tossed a dog biscuit to Cheese on her way out the door, but Nacho grabbed it first.

In the confession box, Grace had told Father Tom everything. The affair. Her resentment of Robbie. Her guilt since his death. How she cared more about the doves on her windowsill sometimes than the family business. Her anger at her husband for sharing so little about their money problems. Her fury at herself for acting like she couldn't manage their money on her own. That though she had done everything expected of her, life still didn't quite fit. How prepping made her feel powerful and safe. Her desire to run away from all of them. That she had run away but then came back. Her epiphany about her fellow preppers and her own single-minded selfishness. "After dinner some nights, I sit in my car gripping the steering wheel. I make myself a deal that I can sit there all I want if I don't start the engine. Sometimes I smoke too. Is that sin?"

"Which part, Grace?" Father Tom had said through the tiny mesh screen.

Now the cross on the rosary dug into Grace's hand as she drove. It had been her mother's. As a young girl, she'd watched her mother's lips move in silence as she worked her worries through the beads.

First, Grace went to the bank to sign the bed bug loan papers herself and put the house up for collateral. She'd read Maggie's business plan, even if she hadn't said so. The business had barely survived, but her daughter was smart and it showed. She deserved a shot. Mrs. Cooper wasn't that surprised to see her. "It's what Robbie would have done," she assured her, sliding the pen across her desk. Grace didn't ask how many times he had borrowed against the house over the years to keep them afloat. He'd used the butcher shop for collateral and never told her. She could see now the burden he'd carried agonizing over how to pay what with what, when to borrow more, how to pay things off, and how to earn everything they needed and asked for.

After the bank, she drove to Wade's parents' house to sit on their couch and not sip the weak tea they offered but instead to insist their perfect son marry her flawed daughter. "We love Tammy, we really do," Wade's mom said, patting Grace's knee. "But we have to think of Wade's future too."

"Wade chose his future when he got her pregnant. Tammy would like a formal proposal, and I'm here to give my blessing and my ring." Grace slid the band off her own finger and placed it in the center of their coffee table. The ring had begun to slip side to side as her finger slimmed and aged. Each time she straightened it, she felt a pang in her gut. "Since her dad can't give his permission, it's my duty. I'm sure you've raised your son right. Father Tom is looking forward to officiating the ceremony and baptizing the baby. Father and I had a good long talk about everything, and it's all set."

Next, she went to Bryan's tiny apartment to buy his share of the business. She offered him what was left of the life insurance money. "Family is family," Grace said, putting her arm around his shoulder. "But you have never been bug girl material." At least he had a river view from downtown Cape, but she hoped the money might get him a decent place, especially if he ever hoped to have a girl over.

Bryan nodded. "I loved Uncle Robbie, you know?"

Grace had learned exactly what to say in this situation. "He thought highly of you too." It put people at ease when she spoke on behalf of Robbie and granted his appreciation, even when she knew it wasn't the whole truth. She wasn't lying to Bryan though. Her husband had adored him so much that he'd left him part of the business he should have given her. She wondered if that would ever not sting.

"One time when my dad was telling me to 'man up' because he said I was becoming a 'girlie academic,' Uncle Robbie stood up for me. He said, 'There's more than one way to be a man, son,' and it stuck with me."

Grace thought about how Robbie always said, "To each his own"—and usually meant it. It was part of his pride to take care of himself and his family, so he hid the hard parts. She wished he was beside her now to watch her "woman up." Maybe he would be proud of her.

After she left Bryan's apartment, she called Jules and offered her the freedom Grace couldn't have. "You want my share in exchange for tuition?" Jules asked. "It's not worth that much."

"It is to me. Survival skills are for living, kiddo, not for waiting and wanting."

"But if I don't have a share in the business, what do I have?"

"A home, Jules. You can always come home. It's not a small thing after all. Maybe you'll get rich and buy your share back from me someday."

When Grace pulled into her driveway that night, she sat in her car the extra moment and lit a cigarette. She'd earned it. She'd missed three phone calls too. One was from Prep U telling her since she violated the legal agreement and left camp early she wasn't eligible for the Entrepreneur Prepper Showcase prize. Like she cared about that now. One was from the school reporting Tammy and Kate absent and truant for the afternoon, even though they clearly weren't wanted there. They were probably trying to build a case for expelling them for another reason besides the pregnancy. Father Tom said Tammy was welcome to return after the baby. He'd appreciate if she didn't talk about it to the other girls, as if pregnancy was contagious or she could hide the fact that she'd become a mom. She assumed Wade wasn't getting the same talk. The last message was from a Tampa, Florida, number she didn't recognize. She was annoyed to be bothered but curious enough to call back.

"This is Grace Fehler," she said. "Someone from your office called me."

"Please hold."

"Mrs. Fehler? I'm Jaime Winters with Preppers United." Grace took another drag off her cigarette and had to admit she still loved the excitement of prepping and thinking about the end, whatever that meant.

"I was one of the judges who gave you feedback on your project idea—the BOB for liberal ladies. I wanted to talk to you about how to market it to feminists and see if you're interested in expanding your business."

"To be honest, Mr. Winters, I have enough business on my hands these days."

"Would you be willing to consider an offer then? Sell the idea to me. I assume you have a lawyer and a patent pending, yes?" She caught sight of Maggie watching from the front window and waved to her frantically.

"I do. I have both," Grace lied. "I'll put you in touch with our family attorney. Can you hold on a minute? My business partner just joined me and has some questions."

"Mom, you smoke?" Maggie stared in disapproval as she slid into the passenger seat. Grace thought about how many more times in her daughter's life she'd disappoint her. But not today—apart from the smoking.

Grace put her hand over the receiver and whispered, "They want to buy the rights to the Little Women Survival Tote I made for your aunt."

"What? Who? They want to offer you money?"

"You'll need to make it worth my time, of course," Grace said into the phone, like she'd seen shrewd businessmen say in the movies. "We run a family pest control business, and I have four daughters to raise. My husband recently passed away, you see."

"I'm so sorry for your loss, ma'am."

"Thank you, Mr. Winters. I appreciate that."

"We're prepared to offer you fifty thousand dollars for the patent, and you'll maintain fifty percent equity. If you say yes, we'll continue the conversation we began about the product with one of our distributors."

Maggie grabbed the receiver out of Grace's hand and held it out so they could both listen. "Who is your distributor?"

"Costco."

"Jesus, Mom. Do you know what this could mean?" Maggie whispered. Then back into the receiver, "Thank you, sir, for your phone call. We're happy to move forward with the negotiations in good faith. Please keep us updated on your progress."

"We have a deal? That's fantastic. I know a good businesswoman when I meet one. I'll send some paperwork over right away. Please hold for my assistant."

Maggie stomped her feet on the car floorboards in delight. Grace felt relieved. She'd known all along that her prepping skills would pay off. This is why she'd worked so hard. For them. For their survival. And she'd done it on her own.

"Let's get your sisters," Grace said, stubbing out the cigarette. She got out of the car but only leaned through the front door to call, "Girls! It's Holy Monday. Close enough to Palm Sunday. It's time to clear the temple. Get your coats. We can still make it to evening Mass. We have a Savior to celebrate!"

When the Fehlers reached their regular pew, it was vacant, but branches were waiting on their seats, as if they were all making the procession into Jerusalem along with Jesus.

23

Maggie

On Good Friday, Mrs. Cooper called to let Maggie know her loan had been approved and she could come in that morning and sign the paperwork. They were even going to get a big tax write-off because Obama's stimulus bill included a break for small businesses. Jules had already submitted the documents. That would mean even more money in their pockets and maybe they could hire again. Maggie decided not to mention it to her mom, though. Fehler Family Exterminating was closed for the holiday, of course, but the board members were all gathered around pans of Grace's homemade corn bread and fried catfish. Nothing made Maggie feel more Catholic than abstaining from meat on Fridays during Lent and gorging instead on fish. "Survival is about knowing when to be safe and when to risk," Grace said. "Now is the time to take a chance. All those in favor of letting Maggie move forward with her purchase of the bed bug rig, raise your hand."

"But, Mom, you can't vote," Maggie said. It was embarrassing to bring this up again. "And my sisters have all been clear that they think my idea isn't worth much." It was true, and she hated to know it. Their lack of faith had the same edge as her dad's, dull but a knife nonetheless. The bank thing seemed desperate to her now, and she was shocked when Mrs. Cooper changed her mind about the loan. She had overheard Tammy and Kate say that they didn't think things had to change at work when so much had changed at home. They were too young and too wrapped up in themselves to understand. Maggie had gone over the numbers again and again with Jules. They needed a new track for income, and fast.

"I can and I will, actually," her mom said. "The only interested buyer of the business shares was me. I now own forty percent. I signed the paperwork yesterday with Mr. Bly. Turns out hiring him was the best way your dad could have taken care of us. With your vote, Maggie, that's a majority."

"But why? You hate the business." Maggie was defensive and confused. Wasn't this what she was asking for—family support? She never expected this much from her mom, but maybe her dad had been in the way of it.

"I don't hate Fehlers'. I am a Fehler. I hate that it always comes first. At least it did with your dad. But if you want to give it a go, knock yourself out. Maybe you'll do it different. Maybe change isn't so bad. Maybe fear drives us too much. I'll stay right here with my one business line that rarely rings. And now I'll be in business for myself."

"It rings, Mom. You just don't answer it," Tammy said. Kate and Jules high-fived each other. It was true.

Grace looked at the yellow phone hanging on her kitchen wall. One of Maggie's first memories was trailing the plastic curly cord around the house as her mom talked on it about pest control treatments and termite inspections. "That probably won't change," her mom said, and Maggie knew it was true. But maybe her family would finally see that leaders lead best by doing rather than talking about doing. She wasn't her dad, and she didn't want to be. Being Maggie was good enough, and she didn't need anyone's permission for that.

Cairo, Illinois—where they were picking up the bed bug rig—had seen better days, Maggie thought. Not many. But a few. The storefronts were abandoned now and most of the brick facades hid crumbling staircases and caved roofs. The 150-year-old town had dwindled to a few thousand stubborn townies. The more the threat of their extinction grew, the tighter they held to memories of grandeur and glory that weren't entirely true and wouldn't return if they were. Maggie had agreed to meet the salesman from Thermic Fix on 8th Street, around the corner from the once majestic Gem Theatre and decaying Chamber of Commerce, to pick up the bed bug rig and hand over the check.

Wade, who was back to fawning over and pawing her sister, had driven Maggie and Tammy down so they could caravan back. He and Tammy were suddenly and firmly engaged, their parents insisted, though neither family seemed all that thrilled about a wedding. It wasn't until Kate suggested the honey theme that the Fehler sisters got on board. Tammy was now calling herself the Queen Bride. Bryan had told them that even Mark Twain loved bees, so much so that he designed his guest room in them. "There is a wallpaper at the Mark Twain House in Hartford in the Mahogany Room, and the print is honeybees from Candace Wheeler's design 'Honeybee Wallpaper and Frieze' from 1881. It was hand-printed in New England and has off-white with light-yellow honeycombs and these metallic gold and green spider webs that glow in the dark." The Fehler sisters just stared at Bryan when he shared stuff like that, except Jules. She craved what she didn't know, and Maggie found it exhausting sometimes. Maggie understood the wanting, but her goals were tangible. Jules wanted to know stuff just to know stuff. But Jules was energized by making money, even if going back to college and Niko were her biggest motivations. Maggie's immediate goals were to get both the bed bug rig and the Queen Bride back to Cape safely.

A rolling fog had covered the peninsula; they couldn't even read the "Historic Downtown Cairo" on the arch, but they all knew it was there.

"What a sad little ghost town," Tammy said, leaning against a lamppost Maggie feared wouldn't hold her weight. Tammy had complained the whole drive about cramps, but Maggie was used to her sister's melodrama.

"Used to be something. Once the railroad came in," Maggie said, looking up and down the streets. "Dad said at one time they thought the town would be the biggest in Illinois."

"What happened?" Wade asked. He seemed spooked to Maggie, and she worried about his endurance when things got tough.

"They died because they wouldn't change, I think," Maggie said, checking her phone. The Thermic Fix folks were ten minutes late, but the weather could have delayed their drive up from Tennessee. "Progress happened, but the people didn't progress. A Southern town stuck in a Northern state, I once read. They refused to integrate. Corrupt, racist police too. There was even a mob lynching. But really, it was the economy. Hard to make money when you're stuck in the past and don't adapt." Then Maggie saw the bed bug rig crawl down the street in the fog, and she thought it was lovely. A black Ford truck followed it. She waved at both, and Tammy told her to stop looking so eager.

Maggie put both hands in the air like she was a cheerleader. "That's our future right there, sis. Driving right at us."

An hour later, after a brief orientation and a lot of paperwork, Maggie drove the truck slowly away from the tiny town and began retracing her way back up the Mississippi River toward home.

"I need to pee. Can you pull over?" Tammy asked, grabbing the door handle.

Maggie held tight to the steering wheel. She wasn't used to

driving a vehicle this big and heavy. It felt like she was dragging weight—like when her dad used to make her back the boat in for practice. "Not really. Not in this fog. Can you hold it?" She adjusted her rearview mirror, but the visibility was zero. Robbie would have kept driving, and he wouldn't have expressed or felt the caution Maggie did. Maybe hesitating and assessing before rushing in was a kind of sacred pause rather than a weakness.

"I don't think so. It feels like my butt is about to explode," Tammy said. "I gotta go."

"Like on the side of the road? You want to pee on the side of the road? Seriously, Tammy? You should have gone back in town."

"You sound like Dad," Tammy screamed. "Wait!" She put both hands on the dashboard to steady herself. "Something is wrong."

"What? What's wrong?" Maggie yelled back, flipping on her hazards and pulling onto the shoulder.

Tammy wiped her hands down her sweatpants. "I'm soaked." Then she stuck her hand between her legs. "I thought I peed myself, but my water broke."

"Okay. Okay. Okay. The hospital is about thirty miles away." Maggie started pulling the rig back onto the highway.

"Ahhh! I can't make it."

"Can't make what? Breathe, Tammy. Babies don't pop out because your water broke. That's only in the movies."

"I have to push."

"You have to what? No, absolutely not. Don't do that. You are not having that baby until we get to the hospital." Maggie pulled back over and dialed Wade. She wished they'd caravanned like they had planned, but he had to get back for basketball practice.

Of course there was limited cell phone service. The fog made it impossible to see any signs ahead to know if there was a turnoff. She tried 911 but didn't have enough reception for the call to go through.

"I can't stop, Maggie. It hurts!" Tammy held on to the oh-shit bar with both hands like she was trying to jump out of the seat. Then she pulled her legs up to the dashboard and slid off her wet sweatpants. "It feels a little better like this. You're going to have to look."

"To what?"

"Oh, come on. You've seen worse. I swear to God I can feel the baby's head. Maggie, look." Tammy writhed like Nacho when he rediscovered a bone in the backyard he had buried, frantic and overcome.

Maggie unbuckled her seatbelt and climbed over the console to Tammy. She leaned over her front and looked upside down between her legs. "Shit, it's the head."

Tammy screamed again. Maggie tried 911 again. She rolled down the window, and soupy air rolled in and between them. They were stuck in a cloud.

"I'm climbing in the back to lay down," Tammy said. At least there's benches and blankets. I can't sit here anymore. I have to move."

"Nine-one-one. What's your emergency?"

"My name is Margaret Fehler. I'm on the side of the road between Cairo and Cape, and my sister is having her baby—*now*."

Tammy became a caged animal. She squatted and roared. She cried and moaned. *If she'd just calm down, we could keep driving, maybe*, Maggie thought. But the operator suggested they stay put and wait for the ambulance. A rumble of thunder rolled toward them. Not a single car had passed in the ten minutes they had been sitting there. Tammy alternated between screaming and panic. It was clear to Maggie that it wasn't safe to drive and even clearer that Tammy needed a doctor. She found some tarps in the back of the rig, tore off the sheet of plastic that covered the generator, and made a kind of nest for her sister.

"Maggie, it's coming out!" Tammy screamed.

Maggie reached her hands under her sister and caught a head, then a body with a quick, tight scream that matched her sister's. A beautiful pink chubby little girl with a head full of ginger curls. Then out gushed fluid and pink stuff and a fat gray pulsing umbilical cord. The baby opened her eyes to see them both.

Maggie held her niece up to Tammy and nodded toward her breast. She'd seen her mom do this part plenty with her sisters.

"Oh," Tammy said and pulled the baby to her chest. Maggie tucked her sweatshirt around them both as the baby latched on and closed her eyes.

"Mom is going to make you bring her to Easter Mass," Maggie said, smoothing back Tammy's sweaty hair.

"I just had a baby in a bed bug truck," Tammy whispered. "Surely that gets me out of Mass once." The baby looked like a fish opening and closing its mouth.

"It's going to be Easter Sunday. You'll both be there," Maggie said as flashing red lights came through the fog. She was relieved to see them, but she didn't need their rescue. She could do even this on her own.

As Maggie suspected, the local news station was interested in the story of her sister giving birth in a bed bug truck. The evening host shared that Fehler Family Exterminating was officially in the integrated pest management business, fighting Cape's growing bed bug population with women in the lead.

24

Tammy

Tammy made Wade buy the spray-on glue to hold her squishy butt in place, but she needed Maggie to do the adhering. At first Tammy thought a glue stick might work just as well, but Alexis, one of the other contestants, told her about Firm Grip. "You'll need baby wipes to get it off," Alexis had said when they stood in line together at the rehearsal. The armory would turn the air conditioning on only during the actual pageant, so the girls sweated backstage, then swayed under the lights. "You can borrow some of mine. My mom uses baby wipes for everything." Tammy had plenty of baby wipes, though. Alexis taught her about reusing fake eyelashes, Velcro hair rollers, and how to use Scotch tape to take off eye shadow to avoid red splotches sometimes left by makeup remover. "Did anyone tell you about wearing a strapless bra under your swimsuit too? Trust me. Mom bought me a bombshell bra from Victoria's Secret at the mall. The extra lift goes a long way."

Tammy read the side of the Firm Grip can. "It says a light coat on each cheek, then pat the swimsuit gently into place." Maggie, Jules, and Kate were huddled in a corner of the pageant dressing room staring at their sister's butt even though the rules clearly stated only one attendant was allowed. Most of the contestants had a professional coach. Tammy couldn't choose among her sisters but knew Grace was no pageant mom. Best to leave her busy with the baby. Wade would be there soon and had promised to pick up extra diapers. Tammy figured it was easier to beg forgiveness from the event staff than ask permission.

"You've got looks that will open doors," Robbie had always said, as if she wouldn't need much more than that in life. Tammy wanted more though. Motherhood had split her open. She could feel herself being reorganized, and she didn't mind it. Maybe being a young mother means you're still malleable. You have no idea who you are, so you might as well be this.

The world was different with another little woman to look out for. She noticed that the other drivers were suddenly reckless as Wade drove them home from the hospital. She hopped into the back seat with the baby and used her own body to protect the car seat. Who else would do it? The pediatrician was too rough during Piper's first examination, squeezing white spots onto the baby's plump, blushing skin. What if he bruised her? Every customer who insisted on ringing the home business line threatened precious sleep. Why not forward the calls? Grace had said Tammy had tiger in her, and she didn't deny the growl of motherhood growing inside. She couldn't imagine a moment without Piper and wouldn't remember at all that she once considered the pregnancy a huge mistake. She was only sorry Robbie wouldn't know his grandchild. But if her dad were still here, the family's whole future would be different. Piper might never have been.

Grace had said the swimsuit was tacky when Tammy brought it home from the JCPenney sale rack. She chose the red-and-blue one-piece with the stars for this dumb part of the pageant because it reminded her of Wonder Woman. She felt like one these days. Even Jules had said it was a bold look and agreed to bite her tongue after her "pageant patriarchy" talk. Besides, Jules's bags were packed again, and she was moving back to Columbia to share an apartment with Niko. She had two jobs lined up and summer school. Jules was helping with costume errands so Tammy wouldn't tell on her for living in sin.

When Tammy had modeled the swimsuit in their kitchen, Grace said, "Those cutouts are inviting attention, if you know what I mean."

"I'm parading around half naked two months after giving birth, Mom. Seems I'm inviting a few stares, don't you think? Besides, I'm already down ten pounds." Tammy lifted her breasts a full inch to where they used to be located before they doubled in size with milk. "And this is probably the best chest I'll ever have." Wade couldn't disagree, but he was on strict orders not to go near them, which seemed an enormous waste of resources to him. There wasn't much opportunity anyway, with Tammy moving back to her house when Piper was only a week old. "I can't sleep here," Tammy had complained about the new bed in the basement rec room Wade's parents had fixed up for them. But Wade thought she missed her sisters, and he seemed grateful to sleep through the night again before his morning basketball practice followed by an eight-hour shift at Fehlers'. "Besides, Piper likes the crib at home better. It's special. All of the Fehler girls slept in it."

Wade had pouted, but he didn't seem to mean it. "But I want my girls with me, Tammy. This better be temporary." He had even agreed to burn the stupid breakup note he'd written. He stomped out the fire in the parking lot after school with everyone watching. Tammy was grateful. He was willing to shout his love publicly so that the dumb gossip girls saw that they were for real and not stuck together for the baby's sake. She promised after the pageant and Piper's teething, they would think about their own place. Maybe an apartment down by the river. Or they could move into the back of the Fehlers' garage, where there was a makeshift studio. They would make it work, and not just because they had to but because Tammy wanted to. She wanted to be with Wade. But first, she wanted to be Miss Cape.

Maggie caught Tammy's hips and leaned over her sister's backside. "Hold still. I can't spray the glue right when you keep moving. This stuff says it's wedgie proof."

Kate read the side of the adhesive bottle too. "This says the glue could last three hours. What if it gets stuck between your outfit changes? Isn't evening gown next? You may have to wear yours over the swimsuit." Tammy would hardly call Jules's hand-me-down prom dress an evening gown, but at least she'd been able to talk Grace into bedazzling it for her.

"It burns. And now I'm leaking. Jules, get me a tissue." Tammy applied pressure by smashing each nipple with a palm. She thought about baseball—anything but the baby, or the milk would flow. "This is stupid. Why does the swimsuit have to stay in place anyway? Aren't they meant to move when you walk? Seems dumb that something meant to go in the water is supposed to look like it's never been wet. Who makes these rules anyway?"

"Men," Jules said, stating the obvious.

Maggie nodded. "You don't have to follow these rules."

"Seems a little late for that," Kate offered quietly.

Tammy stared at the clock and held still while her sisters preened her. Twelve minutes until she had to suck in her gut for the audience. It was only a thirty-second stroll across the platform. She didn't need to breathe for that. The sisters all agreed that the metallic gold headband Jules had found for her at Dollar General was the perfect complement for her superhero look. Maggie settled the band into Tammy's curls, and it shimmered when it caught the light. She already felt like Miss Cape Girardeau and decided she cared more about showing up than winning. Who says a teen mom can't shine? She would show them. Or at least, she would finish this thing she started that was maybe a little ridiculous now, but she couldn't very well call her own bluff. She kind of wanted it over with so she could take a nap and schedule Piper's two-month baby pictures. Maybe she could even enter her in the little tot contest next year. There was an elastic baby tiara waiting for the occasion.

While she stood still, Tammy thought back to the delivery and the one visitor she never expected: Laura, the nice ER nurse who was there when Robbie died. She had brought a stack of chocolate bars instead of a teddy bear, and Tammy loved her instantly for it. Laura sat on the side of the bed while the baby dozed, milk drunk. "You're good at advice," Tammy said. "Give me some before all the meds wear off and I stop listening."

Laura opened a family-size bar and broke it into squares. She popped one into her mouth and held out the rest. Tammy took three chunks. "It's hard to raise someone else when you're still raising yourself," Laura said. She looked different out of her nurse scrubs—like a regular mom, but you couldn't actually tell she was a mom. She wore a black T-shirt that said "Hannibal, MO: America's Hometown" and jeans with her cowgirl boots.

"You think I'm a kid because I still like candy?" Tammy asked, popping in one long strip of the bar without splitting it. The chocolate was creamy and welcome. The hospital food had been awful. They kept feeding her powdered scrambled eggs and cartons of 2 percent milk, so she'd made Wade bring in fried chicken and mashed potatoes. Nursing made her hungry. She'd eaten four drumsticks and a biscuit before she even said thanks.

"No. I still like candy too. You wanted advice. Here I am. Your baby will be fine. She's got love all around her. You don't need to lay down your whole life for hers. She needs to know you are a person too. Talk back to that 'selfless mom' praise. Show your daughter that you matter too." Laura held out the Styrofoam cup of water and pointed the straw at Tammy. "Drink."

She took a sip but used her tongue to keep the wad of chocolate melting on the roof of her mouth. "My mom says the opposite. She says I made my bed and now I have to lie down in it."

Laura wrapped up the rest of the chocolate and filled the water cup. "That's true too. You remind me a little of my best friend, Rose. She had a baby when she was about your age. He turned out pretty good, but Rose still acts like she's sixteen sometimes. She's the most loyal person I know, but she drives me crazy too, because she's stuck, you know? Babies don't stop you from moving forward in your life. They teach you what matters."

Piper was making funny faces in her sleep. She pursed her lips into an *O*. "What's Rose doing now?"

"I hardly believe it, but she teaches Zumba. She went into the nutritional supplement business with my mom for a while during the recession, but there was no money in it. Now she gets to have people stare at her for a good reason. Good ole Rose." Laura swaddled the baby tight and kissed her on the forehead before she left.

Tammy was thinking about Rose as she lined up with the other contestants. She had made the same mistake getting pregnant, but that didn't have to stop her from going back to school and helping Maggie grow Fehlers'. Maybe she'd be a bug girl after all and make her own daughter proud one day.

Ayla walked on stage. Her black bikini blended with her glossy brown legs. The five judges smiled and nodded. They were all men. All White, mostly overweight, mostly balding local businessmen. Robbie would have fit right in. The judge in the middle, who ran the car wash, Suds, boomed into the microphone, "Tell us about your journey to become Miss Cape." Tammy looked down at her pale flesh and wished she had booked a few tanning bed sessions. The lights would reveal every stretch mark and cellulite pocket.

"It's been hard work," Ayla answered, tilting toward the judge's table with the stiff practice of a mannequin. "I've reached my fullest potential by overcoming many hardships. I hope that I'm following the Good Lord's will."

"God bless." The judge nodded.

"Jesus Christ," Tammy muttered, taking her place as Ayla strutted off stage while the judges assessed her backside. Tammy hoped Ayla had a wedgie.

The fattest judge frowned and looked Tammy up and down. "And how did you prepare for today's challenge?"

It was a stock question. The same one this same judge had asked Alexis when she came on stage moments before Ayla. Tammy thought through what she was supposed to say: studying Missouri history, visiting local landmarks, meeting Cape residents, practicing her answers, praying for guidance. "I had a baby," she blurted, and the audience became still. "I mean, I'm a mother now. It's not what I planned when I signed up for the pageant. But I'm not sorry either." The judge shook his head and scribbled on the scorecard in front of him. "I don't recommend teen pregnancy or anything, but I've learned that I'm more than what people think of me. And most people think only about how I look and not who I am." Tammy couldn't seem to make the words stop. Then she saw Grace rocking the baby in the aisle and beaming at her like she had already won the prize. Grace moved the baby to her shoulder and made the sign of the cross. "Moms are tough. They have to be. And if I'm strong enough to be a baby's mom, continue my education, and become a family with her daddy, I sure can represent a town like Cape. I think we're both more than anyone expects of us, and people should expect a lot more."

In the back row, Maggie, Jules, and Kate stood up and clapped. They pulled Wade up from his seat too, and he joined their cheers. From the stage, Tammy heard them. She'd know her sisters' screams anywhere. Who cared about a bunch of strangers loving you when your own people already did?

25

Grace

Grace had traced and retraced Robbie's final days, and they still didn't make sense. He'd had indigestion the weekend before, but he had also eaten too many BBQ chicken wings at the Thompsons' cookout. "Fried food makes you feel worse not better," Grace had reminded him, but he wouldn't listen. Ever. He was in a bad mood. That wasn't unusual. He had claimed to have lost three pounds and increased his water intake as the doctor recommended, but Grace didn't know if sugary iced tea counted. Beer didn't, but he'd had plenty.

Looking for more clues, Grace developed the film that Kate shot the night of the Chamber dinner. She needed to see Robbie's face, to read anything she might have missed. It was a gruesome series. Candid snapshots of her daughters. It touched her to see their energies turned toward each other in the pictures. A photo of Maggie's panicked face replayed the details in her memory. They say moments like these can be such a blur, but Robbie's death happened in slow motion, frame by frame. The final picture Kate took before she ran to her sister's arms was Grace's hand on her husband's cheek. She wasn't trying to wake him up; she already knew he was gone, but she didn't want to let go.

Grief was a punishment. When she woke up most mornings, she stayed still before opening her eyes. She'd feel for the weight of him on the other side of the bed. Robbie was gone, and so was that half of her. Guilt hogged the covers. She had so many things to say and no one to say them to. This morning, she decided to make a list. It was Pentecost, after all, fifty days after Easter, and the right time for a reckoning. Direct communication, like the apostles had with God, was suddenly possible. The portal was clear and open.

Stuff Robbie Needs to Know:

Tammy had a baby

Maggie bought a bed bug truck

Maggie is training Wade to be her bed bug guy

~~Kate might like *like* girls~~

Nacho picked out a partner

The new dog's name is Cheese

Bryan does the dishes after dinner

~~Obama is president~~

John McCain is president

Jules is probably gone for good ~~with a Black guy~~

Jules is majoring in ~~Art~~ Management and going to Spain

Kate is the real bug girl

~~I'm lonely but happier alone~~

You were the love of my life

Grace tucked the list into her nightstand and glanced over at Robbie's, which she hadn't touched in the six months since his death: his readers, a half empty bottle of Tums, crumpled receipts from his last purchases, a paper program from the Chamber dinner celebrating Maggie that he had asked to see early and printed to study. He wasn't preparing to die. He was a proud dad happy to be alive. Grace took two slow, deep breaths, as Father Tom taught her to do when the tears came. She didn't want to show up at church puffy.

She could count on Kate to be the first in the car, especially on Sundays. Grace found Maggie waiting to drive, Tammy putting on mascara, and Piper already asleep in her car seat. She thought of Jules and hoped she'd go to Mass on campus. But Kate wasn't in the car.

"Where is your sister?" she asked, with an accusation pointed at the oldest, always the oldest.

"She went to check the hives," Tammy said, blinking away an ink smudge.

"Before church?" Maggie asked, shifting the blame.

Grace looked toward the back acreage and listened for buzzing. Nacho barked from the back door, and Cheese whined. Something was wrong.

"Let the dogs out," she called to Maggie. Dogs run to danger, and Grace felt it. She blinked twice and sprinted when she saw Kate stumbling toward her. Nacho jumped in the air trying to eat the bees trailing Kate in a black cloud. Her swollen eyes must have made it hard to see, but she lurched toward Nacho's bark. Her hands hung heavy, as if they were weighing her whole body down. She looked sunburned, but that wasn't possible; the sun had barely risen yet to announce Pentecost. Kate wheezed, and Grace caught her fall.

"The bees," Kate said in thick syllables. A swarm followed them, and the family ran for shelter, the screen door slamming with a *whack* at their back. "The dogs!" Kate cried.

"Jesus, Mary, and Joseph. Why didn't you wear the bee suit?"

"I did, but I took it off." Grace couldn't tell if Kate was crying or sweating from the pain, but her face was soaked. "The suit smells like Dad."

Grace took talking as a good sign. Kates lips weren't swollen. "Can you swallow?"

Kate nodded and gulped. Maggie ran to the garage to meet Nacho and Cheese, who were now running from bees. Nacho yelped and must have gotten stung. Tammy stood in the kitchen, stunned, without her own baby. Grace had to give orders. Motherhood was the best prepper training possible.

"Grab the oatmeal," Grace ordered. "Keep the baby in the car with the air conditioning on. The bees will still be active. You have to protect Piper. I've got Kate. And check the dogs."

Maggie rushed to the kitchen for the oversized Quaker tub Grace bought once a month at Walmart. "Get the Benadryl too. And the first aid kit—the big one—from my bench in the basement."

"Kate isn't allergic, is she?" Maggie asked as she handed Grace the oatmeal.

"Not that I know of, but I've counted twenty stings." Grace started running a bath and poured the dry oatmeal into the water. "Mix me a paste of baking soda and honey."

"Honey?"

"I know. It helps, though. We should get the stingers out first." Grace grabbed the tweezers and searched Kate's body, attacking each entry point. "You're fine, baby. Just keep breathing, and I'll do the rest. Hold still. Pulling on the stingers is going to pinch a bit." Grace remembered from her first aid course at Prep U that when the barbed stinger pierces the skin, it injects venom, apitoxin. The sting requires part of the bee's abdomen too, often its digestive tract, muscles, and nerves. Bees don't survive their attack, but their victims usually do. Kate would. "We have to get the stingers out quick. They can keep pumping venom, even without the bee."

"Okay," Kate whispered and closed her eyes to let Grace do the rest. "But it will kill them." Kate lips began to swell. She grabbed her throat.

"Get my BOB, Maggie. Hurry! Hold on, Kate. Focus on your

breath. See if you can swallow again." In the twenty seconds it took Maggie to run to the basement and grab the BOB embroidered "Mom," Grace had pulled out three more stingers, said two Hail Marys, and turned off the water to the tub they clearly weren't going to need. Maggie dumped the contents of the BOB on the floor. "I need the EpiPen. Side pocket on the right." In a quick grab, Grace popped the cap off the needle and then shot it into Kate's leg. Kate gasped.

"What happened?" Bryan said, appearing in the bathroom doorway. "Your church pew was empty." He wrung out a washcloth in the sink and put it on Kate's forehead.

"The hive defended their queen against Kate. You can drive us to the hospital. It'll be faster than waiting for an ambulance. Help me carry her, Bryan."

In the car while Bryan drove, Grace continued her own assault on the stingers, rubbed her homemade paste on each wound, and prayed. Later, she would remember to be pleased about their rapid response and coordinated efforts. Their time was outstanding. That's why they had practiced the drills. But for now, she was focused on wanting her baby to survive.

After six hours at the hospital where they monitored Kate's breathing and did far less first aid than Grace had done, they released the Fehler family to return home. Tammy, for once, had put the meat loaf in the oven and made mashed potatoes, even though they could use more butter. Maggie had put on water to boil for the corn on the cob and set the table. Piper was asleep on the couch, and Grace didn't remind Tammy that the baby would be inching around soon and that wasn't a safe place to leave her. She would figure out a way to tell her tomorrow. Not today. Today, she would tuck Kate into bed to rest, be grateful that Tammy made dinner, thank Maggie for her quick reflexes, and award Bryan with two desserts. Then she'd call Jules to ask about her class and pretend she didn't know she and Niko were living together.

Later that evening, when she got back into her bed, Grace returned to the list and added:

Kate almost killed herself with your damn bees

~~My prepping skills paid off~~

~~You were wrong: $200 was not too much for that EpiPen~~

I miss you

Before she turned off the light that night, Grace saw something else on Robbie's nightstand. It had been hidden by the curve of his lamp and the mess he'd left. She had kept her distance, afraid that each time she cleaned up the last thing he'd touched, more of him might fade. In a miniature ivory frame was Grace's high school yearbook photo.

EPILOGUE

Fehler Sisters

At the end of their first summer without Robbie, Piper will learn to crawl on the dock at the Fehler Family Fish Camp. She'll be wiggling on her blanket next to Grace's lounge chair and scoot three tiny times toward Aunt Maggie before rolling over onto her back. Kate will film it on her phone to show Tammy and Wade later when they both get out of class. They'll all agree that every single thing the baby does is the best.

Grace will look away when Jules's T-shirt rides up again and her tattoo of the word *hope* peeks out. "It's a thing with feathers," Jules will say, and Maggie will tell her to stop because they've both found their voices and learned when to raise them and when to whisper. "Did I tell you all that Niko has the same tattoo?"

"Yep," Kate will answer when it's clear no one else will.

"Several times," Bryan will add. "Cool."

"Is Niko coming to camp this weekend?" Grace will ask. "He's welcome anytime."

Niko will visit that weekend, and he'll gift the family a giant papier-mâché hive he made in his studio fine arts class with *Fehlers* spelled out in honeycomb holes. "It will be a perfect decoration for the reception!" Tammy will say.

On the dock that summer, they'll talk about the upcoming August bee-themed wedding and how to transform the office garage into a party space. Grace will offer to do the flower arrangements since she planted lavender, clover, buckwheat, vetch, and other pollen-producing plants to please the bees.

Lila will be Kate's plus-one at the wedding, and they'll build a skateboarding ramp in the office parking lot. During the final song of the wedding, "I'm Yours" by Jason Mraz, Maggie will be asked to dance by a sweet boy named Bobby. Bryan invited him because he was in town talking Twain, and Maggie will remember that they'd met before and will lean in close to make her intentions clear. Tammy'll wear the same dress she wore for the Miss Cape pageant, where she won first runner-up and a $1,000 scholarship to the Trend Setters School of Cosmetology and walked the celebratory runway with Piper proudly on her hip.

After the happy stress of the wedding, the family will pack up and head off for a whole week at the Fehler Family Fish Camp. As the first car arrives, Grace will yell out Maggie's front seat window, "Wait until you see! I've been planning this for months."

Kate will call it. "Are those solar panels, Mom?"

"Sure are. We're off the grid! That old thing needed new stilts, too, for the flooding that's coming." The sisters will be impressed and relieved that their mom's tension, fear, and fight will have melted into something closer to living. Grace will even splurge for a new screen door, and it'll slap against the trailer frame with the same soothing sound as the broken one.

The bed bug business will boom, of course, but the BOB business will bust with Obama's reelection and the liberals settling into false security. Grace will design a higher-end BOB that sells much better for the 1 percent who want something more signature to don the hooks in their steel bunkered vacation homes. Fehler

Family Exterminating will give their first annual employee of the year award to their newest addition, Valerie, whose bed bug hunting dogs will help establish the integrated pest management division, which quickly doubles their customer base beyond the borders of Cape. The Fehler family, having lived through and sustained loss, will be a stronger hive than they could have imagined a year before.

By September, when the Fehlers begin planning a small family service for the first anniversary of Robbie's death, Piper will be scooting as she pulls herself between the sisters. Then she'll move on to stumbling and discover she can talk. When she hears tree frogs croak, crickets chirp, or a bird song from the banks of the Mississippi River, the baby will remind them to pause and listen. Piper's first word will be "bug" and Kate will say she heard "butt" instead, and they'll tell that story for years.

One day, when Piper is a teenager, she'll be restless on the drive to family camp, and she'll reach down into a backseat pocket and find the dog-eared *Adventures of Huckleberry Finn.* Maybe she'll be wise enough to read it as the revolutionary book it is: a manual and remedy for the ills of American life. Or maybe it will take her fifty years of rereading to get Huck's life lessons: break free, take adventures, accept risks, make choices, have hope. The Fehler family women will pile on their wishes and pray that Piper learns from the novel to follow her own directions.

"Know what moment matters most?" Grace will ask every time her family gathers on the dock that summer and the ones after that too. "This one."

AUTHOR'S NOTE

Dear Reader,

Political and personal struggles are rifting our hometowns, our communities, and our families. They are occurring on the dirt road I grew up on in rural Missouri near the banks of the Mississippi River and near the campus where I teach in Washington, D.C. In *The Hive*, the Fehler family endures similar threats and they must find what they have in common to rebuild the foundation that has been quaked. To survive, they must investigate their differences and consider the line between preparedness and paranoia. As research for the book, I attended Prepper Camp, a survivalist training weekend in North Carolina, and learned about the precarious crossover from fear that protects us to dangerous delusion that spurs violence. The queen bee of the Fehler family, Grace, travels in apocalyptic prepper circles and comes dangerously close to trading responsibility for romance.

Like the Fehler sisters, I was raised in a family pest control business in rural Missouri, but this is not my family's story. I have brothers. My parents are happily retired in Florida and Dad fishes daily off a dock on the St. John's River. I don't write about the people in my life, but you'll see their spirit on every page. This is the complex Midwestern community that raised me; I'm proud to call them my own. I didn't set out to write the familiar as fiction though. I wanted to tell the story of feminism rising from rural roots and to wrestle with the politics of family business succession. I intended to explore sudden grief and those left to pick up the pieces. My greatest hope for *The Hive* was to write characters with compassion and to welcome readers to homes they don't occupy but with which they can empathize.

I have always wanted a sister. When I wrote the Fehler sisters, I imagined how their bond would be complicated and deep. Their griefs are common: the loss of their beloved patriarch, the financial threat to their family business, Midwestern political fear and resentment growing around them, and their absent mother who has her own agenda to save them all. But sisterhood endures.

Thank you for reading *The Hive*.

Best wishes,
Melissa Scholes Young

ACKNOWLEDGEMENTS

A story has many lives before it finds its way to a reader, and I am in awe of the hands that helped this book find a home.

Thanks to my Turner Team, especially my editor, Stephanie Beard. I'm grateful to my agent, Claire Anderson-Wheeler, who said yes to my voice years ago. To Lauren Cerand, thank you for joining me on this journey with grace and style.

Deep bows of gratitude to my roots and the community that raised me. Love always to my parents, Gene and Kathy Scholes, and my hive of siblings, nieces, nephews, aunts, uncles, and cousins.

I've been blessed with mentors, especially Mark Eggleston, David Suda, Stacy A. Cordery, Beth Lordan, and Allison Joseph. Rest in poetry, dear Jon Tribble.

All hail the Buzz Team of early readers and cheerleaders. Thanks for making noise for the Fehler family.

I'm grateful to the Sisterhood of Grace & Gravity and the entire D.C. Literary Community.

The support of American University, the Department of Literature, and the MFA Faculty means so much. Love and praise to my students who teach me the most.

For pandemic happy hours that buoy my soul, cheers to Jared Yates Sexton.

Hugs to my best bees: Wendy Besel Hahn, Kate Kile, Kristen

Beracha, Caron Garcia Martinez, and Catherine McGrady. Thank you for knowing my heart and caring for it.

Again to my daughters, Isabelle and Piper, being your mom is the honor of my life. You are more than enough. Your lights are so bright. Shine them with kindness for good.

To Joe, my love, who endures many drafts and supports me when I run away to write. I will always come back and walk the dogs with you.

ABOUT THE AUTHOR

Melissa Scholes Young is the author of the novels *The Hive* and *Flood*, and editor of *Grace in Darkness* and *Furious Gravity*, two anthologies by women writers. She is a contributing editor at Fiction Writers Review, and her work has appeared in the *Atlantic*, *Washington Post*, *Poets & Writers*, *Ploughshares*, *Literary Hub* and elsewhere. She has been the recipient of the Bread Loaf Bakeless Camargo Foundation Residency Fellowship and the Center for Mark Twain Studies' Quarry Farm Fellowship. Born and raised in Hannibal, Missouri, she is currently an associate professor in Literature at American University.